Moment of Freedom

Moment of Freedom
The Heiligenberg Manuscript

Jens Bjørneboe

Translated from the Norwegian by
Esther Greenleaf Mürer

Norvik Press
1999

Original title: Frihetens øyeblikk (1966). © Gyldendal norsk forlag.
© Esther Greenleaf Mürer 1999: English translation of Jens
Bjørneboe: Moment of Freedom.

A catalogue record for this book is available from the British Library.

ISBN 1-870041-41-0

Cover illustration: Frans Widerberg: Selvportrett (Self Portrait), 1976.
91.5 x 76 cms., oil on canvas. Property of the National Museum of
Contemporary Art, Oslo. Photographer Morten Thorkildsen.

First published in 1999 by Norvik Press,
University of East Anglia, Norwich NR4 7LY, England.
Managing editors: James McFarlane, Janet Garton, Michael Robinson.

Norvik Press has been established with financial support from the
University of East Anglia, the Danish Ministry for Cultural Affairs,
The Norwegian Cultural Department, and the Swedish Institute.

Contents

Doch in dir ist schon begonnen
was die Sonnen übersteht

Translator's Introduction

Moment of Freedom (1966) is generally considered to be Jens Bjørneboe's masterpiece. It is a complex work, presenting many difficulties for the reader. Two extended discussions in English are to be found in Janet Garton's excellent introduction to Bjørneboo's life and work, *Jens Bjørneboe. Prophet Without Honor* (Greenwood Publishing Group, 1985) and Joe Martin's recently published study *Keeper of the Protocols: The Works of Jens Bjørnehoe in the Crosscurrents of Western Literature* (Peter Lang, 1996).

Moment of Freedom marked a new departure in Bjørneboe's literary production. It represents a synthesis of several strands in his previous work: the mystical orientation of his early poetry, the social criticism of his early novels, his fascination with Germany and Italy—all are richly interwoven here. As before, the spectre of Nazism, which had haunted him since he first read Wolfgang Langhoff's book on the Oranienburg concentration camp at the age of fifteen, looms large; the themes of injustice, authoritarianism, and the violence of power are pervasive.[1]

Bjørneboe increasingly felt a need not only to place the mystery of human evil in broader historical and philosophical context, but also to make a more personal statement of a vision which sees beyond evil to the fundamental goodness and beauty of creation. He wrote in 1967:

Much of what I have previously written has been morally covered and grounded, so to speak morally defended, by the fact that I have continually treated *other* people's problems. I have been dependent on finding a moral defense for writing at all; I have thought of what others thought or would think, believe and say.... I have felt the past fifteen years as a moral and social *military service*, which I as a writer did not have the right to shirk.

But one day you get too old for military service.

And I know that if I am to be of use in the future, this usefulness will consist in my writing the truth which is my own truth, which only *I* know—because only I am I, only *I* can see the world in *my* way.[2]

Moment of Freedom had been a long time in coming. His inner resistance to finishing it informs his previous novel, published in 1964 after a four-year hiatus—the longest in his career. *The Dream and the Wheel* is a fictionalized biography of the Norwegian writer Ragnhild Jølsen (1874-1907), with whom Bjørneboe obviously identifies strongly. Ragnhild is portrayed as incubating a magnum opus, *The Red Autumn*:

...[The other books] did not distract her, for they were merely books, but *The Red Autumn* was *the book.*

It lay there and waited, against the time when she should be strong enough to write the truth as it had not been written before. If she touched it, the other books would die. And they must be written first.

The Red Autumn could wait, for when she wrote it, she would be finished with herself. It meant an annihilation of herself, and perhaps also fertilization and new life. Not a single word of *The Red Autumn* could be put on paper yet, because the hour of complete self-destruction had not yet arrived. Before it came, she must have exploited herself more.[3]

✧ ✧ ✧

Unlike his previous novels, *Moment of Freedom* has little discernible story line. We learn at the outset that the narrator is a "Servant of Justice" in a tiny Alpine principality. The Norwegian word *rettstjener*, translated as "Servant of Justice," has a more prosaic meaning—court official, bailiff; and he does indeed earn his living as a sort of courthouse factotum. Elsewhere Bjørneboe has written, concerning a judicial hearing in which he was involved:

> ...it was a purely absurd, formalistic stage play. The last thing I remember from it all was that as I was leaving, an elderly *rettstjener* came over to me unbidden and declared, utterly shaken, that he had never witnessed the like in a courtroom. (I'm eternally grateful to him: he gave me the idea for the *rettstjener* in *Moment of Freedom*.)[4]

But the word *rett*, "court," can also mean "right" or "justice"; and in fact the first page of the novel is loaded with puns on that word; *urett*, "injustice," could also be read as "kangaroo court," etc. The puns are the author's way of signaling that the word *rettstjener* too is to be taken in a double sense; and indeed we learn that in his free time the court official/Servant of Justice is working on an "enormous, colossal twelve-volume work on The History of Bestiality." [22]

The novel's present tense is soon abandoned; in what follows it surfaces now and then amid all the memories and reflections like wisps of basting thread which didn't get removed. This plotlessness can be very frustrating because, among other things, the title leads us to expect the narrator to undergo a single dramatic, life-changing revelation. To what does the title refer? Although various commentators have come up with various answers—the dream of the tunnel through the mountain, the vision in the catacombs, etc.—the only explicit identification of "the Moment of Freedom" in the novel refers to the use of atomic bombs on Hiroshima and Nagasaki:

.... In August came the great change.

The planets Uranus and Pluto stood in conjunction in the Sign of the Black Widow, and I decided that it no longer concerned me what the little bears did to each other....

There now reigned complete peace, not least in those two cities.

Meanwhile the deed was accomplished, and many people understood that from now on the little bears had altogether new and unheard-of possibilities for harming each other; no destruction was any longer impossible; the Moment of Freedom had arrived. [148-49]

But if this is *the* Moment of Freedom, what does it have to do with the rest of the novel? It is a collective Moment of Freedom, but not a decisive Moment of Freedom in the consciousness of the narrator. If "I decided that it no longer concerned me what the little bears did to each other" were the narrator's Moment of Freedom, there would be no point in his writing the book at all, much less a monumental multi-volume *History of Bestiality*.

It happens that the Norwegian word for "moment," *øyeblikk*, is one of those words with an invariant plural, like "deer" and "sheep" in English. This means that the title could equally well be translated as "Moments of Freedom." Furthermore, if we look at the word's roots we find it means "eye-look," as in the English phrase "in the twinkling of an eye." So the title could also be rendered "Glimpses of Freedom."

In my view the title contains all of these meanings, singular and plural. To be sure, it is established in the first chapter that the phrase "moment of freedom" is derived from the Spanish bullfighting phrase *el momento de la verdad*, "the moment of truth" [20]. On the other hand, the first chapter of the "Lemuria" section ends with this: "...our brief moment of consciousness is framed by darkness; some few glimpses of light between the darkness before and the darkness after! These glimpses are all one has to hold onto." [159]

Joe Martin offers a useful key to the puzzle in his suggestion that "the developments in this new sort of *Bildungsroman*...are not 'moments' which occur in our familiar linear time. The moment of freedom is a process."[5] He supports this thought with a quotation from the novel:

> ...it's obvious that time and place are nonexistent, all reckoning of time is irrelevant, the whole thing is only a glimmer. Even the most intense awareness of existence here and now means simply that this "here" is all places, this "now" is all times. [171]

The novel's moments of freedom occur in several different kinds of time: besides linear time there is the decisive moment of the "once to every man and nation" sort, exemplified by the atomic bomb; and the "eternal now" of the peak experience, when all sense of time dissolves into intimations of eternity. The narrator spends a fair amount of time trying to recapture peak experiences, such as the early childhood memory of soap bubbles in the "Praiano Papers" section of the novel: "I was a little child and stood looking into all the color and all the light in the world...." [93]

There are many descriptions of works of art in which the linear motion stops. And indeed one autobiographical thread running through the book concerns Bjørneboe's transition from painter to writer. In a 1971 interview he is quoted as saying:

> ...I remember clearly my last period as a painter. I struggled with a recurrent problem: As I painted, and was strongly absorbed in the picture which was to be created, there was always a dialogue buzzing inside my head about quite other things than working out the

subject: About cultural, political, social, psychological
and other problems. At times I despaired because I
couldn't put the brakes on this unstoppable dialogue
while I was painting.... But when I was 28 years old I
went over to writing. For when I write, I'm not plagued
by this schizophrenic feeling that I'm busy with something else at the same time, this disturbing mental split.[6]

And in *Moment of Freedom* we read:

Today it's rather remarkable to think that I walked
around Stockholm painting flower pots, apples, and
landscapes while the whole world was aboil around me:
it was revealing itself with terrible clarity as the combination of latrine and torture chamber it is. And my own
inner pictures of the world were also an apocalypse; I
knew very well that the world was a crematorium.
    But I didn't dare to say it. [147-48]

It seems that for Bjørneboe painting was an essentially
contemplative mode which he felt compelled to abandon for
the active, linear medium of language. For the narrator of
Moment of Freedom (who, though he has much in common
with Bjørneboe, is not to be regarded as identical) the central
problem is to learn to "paint his own picture," speak his own
truth. He feels a real call to write *The History of Bestiality*.
Moment of Freedom is not so much a record of how he learned
to overcome his inhibitions in the past (although it contains
elements of this) as an ongoing struggle in the present. The
resistances to writing it down, the many dodges he uses either
to get it said or to avoid saying it, form the book's driving
energy. And in fact Bjørneboe draws upon his early experience as a painter in profound ways; the novel's very form is
that of a painting, a collage.
    For example, the incident with the judge's pornographic
pictures in the second chapter might have become a tale of a
battle to uncover vs. cover up malfeasance in high places;

Bjørneboe was no stranger to such battles, but that is not his purpose here. Once the narrator hides the photographs, they are never mentioned again. Why bring them in at all, then—is it sheer prurience? The point, I suggest, is the narrator's almost painterly attempt to capture as precisely as possible the complex feelings of shock, disorientation, and horrid fascination which the photographs arouse in him. Throughout the first chapter he boasts of having achieved an olympian detachment; now he finds that that detachment is specious, and that he has much more inner work to do in the way of joining the human race before he will be able to proceed with following his call.

In what follows he struggles with a variety of strategies for dealing with the horrors he feels obligated to describe. "Florentine laughter" looms large. He muses on "the equivalency of all things," and on the need to gain distance, "become irrelevant to himself." The recollection of past dreams and visions forms inner connections which help him get beyond the one-dimensional world of the "little bears." He returns again and again to the importance of the awareness of death as a precondition for transcending this one-dimensionality.

Many readers are left with the feeling that the narrator wallows in cruelty but has no sense of his own participation in the mystery of evil. For example, John Hoberman finds in Bjørneboe's work "a peculiar absence of the confessional dimension."[7]

It is clear that *Moment of Freedom*'s two sequels were afterthoughts; Bjørneboe himself may have felt that "the confessional dimension" was unfinished business. The narrator's struggle to "join the human race," to come to terms with his own participation in evil, continues throughout the trilogy. In *Moment of Freedom* he gradually moves from the bogus detachment of the first chapter to the beginnings of a genuine detachment in the last.

The importance of the final chapter has been overlooked; if there is a culminating moment of freedom, I suggest that it is here. In particular, the third paragraph from the end repays

closer attention than any of Bjørneboe's commentators seem
to have given it. What has happened to the bell-ringer? In my
view that paragraph tells us the state of mind in which the narrator has been writing the whole chapter: the reality of human
evil has been brought home to him with such immediacy as to
produce the yearning vision of the New Jerusalem with which
the chapter opens.[8] The distance this vision gives him makes
it possible to describe the horrors which fill the chapter in the
low-key, factual style he manages to adopt. But the final, ten-
dering event is one for which he has no words—a state which
he is able to accept as mercy.

❖ ❖ ❖

I cannot adequately express my gratitude to Norvik Press and
Dufour Editions for undertaking the republication of this
work. Thanks are due especially to my editors, Janet Garton
at Norvik and Tom Lavoie at Dufour.

It is likewise impossible to list all the people who have
encouraged me over the nearly thirty years since I embarked
on these translations. Some, such as Bjørneboe himself and
Kurt Hellmer, our agent who arranged the original 1975
Norton publication of *Moment of Freedom*, are long dead. Since
then I have gained a sense of being part of an ongoing community which has formed around the long struggle to get
Bjørneboe recognized in the English-speaking world. In particular I want to thank Tone Bjørneboe for her unfailing
friendship and support over the last twenty years, and
Elizabeth Schultz, Todd Bogatay, Joe Martin, and Alison
Lewis for their continued faith in the project.

And thanks above all to my husband, Erik, who intro-
duced me to Bjørneboe's work, went over the manuscript for
errors of translation, provided much indispensible help with
contacts in Norway, and has faithfully put up with all my
vicissitudes over the years.

Esther Greenleaf Mürer
June 1998

For more information about Jens Bjørneboe and his work, visit the "Jens Bjørneboe in English" online archive at http://home.att.net/~emurer

Notes

1. Wolfgang Langhoff, *Die Moorsoldaten* (Zürich: 1935); English translation: *Rubber Truncheon* (New York: E.P. Dutton, 1935). Bjørneboe recounts this incident in *Ere the Cock Crows, Jonas,* and *The Silence.* See Janet Garton, *Jens Bjørneboe: Prophet Without Honor* (Westport, CT: Greenwood Publishing Group, 1985), 5, 36 and Joe Martin, *Keeper of the Protocols: The Works of Jens Bjørneboe in the Crosscurrents of Western Literature* (New York: Peter Lang, 1996), chap. 1.

2. "Istedenfor en forsvarstale" (Instead of a defense speech), *Samlede Verker: Uten en Tråd* (Oslo: Gyldendal, 1995), 147.

3. *Samlede Verker: Drømmen og Hjulet* (Oslo: Pax, 1995), 145-6.

4. "De rettferdige og de uskyldige" (The just and the innocent), *Samlede Essays. Kultur I,* (Oslo: Pax, 1996), 71; originally published in *Norge, mitt Norge* (Oslo: Pax, 1968).

5. Martin, 51.

6. Jens Bjørneboe, interview by Odd Berset, *Morgenavisen* (Bergen), 2 January 1971. In *Samtaler med Jens Bjørneboe,* ed. Håvard Rem (Oslo: Dreyer, 1987), 145-6.

7. John Hoberman, "The Political Imagination of Jens Bjørneboe: A study of *Under en Hårdere Himmel.*" *Scandinavian Studies,* 48 (Winter 1976): 67.

8. The sun as a Christ symbol is a vestige of Bjørneboe's early involvement with the Anthroposophical system of Rudolf Steiner; all three volumes of the trilogy have quotations about the sun by German poets (Rilke, C. F. Meyer, and Goethe) as epigraphs.

THE CITIES

ONE

During the several years that I've now been a Servant of Justice, I haven't been able to avoid acquiring a certain perspective on life. The varied and wandering existence which I've led, the age I have reached, the enormous number of different kinds of people I have met; in short: the countless impedimenta of experience which I've accumulated in the course of time—these have been sifted through and sorted out over the last few years during my daily attendance in the courtroom.

I've always had an uncommon ability to adapt to the most varied milieux, regardless of poverty, wealth, language, nationality, race or religion—over large parts of the globe, from Africa to Canada, New York, Moscow, Leningrad, Paris, Naples, and London. I've met people everywhere, from the Arctic Coast to the Equator, from Montreal to the Siberian steppes; this is my world. It has often struck me as unbelievable how much a pair of human eyes can see, for I've long thought that as a young man I had already absorbed more impressions and seen far more than one man's consciousness can ever manage to work through. Within me all was chaos and darkness, turbulent and wild, sense impressions all too strong, devoid of concepts. Without concepts, of course, our impressions remain in the form of "raw experience," not subjected to the clarity, order, and discipline of thought. My life was for many, many years a long journey in the land of Chaos.

In my position as a Servant of Justice this changed for the first time, and I was able to see life spread out as a logical chessboard in large, coherent images and patterns. My presence in the courtroom, at the daily rites of justice—or better, the daily wrongs—gradually became the strength in me which brought order and meaning into the land of Chaos.

My patient attendance at the bar of injustice, my silence in the face of unrighteousness, my ability to *endure wrong*—not only my own, but also others' wrongs—was transformed, in the course of these silent years, into an uncanny power. Naturally this happened only because I never for a moment lost the ability to suffer at the sight of this all-pervasive injustice. The daily sight of it, the perennial spectacle of wrong as a principle of existence, gradually changed my whole attitude towards life. From being a pilgrim in the land of Chaos, that is: at the bottom of an unsurveyable landscape where I could see no further than to the nearest ridge, I was slowly lifted up by a kind of spiritual levitation until I saw the landscape under me—a geographical map, a map of the world, divided into continents, countries, mountains and valleys and plains, rivers and oceans.

This incredibly modest position in the courtroom, not as a member of the jury, not as an armed guard, not as a lawyer or judge, not even as a defender or reporter or witness—*not even as the most degraded, most wretched figure of all: not even as the accused!*—but as the only completely insignificant person, as a Servant of Justice, a man who carries files, sweeps floors, runs errands and fills inkwells, lays out clean paper and takes care of the judges' robes and wigs; who never expresses himself about anything, but is simply *there*—in this position, as the years went by, large and coherent pictures slowly began to form inside me.

I am a born Servant of Justice.

It's the purpose of my life to be in the courtroom while the proceedings are going on. And here in this small, dusky and somber, old-fashioned courtroom, here life has been unrolled for me again and again, the land of Chaos is eternally coming into being in here: ink, records, men's fates. Every passion, every peculiarity, the meanest and the noblest: here in the courtroom all is subject to the same eternal, imperturbable and holy injustice.

❖ ❖ ❖

I'm a Servant of Justice in Heiligenberg, in this Alpine city in this tiny principality. High mountains surround the valley where the city lies, and over the whole landscape all the houses and all the walls and fences are built of the same gray stone. The whole city is like that. The whole country. And the Palace of Justice, where I have my daily work, is no exception: it's built of the same kind of stone.

The people in this valley can hardly be said to be filled with the Holy Spirit. Within sight of the immense mountain peaks and eternal glaciers they haven't grown to greatness. They don't think clear and far-sighted thoughts. The people here, in the villages, in the valley or down at the inn where I drop in and drink my daily glasses of oblivion—they're a people without songs, without folklore, music or dance. They have their chapels, but no religion. At the same time they are—in their way—sharp, almost intelligent. They are crafty. They live in this valley, and they have mountains and eternity all around them. Now and then they think. You can see it in their eyes. Then they're doing arithmetic. They're adding or subtracting in their heads. The craftiest of all can multiply, or even divide. The people here are, as a matter of fact—yes, to tell the truth: so to speak, more or less, in their way, and to a certain degree, they are rather like lemurs.

When they read, it isn't the Kabbala or the Vedas or the Psalms they study. They read their bankbooks. Or if need be their laws—to find out what they can allow themselves to do to their neighbors. Everybody fights with everybody else, but in a strange way they stick together all the same. It's a union of lemurs. They've produced judges and even doctors, not to mention master engineers. But they don't relax by reading Dante.

As I said, they have no folklore.

All the same, they do their part to maintain the world's population and balance. They're a flock of shaggy little bears.

There is positively no innocence in them. They're capable of doing absolutely anything to their fellow man. At the same time they are mighty skiers, and in the winter they get themselves pulled up the mountainsides with steel wires, high up—whereupon they skitter down the mountainsides all the way to the bottom of the valley. This they do over and over again. They keep it up for weeks and months—up and down, up and down. And they have their joy of it, but they aren't joyful.

Of course I'm in every sense inferior to them, and when I slander them so basely it's doubtless due to a measure of envy and spite. Their useful for their purpose, but they charge me too much rent. They always con me into paying out too much of my humble salary. They all want a cut of what I earn. And I pay. They cheat me on everything—on wine, meat, cheese, on my electric bill. The tax authorities enter my income twice, so as to take more taxes from me. They put down other people's incomes under my name, since they all see it as their manifest right to get rich off others. They've been known to kill people by choice and painful methods, just to amuse themselves and pass the time. But their own courts acquit them.

Of course there are exceptions, but by and large that's the way they are.

And here in this Alpine valley I—sailor and wanderer, singer, apocalyptist and troubadour—*I,* of all people!—have become a Servant of Justice.

If I can only remember it, I shall soon tell you my name. It isn't easy to recollect, but now and then I'm on the point of calling it to mind and then it slips away again. But I have a name. That I can't hit upon it is an aftereffect of long years of wandering. Otherwise I remember a great deal.

First I shall tell about The Long Journey in the Land of Chaos. It took forty years, like the Children of Israel's wanderings in the desert.

At present I am rounding out my forty-sixth year, and my beard has turned gray.

The hour of truth has arrived.

Of course it's possible that you have to be old enough to have a gray beard before you can speak the truth. Or perhaps it's something else: that you've gotten too old to think up excuses, too old to pretend, too old to lie anymore. Here in this Alpine valley I have a prominent name, a nickname, naturally—not my right one, which I can't remember—a nickname, completely nasty and spiteful, of course—for nobody knows my real name, even if it's certainly there in the records, on yellowed and rather brittle paper, and in ink that wasn't altogether indelible, but which will still hold out for yet awhile. The main thing is that I have a prominent name in the valley, and have reached a certain age—and that the hour (or moment?) of truth has arrived. I believe it was Socrates who also built up his dialectic for his own defense in this fashion; when, after his conviction but before his execution, he was urged by his friends either to lie or to flee, then he uttered something like this:

"No," he said, "I can't do that. A man of my age and with such a prominent name!"

✧ ✧ ✧

One needs a dialectical superstructure in order to speak truly, and he knew it. One needs it in order to die as well, because these two things hang together: there's a smell of death associated with all truth, something of death's shamelessness. Falsehood likewise has its relationship to death. No one knows that better than I myself, who have lied so much. But it's a different relationship. It isn't so inexorable, because a lie can be made right again, it can be corrected with a new lie, it isn't final and absolute. But a *truth*—once it's out, then it's inexorable—a brother to death.

You are naturally curious to know what kind of man I am,

and what I look like. Well then, I'm a Servant of Justice, and therefore a man with a prominent name in the valley. For the most part they make Servants of Justice out of the kind of people who are easily noticeable, and who can't be used for anything else. That, in fact, is the point: for a Servant of Justice they need a man who is distinctive in appearance, and otherwise useless. By preference they use a nearby village idiot for the job, or a mental defective from the city who is generally unfit for work, often of good family, because he needs only one qualification—a solid and thoroughly honest character, so that he won't drink the ink or steal the toilet paper, but will take good care of the judge's robes and see that the pieces of soap are in the right place in the washroom. Because of my taciturnity I fit the image very well.

I'm of medium height, not particularly stout, but powerfully built. My face is dark, more precisely brown, and my hair is black as a crow—even if my beard, as I said, has begun to go gray. I limp a little because of an old bullet wound and a deep knife thrust (strangely enough) in the same leg. On my abdomen, under my navel, I also have a large scar. Over the years I've had three front teeth knocked out and have two fractures in my hands from long ago. On my right hand I once broke a metacarpal bone, and on my left it's the ring finger that got broken another time (on a similar occasion). The two fractures aren't so dangerous, for they've healed in the course of time, even if they're both a bit crooked. It's worse with the broken teeth, because they won't grow out again, but have to be replaced artificially, by an odontologist. The first of my teeth was knocked out a long time ago by a drunk; the second met its fate in an auto accident on a highway somewhere in France. I lost the last one during an international trades union congress in Marseilles, because some of us left the meeting and went to a brothel and drank grappa until we got into a fight with the pimps and were arrested. At the station I said I was a Servant of Justice, with the result that the police knocked out my tooth and then played soccer with me while I lay on the floor and quoted Socrates: *Don't you know that a man like me can read the future?*

Before my beard turned gray I would have been rather embarrassed to tell about this, but now the moment of truth has arrived, and there's a slight smell of death from my fingers; so today I'd be more ashamed to speak untruth than to speak truth. But I don't know if you have any picture of me yet. I've also gotten a slight paunch since I became a Servant of Justice; my clothes are sometimes rather sloppy, and I haven't had my teeth replaced properly because I've become indifferent to that sort of thing. So when I open my mouth you can see that I'm missing some teeth behind my beard. It's very obvious when I eat chicken or laugh. Although I rarely do either now.

The daily wrongs in my and the little bears' lives don't serve to encourage gaiety. In the old days, when I was a sailor and vagabond and troubadour, then I laughed often. At the same time my dress is usually fairly correct. Rather ordinary. Never elegant at any rate.

And then I wear glasses when I read. But I rarely read when people are looking, so most people know me without glasses. And I don't need them to carry a file or sweep a floor.

What else is there to tell about myself today, and about my way of life? It certainly isn't this that you're interested in: that I live by myself in one room and cook in the landlady's kitchen? No.

And then I have a number of books, but not too many. One important thing, perhaps, is that I can change myself completely, so that people hardly recognize me. I change with the weather and the wind, according to the latest court case, or what I'm reading at the moment, or how I'm dressed. Sometimes I'm without a beard, but then I let it grow out again. It only takes two or three weeks before I have a full beard.

Meanwhile I must explain what I mean by the moment of truth. I came to understand it in Spain, where I was engrossed in the fine symbolism and the sacred mysteries of bullfighting.

I shudder when I think what it means—that a man of my

age and with such a prominent nickname—

Luckily I can postpone the truth a bit, I can allow myself yet another digression. This is *my* book, and *I* decide what goes into it. Every word. I'm a Servant of Justice in the little bears' courtroom, but they're not the only ones I've known. Later on (perhaps) I will talk about another type—the ideologists. Broadly speaking I divide them into these two principal groups: the little bears and the scholastics. Almost everybody I've met belongs to one of these two varieties *of Homo consumens*, but I don't know which group is the sickest and greediest—the scholastics or the bears. The scholastics are more intelligent and more dangerous. Later I'll tell about them.

It's possible that there's a third group, perhaps less sick: the eschatologists. But I don't quite remember. If I can think of my name, then maybe that will come to me too.

At the same time I must add something about myself, in order to correct whatever imprecise, slightly skewed picture I may have happened to sketch. It's true that I've bummed around a lot, as seaman and hurdy-gurdy enthusiast, around this apocalyptic idyll and snake pit of a world, but that isn't all. It's true enough that in recent years, in my position as Servant of Justice, I etc.; but that isn't the full and complete truth, and even if every word I say will be used against me as usual, I must complete my self-portrait by saying that I also traveled around for a number of years as a well-known and respected man, in comfortable and economically independent circumstances. During that period I wrote a series of books, of which some won recognition and were translated into several languages, but which still had this singular characteristic in common that nothing they contained was particularly new or significant.

They were written in the land of Chaos, and were children of the time. Like most other books which aren't about Socrates or by Lichtenberg or Stendhal or Stirner or La Rochefoucauld or by the ancient Romans or by Swift.

Of course there's only one thing which counts when it comes to books—and that is, whether they're written on the

island of Patmos, in other words whether they've come into
being during an effusion of the Holy Spirit. Naturally not all
books can be written during a spiritual outpouring, inasmuch
as thousands of books are written outside of Patmos every
year, and inasmuch as the Holy Spirit can't possibly have
time to shed Grace on everything that's intended for print.

From the civil war following the Russian Revolution
there's a description of how the noble-minded participants
treated their prisoners: they took a prisoner and ripped his
belly open a little way, so that they could get hold of his small
intestine. This they nailed to a tree, and with white-hot bayonets—heated up in a small bonfire lit solely for the purpose—
with these glowing bayonets they forced the prisoner to run
around the tree until his small intestine, and in the best cases
part of the large as well, were wound around the tree like
thread on a spool. Then the prisoner was left hanging by his
bowels until he expired in the fresh woodland air.

I don't know whether it was the little bears who treated
the scholastics in this fashion, or whether it was the scholastics who treated the little bears thus. But judging from everything I've seen of both parties during my long journey in the
land of Chaos, either would have been capable of it.

Such a description may have a bit of the Holy Spirit in it,
because it does say something about the little bears' underlying nature.

And while we are nevertheless talking about freedom, I
must confess that I've brooded just as much over the expression Moment of Freedom as over the Moment of Truth. The
rabbi Joshua ben Josef, who was crucified in the year 33, is
quoted as saying that "the truth shall make you free," thereby
presenting freedom as a function of truth. This sounds as if it
corresponds to my experiences from the courtroom and the
bar of injustice, where it is demonstrated that un-truth makes
you un-free. After the moment of truth comes the moment of
freedom.

In my position as Servant of Justice I've naturally had
occasion to ascertain that freedom is the only thing in the

world which is even more terrifying than truth. It can only be borne under Grace and the Holy Spirit. The term "Holy Spirit" may possibly include Prometheus or Lucifer, both of whom did in their time steal light and freedom from the gods and give them to mankind.

It was a dubious gift, and among specialists there are those who think that freedom came too early, that is to say: *before* truth, so that the little bears found out that they could get away with *doing* whatever they wanted, but not that freedom can only be found in back of our illusions.

For the same reason True Grace was something the little bears could never attain, because it can't be separated from a truth which is totally unambiguous and indivisible: namely, the *perfect awareness of death.*

Of course I can never mention this sort of thing in the courtroom in my capacity as a Servant of Justice, and have therefore become a silent man in the course of time. From day to day my beard gets grayer.

If the little bears had the consciousness of death, they would be human. Amid this heap of stones and before the face of Eternity they would be filled with the Holy Spirit.

The Moment of Truth—*el momento de la verdad*—is taken from the terminology of Spanish bullfighting: the expression signifies the decisive second in which the ritual of the bull-fight has reached its turning point, in which the dance and the elegant, stylized forms are relegated to the past, and the bull-fighter aims at bringing the fight to a close. The moment of truth arrives when the fun is over, the game is ended, the man takes off his mask and the bull shall die: the truth is revealed.

El momento de la verdad is the most important turning point in all court cases—the moment which unmasks the true character of the fight; that it's ultimately a struggle of life and death. It also shows the true face of the court: in the course of the trial's phases the truth becomes clear step by step, and with every meeting with the truth there dies a lie, a hope, a wish.

A bullfight is not a sports event, but sublime, highly cultivated, ritual-aesthetic theater, and the newspaper accounts of the fights are not sports stories but art reviews—aesthetic critiques, in which the bullfighter's execution of the different phases, rituals, and steps of the drama are analyzed and praised or disparaged. The symbolic language has such a high degree of beauty and perspicuity that it needs no commentary, and the expression *"momento de la verdad"* has a manifestly archetypical depth. If one considers for a moment what it is that gives a trial its dramatic and aesthetic dynamics, one cannot but recognize that it's the *conflict,* modified from the simplest of all forms of theater—the wrestling match—to the most refined, intellectual contest, from the battle of the sexes and a clash of nerves and brains to the professional and ritual combat between ice-cold specialists in a courtroom. Without conflict there is no theater; in all genres it revolves around this: that the spectator is witness to a fight. In all the forms of justice: farce, comedy, drama, tragedy—and in such varieties of jurisprudence as operetta, opera, and musical comedy, the central motif is the same: there is someone who triumphs and someone who must die. *El momento de la verdad* arrives in the court with the same beauty and precision as in the bullfight—when the condemned is to be killed. In the courtroom *war* is the father of everything.

Every play is a hearing, a court case, and every court case is a war. The last phase is of necessity death.

At the same time one must never forget that the core of justice is injustice.

It's impossible to describe the truth of the bullfight to someone who is unacquainted with it. The sun and the blood on the sand, the shiny, bloody streamers on the animals, the rage and the savagery, the stormy, unsuspecting passion in the bull, who is subject to the man's grace and technique, his art and facility, his capacity for abstraction. The rapier which glitters in the sunshine like thought made visible, the dance steps, the turns, the ritual—and all the while the blood which trickles and drips, while the sand turns to iron and the sky to copper over the arena. All this is almost hideous, until the moment comes when the man kneels before the raging, exhausted bull, when the man is down on his knees in the sand before those horns and lifts his rapier above his head, without the animal's being able to attack him because the man has played with the bull until it is dying of rage, tired to death; because the bullfighter has *danced* the bull into impotence, until blood is coming out of its nostrils.

And then the moment, the Moment of Truth, when the man rises to the kill. Now it's the man who chases the bull.

It is the last figure in the dance.

The bullfighter and the judge, the arena and the courtroom—this temple to the necessary injustice in the world!

It's a good thing that the little bears don't know who I am, or else they would disturb me in my real work, which I do when I've discharged my last duties in the courthouse—when I've cleaned up, checked the toilet paper, hung out new towels, brushed the judge's robe, and locked up the files. After I've finished by sweeping up the bloody sawdust from the courtroom floor, I don't always go to the inn to empty my bumpers in forgetfulness of the day's injustice. It can happen that I wander straight home to console myself in another fashion. I go home to work on my opus, my enormous, colossal twelve-volume work on The History of Bestiality.

For years I've been collecting material for this work. Ever since childhood I've been doing research, saving, sorting, weeding out, setting aside, investigating, and collecting. It will be the genuine, complete, true history of the world. It will be *the* book about the true face of the little bears, their world-shaking, one and only, historic meeting with themselves. The scholastics (who of course are really bears at heart) also have their richly allotted space in the work, in the volumes on the Inquisition, revolutions, et cetera. The Thirty Years' War is a fine tassel on the scholastics' cap—although they must share the honors with the little bears here as well. I am pleased with the title:

THE HISTORY OF BESTIALITY

By

By whom?
Last night I didn't leave the Palace of Justice until five in the morning. I went through heaps of records, trying to find my name. It must be written someplace. The complete criminal proceedings must be located somewhere, and the transcript of course includes the name of the accused. It would be ridiculous to have trial records which didn't include the condemned man's name and data, and I can't possibly publish *The History of Bestiality* under a nickname. It's really an utterly laughable situation, this—that the only thing one knows about oneself is one's own nickname! And at my age!
Aside from what I remember about the long journey.

I despise the typewriter. *The History of Bestiality* will be written by hand and in thick books, exactly the way it's done in the courtroom, where everything is entered in the eternal records with pen and ink. All of my writing is a keeping of records, and behind the scientific theme you can of course glimpse the less scientific, but just as real, more metaphysical motif: the Problem of Evil.
I'm the one to write it down.
From my life I can hardly remember anything but murder, war, concentration camps, torture, slavery, executions, bombed-out cities, and the half-burned bodies of children.
I remember the bodies of German children after the fire bombs. The remains of walls, like pieces of a stage set; the children ranged on the sidewalks between them. The same thing happened in Leningrad and London and many other places, but nowhere were dead children collected with such diligence and thought and such a pious sense of order. In many places the little bears are highly inconsistent. For example in Italy, where the bears first exulted over Mussolini, then hung him up by his heels in the marketplace, and now once again have pic-

tures and books about him in all the shop windows. Hardly anything has a lasting effect on the little bears—they climb up the mountainsides and slide down again. Over and over again. Upright or on all fours, they go around scratching their flanks as if they always had vermin in their fur, and they start a new collection of twelve of everything: plates, sheets, and a few pounds of future. The little bears have always been clever, and a thousand years ago, in my real fatherland, they used to do something to their prisoners which they called "carving the bloody eagle" on them: they'd bind them with their arms around a tree trunk and cut open their backs, through the ribs and the flesh—then they'd pull out their lungs from behind. The little bears always could get things done!

Concerning the great Belgian king Leopold's operations in the Congo there are still other funny stories which occur to me now. It was a matter of getting the natives to work industriously at the harvesting of rubber. Many a time the Belgians had to take strong measures in order to get the blacks to work, since the blacks had no disposition to regular employment—and when one of the guards had to kill an unwilling man out in the field, then it was the guard's duty to bring home with him the worker's right hand, so that the authorities could keep accurate records. If a native showed insubordination, they resorted to more rigorous methods: they gathered the family together, while the rest of the villagers looked on, and thereafter they crucified the insubordinate's wife and children, whereupon they cut off the sex organs of the man himself and hung them up on a stake along with the hands and feet of the same paterfamilias. Finally they beheaded him and set the head, like a sort of dot on the *i*, way up on the point of the stake. The Belgians also carried on diligent missionary work among the blacks. After some years the Congo's population was reduced from over thirty million to only eight. In return these eight had become Christians.

That was one of the first things I heard about as a child. My father was a well-traveled man and among his other duties he also had to be the Belgian consul. He had a beauti-

ful illustrated book about King Leopold, but in this excellent
book the king was called, not Leopold, but Popold—and the
whole history of the Belgian Congo was described in detail
there. Furthermore, over the years my father received three
uncommonly handsome medals from the Belgian government for his services to the Belgian interests in my fatherland.
He kept the book about Popold not in the bookcase, but
inside a cupboard. He always spoke excellent French, my
father, and used to address me as *"enfant gâté,"* which was perhaps justified. When he died, he looked at me and said:

"You're a nice boy, but what in the world will become of you?"

That was the last thing I heard from the consul.

But now that I've come to my childhood, it's about time to
begin at the beginning of my life among the lemurs.

TWO

The world is full of stars and excrement, and in a way it's easy enough to say "begin at the beginning." But is there any "beginning?"

Beginning?

Putting words in quotation marks has a strange effect on them. Beginning is an entirely different thing from "beginning." You stick something unspeakably ambiguous, false-bottomed and hunchbacked onto a word when you put it in quotation marks. You can do it with completely unsuspecting, wholly innocent words—you could, for example, put conjunctions and prepositions in quotes, just to take the most insignificant and harmless of our brother words. Let us say that I put the words *and, on,* or *toward* in quotes. Thus: the municipal judge "and" his wife. Or: I laid the book "on" the table. One can set something loose on the world that way. One can also say: He went "toward" the city hall. Or if one were nihilistic enough, one could take the most innocent of all words, the infinitive sign, and abuse and ravish it in this fashion: it began "to" rain. Could one possibly look at the world with less enthusiasm?

When referring to the beginning, I nevertheless prefer to write "beginning." It is appropriate.

When I write "beginning" I've said what I think of the word. People for whom nothing is sacred have a tendency to put just about anything in quotation marks, simply in order to throw suspicion on the whole cosmos. That's not what I want.

There are only certain words which I mistrust. For example
"beginning."

My father was a Leo. He had a strong and forceful voice,
was powerfully built and very handsome. He was completely
white-haired, uncommonly masculine, and very fashionably
dressed. He suffered from sudden bursts of joviality, but was
otherwise a silent, morose man, deeply melancholic. He
taught me to read Tolstoy and Oscar Wilde, and he arrived at
the brink of bankruptcy the same month I was born. That was
a couple of years after the First World War, and the happy
days of the bull market had just ended. Peace had definitely
broken out, and the shipping rates on the world market sank
below the freezing point, until there was nothing left but idle
ships, depression, and unemployment. For seventeen years he
kept things going, paying off his debts, until Hitler came and
the shipping market went up again. Then he died with his
debts paid.

When I was born he was as old as I am now; but he was
already completely gray, and I only have a gray beard. He
was forty-six years old when I came into the world, and the
happy years between 1914 and 1918 couldn't last forever—in
fact they were already over, the shipping industry was
merely living on the afterswell of bygone happiness. Simultaneously with me, in the year of Our Lord 1920, depression
came into the world in earnest—and it was the death of him,
not a sudden and merciful death, but as I said a death by liquidation of debts, through bad times and laid-up ships, death
by slow torture, an agony of a death. He died bravely, with
his bowler hat at an angle, with his walking stick with its silver ferrule, with his Egyptian cigarette in his mouth—and
with a gray, curly, devil-may-care lock hanging down on his
forehead. But it was a façade. He died as a businessman—as
a martyr to capitalism.

It has often struck me that he wasn't alone in that: more
than any other group it is the businessmen who suffer from
money's cursed dominance; why aren't *they* the ones, *they*
above all others, who become the real socialists? In reality

nobody has less to lose, nobody suffers so cruelly, so inhumanly, so devilishly much from money's stranglehold.

Every time I see a businessman, my heart flows over with sympathy and compassion: I know his sorrows, his need, his insecurity—I know his anxiety and his dread. I become a real syndicalist, a fervent anarcho-communist, every time I look into a businessman's eyes. For I know of his deep, deep despair, his suspicion that he has built his life on sand. I learned that from my elegant, handsome, and virile father. I know what it means not to dare to claim deductions on one's income tax for fear of coming too far down on the tax assess ment list and thereby jeopardizing one's chances for new credit. Broad-minded liberal and republican that he was, because of him I became a syndicalist when I was still quite young, out of sympathy for the capitalist.

It's a good thing the little bears don't know about this. If they realized that I'm an anarcho-syndicalist, they'd kill me. But as a Servant of Justice I've learned to keep quiet—about this as about almost everything else.

I never saw my father sit down at the table in his shirtsleeves. He wore pince-nez, and a stiff single collar or a silk scarf around his neck. Perhaps I've gotten senile up here in the valley—but in those days there *were* honest businessmen, people in good faith—people "of the old school," as they said in my childhood a hundred years ago. He was one of them. As I've indicated: he never got rich. But in an inexplicable, magical way he *seemed* rich. At a restaurant he'd leave hardly any tip, but the waiters would follow him to the door and bow him out.

For many years after the First World War we children had to listen at every meal to his account of the starvation in Germany and Austria after the war, while the blockade lasted. The minute we opened our mouths to eat, the description of the undernourished children would begin, undernourished even before they came into the world.

"In Vienna," he'd say, "there were children born without any skin."

It was in some unaccountable way *our* fault that we sat there and ate our fill.

I'll never forget his voice. It was deep and rough, with uncommonly clear diction, and a force like a thunderstorm. He had a lion's roar. He could get furious over little things—carelessness, waste, or lack of form.

To this day I still have terrifying dreams in which he has risen from the dead and is coming to see what I've done with my life. But when I wake up, I know that if he could know about my position as a Servant of Justice, he'd take off his pince-nez and laugh. He'd polish his glasses with his silk handkerchief and shake his head. Then he'd say:

"Oh yes, *mon cher ami de la vérité*, you know how to put it!"

He was completely unmusical and knew nothing about grammar, but he spoke a flawless and melodious French. His rage over trifles was disquieting, whereas he took bigger catastrophes and generally more serious things with a surprising calm, almost with humor. He slept in an ice-cold bedroom, because that's what they'd done at the English boarding school where he'd grown up. His equanimity in the face of things which might have irritated others was dumbfounding.

When I was expelled from school at the age of seventeen, I went straight down to his office to tell him the news, and I expected a volcanic eruption.

"I hope you come home to dinner," he said.

A couple of years earlier he had been called in by the police because I was suspected of auto theft. By the time he got there, however, they had cleared up the case and found the culprit.

"How could you think of suspecting my son?" he said.

The policeman smiled deferentially and with relish:

"I'm sorry to say it's because your son was stinking drunk, Herr Consul!" said the policeman, loudly enough so that everybody in the office could hear—including a couple of chance visitors, one of whom later told me about the incident.

There was complete silence for a few seconds.

"My son has been drinking since he was twelve," said the

consul. "In that he takes after me. Good day, gentlemen."

He himself was a man of great sobriety, and I certainly don't get my intemperance from him. He never mentioned to me that he'd been at the police station in that connection.

But these are scattered traits from special occasions. From daily life I remember almost nothing but his melancholy and his rage. That dreadful voice which often came so suddenly, and was a thunderclap. The gray eyes with the carnivorous glint. The long, slender and lovely hands, which could bend a five-øre piece. The silent, matter-of-fact contempt.

I could tell a lot of bad about him, and a lot of good. But what interests me about this man who was my father are the traits which lie beyond evil and good.

He was utterly indifferent to physical pain. He had the root of an eyetooth filled without an anesthetic. Innumerable times I've seen him take a live wasp between his fingers and hold it like that while he opened the window to set "the poor beast" free. Once when he fell over a cliff on the way home from a sail and smashed the bridge of his nose, he didn't say a word about it. He didn't even go to a doctor, but assumed that the nose would knit naturally of itself. When it didn't turn out that way, the fracture had to be broken open again a few weeks later. This also happened without anesthesia. But it was too late. For the rest of his life he looked like a heavyweight boxer—which became him splendidly, as it gave his face an indescribable expression, a mixture of brutality and elegance. It accented his masculine distinction in an amazing way, gave his melancholy still another touch of something devil-may-care and reckless.

Among his other intangible assets he kept a letter he had once received from two girlfriends. It had no other address than: To the handsomest man in town. The letter got there without difficulty, but it belongs in the story that this wasn't a large city, only a rather ordinary coastal town in my original homeland. Nevertheless he was pleased with it.

One time he caught us in the kitchen, eating one of the simpler delicacies of that time, so-called twelve-øre cake. It

wasn't that which was so bad, even if eating cake was naturally objectionable in itself. But what called forth the catastrophe, the thunderstorm, the typhoon of rage, was not the
twelve-øre cake per se, but the circumstance that we had put
butter on it. It happened instantaneously. The air cracked.
The house shook, women, cats, and dogs fled through doors
and windows, while the children still sat there, glued to the
walls in mortal dread, white-faced and wide-eyed. His voice
filled the big wooden house, burst out of the windows, down
into the courtyard and the garden on one side, out onto the
street and into the neighbors' houses on the other. It brought
traffic to a halt.

I've often thought what a mercy it was for him and others
that he departed this earthly madhouse before the Teutonic
occupation took place. He would have died of rage at the
sight, but he would have dragged others with him in his fall,
he would have called forth reprisals and mass executions.
With his rage and his boundless contempt for pain and mutilation he would have provoked disaster even as the Teutons
were making their heroic entry into our small, thoroughly
antagonistic coastal town.

But he didn't live to see the day when the Teutons
ascended into our underdeveloped region to murder Jews
and eat cake; that he was spared. Typically enough he pre-
dicted it time after time. It occurs to me now that he may
have been clairvoyant in this respect. He said it innumerable
times: "This fellow What's-his-name, this Hitler, my boy, he's
leading the world into a new war, *but I won't live to see it.*"

Now and then he spoke English. The first time I came
home totally drunk, at the age of fifteen, I think—he looked at
me with a certain astonishment. When he spoke, it wasn't in
Norwegian, not even in French, he fell back on the language
of boyhood and boarding school:

"My boy, you have got your sufficiency."

He loathed the Teutons with an almost pathological,
inborn repugnance. The only sentence I ever heard him say

in German was, "Ich habe kein Vertrauen zu den Dreck-
säuen." Once in a boardinghouse in Antwerp at the beginning of the century a Teutonic fellow-lodger had made off
with his only suit. But that can hardly have been the whole
reason. Naturally the business with Belgium and "a piece of
paper," as Kaiser Wilhelm had called the non-aggression
pact, played a certain role. The occupation of Belgium had
had indubitable points of likeness with the earlier Belgian col-
onization and syphilisation of the Congo. Still, the thing
which incensed him most of all wasn't their atrocities, I think,
but the Teutons' enormous greed, their senseless *haben-haben*
mentality, their craving for other people's food, others'
money, others' land, others' women, combined with their
peculiar moralizing self-righteousness: *Gott-mit-uns*. Because
of my father's abhorrence of them I myself, in another period
of my long journey in the land of Chaos, later came to study
this people more intensively than any other, I learned their
heavy, grammar-intoxicated language almost to perfection, I
sojourned long and often in Germany, and I studied their literature thoroughly. A good deal of what I know today about
the little bears I can thank Teutonia for. Then when they—
after my father's death—came to my little fatherland, it was
still, despite his teaching, an almost numbing shock to see
their appetite at close hand: in a few hours they ate up all the
cake, all the butter, all the chocolate, and all the pork in the
city. Pork was their greatest joy on earth.

Their most frequently used swearwords, "Schwein" and
"Sau," are not really swearwords at all, but pet names. The
pig is their sacred animal, their Apis. Their occupation of
Belgium was Gothic through and through, and consisted to a
staggering degree of "confiscating," eating, and killing. My
father never got tired of telling stories about their insatiable
greed—and I think that almost without knowing it himself, he
really put his finger on a central trait in the Teutonic national
soul. Mozart's countrymen are not in themselves any crueler
or more brutal than other people, and in *The History of Bestiality* I want to stress this—but they're plagued by their greed

for things, food and money to such a degree that they see it as
their manifest right to exterminate whole population groups,
whole nations, in order to satisfy their innate hunger for other
people's property. You can hardly find any other people,
with the possible exception of the Americans, who admire
wealth and money so violently. Today, many years after New
Teutonia and America won the war against Europe and the
Jews, this is plainer than ever before. It's food they want, endless, indescribable mountains of food. They want to eat the
world, and in order to do it they must have all the money and
all the things, all the cars and all the fur coats on earth. They
are absolutely not militarists, and if they were allowed to own
everything in the world without fighting for it, they'd prefer it
that way. They want. The world is my breakfast.

I'll tell more about this when I get further along with my
description of life among the lemurs.

When I was seventeen years old I was accused and convicted by the lemurs of a sexual offense, and could thereupon
start life in earnest. The case wasn't so deplorable as it
sounds, and the victim unfortunately got away from me alive.
She was half a year younger than I. At that time I was living
in another town because I'd been expelled from all the public
schools and had sought refuge at a private institution. On
grounds of advancing immorality I was finally kicked out
there too. Meanwhile my father had to appear in court as my
guardian, because the accused was legally a minor. He came
on the train, and I stood on the platform waiting to meet him.
My heart lay safe and sound down in my pants, and I was in
no condition to talk when he got off the train with his suit-
case, his walking stick, and his bowler hat.

Without a word we went to the hotel. In the room he
didn't speak either, but rang for the chambermaid and
ordered two bottles of soda and two glasses. She brought
them while he was washing his hands and blotting his face
with his dry, spicy eau de cologne. Then he filled both glasses
with whiskey and soda and gave me one of them:

"A ta santé, mon cher monsieur!"

We drank. Then he took off his pince-nez and looked at me, friendly and twinkling, man to man. Out of sheer democracy and *gemütlichkeit* he spoke Norwegian.

"My boy, is this your first affair with women?"

Masculine frivolity shone from him, brotherhood, shamelessness, and satisfaction: his youngest son, the fruit of his old age, was become a man. He was uncontrollably jolly, gave me Turkish cigarettes and several whiskeys-and-soda. He said I ought to have informed him sooner, so that we might have handled the case better, but what was done was done. I was shocked and appalled, indignant at his frivolity, myself, I'd taken the matter so seriously that I'd planned to run away to England and stay there forever, end up in the colonies, or go under in Shanghai. It was on this occasion that he declared that I spoke French *"comme une vache espagnole"*—like a Spanish cow. In reality he was deathly ill at this point, and he died half a year later. That was one of the last times I saw him out of bed. He was very pale, and the curly silver lock hung damply down over his broad forehead. He was probably in great pain, and perhaps that was also why he drank so much more whisky than usual. He stayed in the town for a couple of days, talked with the lawyer and took me along to a jeweller's, where he bought something for my mother. He confessed that he had lied to her, had said that he was going to a meeting in the capital. I've never seen him so cheerful several days in a row. I often think that he knew he was dying, and that it was this which put him in such exuberant spirits—the thought that he would escape meeting Teutonia on the warpath of righteousness? She was already out to save the world from the poisonous monster of Communism.

The same summer I was there. Teutonia was marching. Even on the whorehouses in Hamburg it said JUDEN SIND UNERWÜNSCHT. Clip-clop, clip-clop, boot heels and pavement. Spirits were high. I remember absolutely nothing but brothels and the clatter of metal sole-protectors. Thrifty and industrious. Obedient, joyous, and thankful unto the mass grave. *Am deutschen Wesen wird die Welt genesen.*

When I said *guten Tag* or *guten Morgen,* the grateful
German people answered as with one voice: *Heil Hitler, sagen
wir bei uns!* It's always been a miracle that precisely these
sanctimonious, obedient, righteous, and thrifty people are so
insanely *lewd.* Today, after so many years' wanderings and
incursions, I'm naturally aware that all peoples, from Eskimos
and Swedes to Tierra del Fuegans and Americans, are lewd
whenever they get a chance. But all the same the Teutons are
lewd in a lewder way. It has something to do with their
beloved animal and their pet names, with *Schwein, Sau, Ferkel,*
et cetera—a kind of deep, pink, Teutonic affinity with the pig,
they're lewd in the same way the hog eats out of the trough,
without cheer—but in wild sorrow and pain because they're
Teutons, and haven't yet been allowed to eat the whole
world. They've only been happy one single time in their history—that was during Hitler's palmy years as master general:
the years from 1936 to 1943 were their happy time, when the
country could wallow in other people's money and pork
roasts. Although today it looks as if Teutonia is in the midst of
an attack of gestation madness. What is Germania about to
bring forth? A new currency, twice as strong? Maybe? During
one of my wanderings, back in my days as a hurdy-gurdy
enthusiast and vagabond, I happened to be there on the
country's new birthday, when New Teutonia was born: I was
there during the very *Währungsreform* incarnate, when the new
mark saw the light of day, when it even at the moment of
birth surpassed the Swiss franc and became just as divine,
miraculous, invincible, and gigantically steel-hard as the dollar. It was a holy moment for the life of the national soul; now
it was possible to earn money: life once more had a meaning.
In the very second that the first new mark-note left the first
bank, in that very second *Germany won the Third World War!*

This—giving them money—is the greatest crime America
has committed against Europe: one day we'll all be eaten up
by Schulze and Meyer and Beck.

❖ ❖ ❖

Oh, Jesus Maria, my perforated memory!

I have a brain like a Swiss cheese, an Emmenthaler. If I could only remember! I'm not so worried about my name and identity and address. What's so horrible is all the *things,* the facts, everything I've seen, been a blood witness to, all the things I used to *know!* You know how it is: you wake up in the morning and you've dreamed infinities, but—as you try to remember the dreams—they crumble, fall into scraps and shreds, dissolve and are lost. The whole thing threatens to sink back into the land of Chaos, where it obviously comes from. But I know that my whole consciousness, my very existence, depends on regaining my memory. Without memory there's no continuity, no reality, no perspective on my life, no *I am.* I lie in sweat and darkness, half-awake, feverish, dreaming, surrounded by scraps of pictures that once were whole. I can't describe how I fight to regain consciousness, to escape going under and being lost among the little bears. I fight like a drowning man. At the same time my memory is enormous. I remember boots and uniforms, the inconceivably disgusting national songs: *Ich hatt' einen Kamaraden...* tramping and bellowing, the mighty enormous yell *Deutschland erwache!* Why should it be *me* who remembers that?

That year my father died.

I remember infinitely many other things about him too. The parties he gave were altogether too expensive. Live oysters imported from America, and bottles of red wine which he uncorked halfway before tempering them. Really great vintages. And the rage which filled him for several days before a party, and which lasted right up until he appeared in the kitchen, five minutes before the guests' arrival, to get someone to polish the little silver matchbox that he always used. From that moment his wrath was gone, and he was gay and cheerful when he received the guests. All this lasted until some time before the war, before his illness made him completely bedridden.

Up here in my Alpine valley I go around thinking about that. I've looked at myself in the mirror to see if I resemble

him, but I don't—not in the usual sense at any rate. He was
taller and white-haired, he gave an impression of being fair
despite everything. I'm just swarthy. Considerably smaller,
with hair black as charcoal and a beard which also looks
black despite the gray streaks. And always in dark clothes,
too. Often in the black suit which is so common in this valley
and this town, because we think that's the most proper, and
because it's been like that since days of old. Or now and then
in a dark brown leather jacket and dark pants, when I'm
sweeping up the bloody sawdust from the floor. No, I don't
look like him. Only when I stand naked in front of a mirror
do I look like him. But then it's in an impersonal, purely masculine way: I resemble him the way one old man resembles
another. Besides, I'm swarthy and dark-skinned, due to the
air and the sunshine up here in the mountains. The sun burns
people to a deep tan, sometimes black as gypsies. Ah, my
blond Germanic brothers, how can I ever forget you! Or as
rabbi Joshua said: *How long am I to bear with you?*
    Oh, this most vital, strongest and sickest and maddest
nation in Europe, these people who have spread the monstrous lie about themselves that it was *nazism* which ate six
million Jews—and who are now trying to convince the world
that it was an abstract idea and not themselves, not the
Teutons, who killed them—that the Jews were killed by a concept, by an ideology, and not by human beings, not by the
same Schulze and Meyer and Beck who will eat us yet again.
I must somehow manage to begin at the beginning, although
there isn't any beginning.
    Shall we begin in a brothel in Hamburg?
    Or in Goethe's house in Weimar? With Hölderlin or with
Julius Streicher? I have the right to do this, because nobody
has loved Germania as I have. There's still nobody who loves
this country as I do. The real reason why I live up here in the
Alps is probably to have Teutonia within range, within my
horizon: There isn't another country in the world where virtu-
ally everything is for sale. Nowhere on earth where everything
is money in the same way. It's the country of checkbooks and

bank notes, where people boil their mothers down for soap, where everything is business. It's one big whorehouse.

The better I've learned to know Germania, the more I understand the necessity of East-Germania.

After they die Germans go to the DDR.

The DDR is Germany's bad conscience. It's a place where no German can sell pornography, buy stocks, speculate in real estate, earn money on Verdun, sell his grandmother. It's a place where Germans are forced to do what for them is worse than death: *to be poor*. If a DDR hadn't been set up, then today Teutonia would have been worse than under Hitler.

East Germany is their only feeling of pain, the only thorn in the flesh of this overfed, overnourished, elephantiasis-ridden people—this sick, deathly sick people—too healthy, too vital and sick unto death.

It was my first meeting with the land of Mozart, with holy Teutonia, our mother—Hölderlin's and Walther von der Vogelweide's mother. Ah, the sweetness of the first meeting! Even in the whorehouses in Munich entry was forbidden to Jews—not because of any official directive, but because of the whorehouses' love for the Führer, because of the proprietresses' devotion to Third Reich morality. No Jewish seed was to be spilled on a Teutonic brothel floor.

As you know, a street in a German red-light district looks like a great big urinal, a sort of prison row with the same comforts of home as a good old-fashioned concentration camp. There's iron and order and guards, and you look around for electrified barbed wire. It's missing. Instead you find officers' boots and ladies with whips. Actually it's comical, and it's amusing that the little bears can be so inventive.

Oh, vé, war sind verschvunden allu minu jar,
is min leben getreumet, oder was es war?

Alas, where have all my years disappeared,
has my life been a dream, or was it real?

I stood there as a child in a street of brothels, knowing my verses of Walther von der Vogelweide—not to mention Nietzsche. He got his syphilis in a brothel, so far as I know—and at the same time began to smoke hashish as well. And what would Teutonia have been without her great, narcomaniacal syphilitics and paralytics? The concentration camps are descended not from Nietzsche, but from *Wagner*—and Nietzsche knew what was coming. He sensed it between the bordello and the madhouse, on that road where so many good thoughts are thought. Whatever would Germania have been without syphilis? Heine, Hugo Wolf.... Or Europe, for that matter: Maupassant, Baudelaire.... What on earth would our beloved, stinking, beautiful Europe have become without our dope fiends, drunkards, homosexuals, consumptives, madmen, syphilitics, bed-wetters, criminals, and epileptics? Our whole culture was created by invalids, lunatics, and felons.

There isn't one normal person who has done a useful or lasting thing: it was the normal ones who built the slave camps in both Germany and Russia.

I know what I'm talking about. To search for a meaning in this lemurian chaos is to look for a needle in a haystack.

I've gotten embroiled in one of those endless discussions with the bell ringer from St. Anne's church.

The bell ringer is indisputably a man of intelligence, and he keeps it hidden for the sake of his reputation. The truth is that he's an old fighter from the days of the Spanish Civil War. We meet every evening down at the inn "Zum Henker," where we drink our daily glasses of solace and oblivion. Almost every time I go there to desensitize myself I have difficulty choosing what drink to seek repose in. I'm constantly having to commit myself all over again as to whether I'll get drunk on kirsch or on Italian red wine—or once in a long while on the excellent white wine from Alsace. The hard sharp cherry brandy has its characteristic, immediate effect, and makes me thoughtful and wise, balanced, perceptive, and lucid—unless I drink too much and have to be taken home by the bell ringer. Red wine puts me into a more lyrical, sensitive, poetic mood, and I never think about *The History of Bestiality* when I've quenched my thirst on red wine.

White wine is something I drink almost only on foehn days, when people in this town and valley are more than usually insane, and when the surgeons don't do operations at the hospitals because the failure rate is twice as high as on normal days. When the foehn has blown awhile, you can see the glaciers up in the mountains turn yellow; that's the dust of the Sahara blowing straight up over the sea from Africa. For that matter they've found this Sahara dust way up in Copenhagen, not far from my homeland. These foehn days are often terribly nerve-wracking, and on such days the judges here in our gray stone city under the mountains mete out sentences of nearly twice the usual length. Half of all crimes of violence, the ones of an emotional nature, that is such as unpre meditated murder, *crimes passionels*, wife-beating, child-battering, and the increasingly widespread cruelty to animals and murder of domestics—occur on these few foehn days every year, and if the delinquent can prove that he committed the act on such a day, when the temperature can rise as much as eighty, ninety degrees in half an hour, he can count on the court's understanding and lenience. Provided that he isn't also *sentenced* on a foehn day. The result, of course, is that the cleverest of the little bears consciously and systematically postpone their crimes of violence until these days, but there's nothing to be done about that. As little bears we are all subject to the same legal process, as our highly esteemed judge likes to say in his summing up.

On such days I drink my white wine, which is unique in that it, to a greater degree than any other drink, directly and immediately deadens the central nervous system. The bell ringer drinks the same; and when the foehn whistles through the mountain passes and down into the streets, and people take off their winter coats and go outside in their shirtsleeves—then there we are, sweaty and peaceful, with our short-cropped beards, sitting inside the inn on the timeworn stools with our wine glasses before us on the ancient table of blackened wood. We smoke our pipes or our bent and crumpled Virginia cigars and speak together in low voices of soothing things, such as war, torture, politics, et cetera.

This time we were drinking kirsch, and got onto more exciting subjects. We were talking about the soul, whether it's immortal and if so, does it wander through the ages.

It goes without saying that an old soldier from the Eleventh Brigade, or *Brigada Internacional,* as he always calls it—or simply "the Brigade"—it goes without saying that he, as an old revolutionary and fighter in Spain, could never have become bell ringer at St. Anne's church without some hard inner battles and self-conquests. That he's a staunch eschatologist and apocalyptist doesn't make it any easier—either for himself or for his superiors. But he almost always keeps it hidden and rarely shows what he thinks. Only when he's really drunk do you notice that he's a sincerely believing Christian, and that now, after many years, he's become reconciled with the church—even if he doesn't view the clergy so kindly. He still regards priests as "swine," but he doesn't think this should affect his philosophical convictions, because that would be confusing the person with the cause.

On this day we were still sitting over our third kirsch, when I happened to say something about the little bears' consciousness—something derogatory about its nature and origin.

The bell ringer put on his glasses and looked at me sharply.

"Even the most pitiful little remnant, the most atrophied and idioticized remainder of an ordinary feeble-minded consciousness is a greater miracle than the mountains and the stars," he said decidedly. He waved at our *Serviertochter,* and a bottle of kirsch was brought to the table.

"Even the most envenomed theological consciousness, even the most paranoid dialectical-Marxist consciousness is a phenomenon greater than the solar system and the Atlantic Ocean."

He stared defiantly at me through his spectacles, with the revolutionary's peculiar arrogance.

"Or the merchant's consciousness!" said I: "All this is fore-ordained by that bit of inflamed and rotting matter which has produced consciousness."

"My friend," said the bell ringer: "My friend, you talk as if you'd completely forgotten science's little multiplication table. Matter producing non-matter?"

"Excuse me," I said; "in this case I have the multiplication table on my side."

"You're forgetting the very basis of all ordered and scientific thinking," he replied, less arrogant now: "The basis of all articulated, i.e. non magical thinking is the so-called causality. The law of cause and effect. Nothing arises from nothing. Consciousness is the most prodigious source of energy we know of, and it's natural to ask where it comes from. Everything else in the world has an origin and a cause, but consciousness as energy, as pure power, is supposed to have arisen without a corresponding reason? It of all things on earth is supposed not to have any origin? No, my friend, I don't believe that the brain, three pounds of porridge and water, can produce a power which has manifested its effects in such things as cybernetics, moon rockets, and the utterly laughable hydrogen bomb—which for all its uselessness still represents a significant accumulation of energy. Pass the bottle!"

He was making me furious, but I gave him the bottle and said: "Energy equals mass. Matter and energy are the same thing."

"No," said he; "intellectual energy falls completely outside this. Energy in the physical sense can be converted to mass, and mass to energy, because it's the same thing. But mass can't be converted to consciousness, not to anything outside itself. The characteristic thing about intellectual energy is that it stands outside physical energy. Physical energy can't manipulate itself from outside and guide itself, only consciousness can deliberately influence natural forces. And consciousness can only come from consciousness. If one believes that consciousness is the only known exception to the law of causality, and that consciousness, i.e. intellectual energy, in contrast to other kinds of energy can come from nothing, then one believes in fairy tales, and has rejected all coherent thinking."

Now I had him in a corner with his back against the wall, so first I emptied my glass and slowly filled it again. Then I said:

"Proof of God?"

I felt like telling him that he ought to stay home in St. Anne's church and ring his bells instead of talking about things he didn't understand, but I didn't dare because he was so wrought up.

"No," he said, "not proof of God, but proof of consciousness. When you observe consciousness, then you simply demonstrate that there is consciousness—and when you observe energy, you demonstrate energy. That's all. Otherwise you believe in miracles—that is, in a breach of the law of causation."

I felt more like talking about Spanish bordellos or about methods of execution; but it was impossible to stop him, so the discussion is still going on, and he sticks to his point: that consciousness is a unique and decisive characteristic of the little bears' makeup. He also counts cats and dogs, pigs and monkeys as partially conscious beings, only not to such a high degree as the bears—even if consciousness in this species as well can vary from individual to individual.

So these discussions too, along with all the liquor they entailed, helped to chaoticize and delay my labors on my life-work. *The History of Bestiality* lay there from day to day, untouched and uncontinued—but at the same time both theme and material gain in suspense when they're combined with the problem of consciousness, and when the little bears' actions are seen in the light of this.

But it was the *third* factor which interfered most strongly with my work, and stopped it completely. The most shocking thing was that this last had to do with the judge's person and intellectual status. I'm thinking about the scandalous things which have happened in this town of late, and which have become a source of anguish for us all.

There's hardly anyone whom I esteem and respect so highly as the judge. Not because I admire his decisions; they're as miserable as anyone else's, and it has to be like that so that injustice can take its course. I admire him for his personal integrity, his subjective morals, and his way of life. And I was the first to discover the scandalous things that were going on.

Through years of wielding a broom and dustcloth in the courtroom, and not least through my job of keeping the wig and robe completely dust-free, I've developed into a keen observer.

I noticed one day during the trial of Polynari that the judge was occupied with something else. He had something hidden inside the protocol that he was completely engrossed in. He sat there through all the witnesses' testimony, through the speech of the prosecution and that of the defense, only pretending to follow them. He let them go on, but he wasn't listening, he was deep in something he had hidden between the pages of the protocol.

It was impossible to see what he was so engrossed in, but it was clear that it absorbed him no end. At the same time he played his role as judge perfectly, and it was only I who noticed

Only when the stream of words from the prosecutor, the defender, the witness, or from the defendant himself stopped for a moment would he look up, apparently sharp and awake and observant; but to me who had seen him in court thousands of times it was obvious that his eye was glassy and vacant. He was occupied with something else, something which I couldn't see, and which lay between the pages of the record.

The horrible thing was that he continued this day after day during the trial, which was not only a matter of life and death for Polynari himself, but which also involved the fate of his wife and children. That otherwise immaculate, conscientious judge—good husband and father and keen, nay outstanding jurist; amateur gardener, alpinist, trout fisherman; but above all the precise and thorough professional—wasn't present with his thoughts, and when he pronounced the awful judgment I know that he had no basis for the sentence. Even as he said the words: *The court hereby determines!*—even *then* his look was absent, as if his eyes were seeking the things he had hidden in the protocol. Even the prosecutor in the case was appalled by the sentence.

The next case he conducted in the same manner. The minute he'd taken his place on the bench he began to look between the pages of the record, and several of those present noticed that something was different from usual—even if I was the only one who realized that he had something hidden in his book, and that he simply wasn't following the proceedings any longer. I could see it because I was the only one in the room with no intellectual task to fulfill.

It was terrifying to witness it, and finally I stole up behind the judge's chair and cast a glance over his shoulder. He was much too preoccupied to be able to notice anything, and I didn't believe my own eyes when I saw what he was doing. The same night I stayed at the Palace of Justice until late in the evening, and I opened the door of the judge's personal locker. I've always been clever with locks.

I took out his book and opened it. At once I found the pictures which lay stuck in between the pages, quite large photographs. And for a moment I had the dizzy feeling that it isn't true what one sees. The world stood still for a moment.

I won't describe in detail what I saw.

But the judge's pictures were such that even an old brothel-owner from Buenos Aires would have blushed and turned away.

Never in my life have I seen the like of those pictures— and I've seen quite a lot. They were so swinish in their inventiveness that I first had to push them away before I could go on looking at them. It was terribly painful, too, because I knew the judge's wife and his grown children, two girls and a boy. I always greeted them with affection and respect when I met any of them. As a Servant of Justice ought to do, and as gradually becomes second nature to him.

There were two sorts of pictures: the one category only with people—the other with people and animals. But the most horrible part of the whole thing was that the people, at least quite a number of them, were inhabitants of the town, well-known and often prominent citizens. This was true chiefly of the older people in the photographs, while the young ones, often mere children, seemed unfamiliar to me.

The first picture I saw was of a very young girl, around fifteen years old, pictured in an unmentionable situation with a large dog which had its paws on her shoulders. Altogether there were quite a number of young people in the pictures, and most of them were around fourteen or fifteen, both boys and girls.

As for the prominent citizens, some were shown in such undescribable situations—with children, with animals and with each other—that I have no desire to discuss them in detail just now, even if I know that I must.

I'll only mention for now that the dean of the cathedral figured frequently in the swinish collection. Likewise the police chief was photographed in an unmentionable situation with a boy. But perhaps the most embarrassing thing was that the judge himself was in three of the pictures, each time in a situation which was contrary to nature. Of the others who had had themselves photographed under similar circumstances I can name the industrialist, Director Kuhnert, one of the leading men in the country's textile industry and chairman of the Skiers' Association; also Herr Staibli, a highly respected man who for years now has been president of the Heiligenberg Commercial Bank. It was likewise extremely embarrassing that the collection included two photographs—obscene to the utmost even in this context—of the popular American ambassador, Mr. L. L. Leonhardt. Finally there were also a couple of pictures of a fat gentleman, a stranger, bald and with a mustache, who was making a naked girl bend over while he amused himself shamelessly with her from behind.

It was for the most part the same children who recurred in the pictures, six or seven girls and boys around the age of confirmation. The big dog, a great Dane, belonged to the dean, I'm sorry to say, and was very easy to recognize because it's the only one of its breed in this town.

As a longtime Servant of Justice I of course shouldn't be
surprised at anything, and as a wanderer, sailor, and troubadour in my earlier years I should naturally be familiar with
everything human. But you have to know the conditions in
this Alpine city to understand my horror: the city is Calvinist
and extremely strict in its view of morality. The people here
have always despised and looked down on the neighboring
canton, which is Catholic, on grounds that Catholics are
lewd—which they are, of course, just like Protestants.
Calvinists, meanwhile, are supposed to be an unusually pietis-
tic and moral group—and I must state here that, aside from
Mr. Leonhardt and the fat gentleman, every one of those pictured belonged to the city's parish council. All were respected
citizens and diligent churchgoers. Well, of course there's
nothing new or sensational about distinguished husbands and
fathers in their fifties and sixties going in for lewd pleasures.
And it's certainly no sensation that the U.S. ambassador also
took part in the orgies. Sexual excesses have always been
very common in the diplomatic corps and among statesmen
in general, which is of course due to their frequent journeys
and long stays abroad, along with their uncontrolled access to
the taxpayers' money as an expense account. Even among
British, Soviet, and Canadian diplomats there have been
extraordinarily embarrassing incidents in recent years, and
for every scandal which comes to public notice there are naturally hundreds of undiscovered, but just as scandalous,
affairs. And among German, French, Italian, and South
American diplomats and cabinet members sexual scandals
are so common that no newspaper will even bother to print
them up for its readers. Of course it's been like that since the
time of Nebuchadnezzar. After all, even King David committed shameless acts in this sphere.

Doubtless the only new thing about these photographs in
the judge's file was the unusually perverse fantasy they testi-
fied to—the mixture of pederastic and sodomitic inclinations,
which one would hardly have expected of the members of
the city's parish council. Besides, there's something dubious

and suggestive about photographing so much of it. It's also indicative of lowered moral standards to use minors in this fashion. Furthermore both *crimen bestialitatis* and pederasty, not to mention relations with minors in general, are punishable offenses here in this Calvinistic land.

As a Servant of Justice I ought to have told myself that from a philosophical standpoint there's neither anything evil nor anything new in this—and the whole thing only confirms my previous view of life: that when all is said and done the little bears are and always will be little bears, whether they belong to the parish council or not whether they're diplomats or deans. Seen against the background of my historical-philosophical work, the little bears can busy themselves with considerably worse things—such as flaying children alive, poking out their eyes or crushing their fingers. They've often done such things.

Just now we up here in the Alps have been receiving rather extensive shipments of little children burned and ravaged by war, maimed and blinded children from a distant part of the world. (One may naturally ask oneself whether it's that part of the world which is distant from us, or whether it's we who are distant from *it*.) Alpine licentiousness is nothing to get hung up on. On the contrary it's fine that the little bears have those kinds of interests at the expense of more harmful ones.

But the fact is, I *didn't* think this way that evening as I stood there alone in my beloved Palace of Justice looking at the judge's collection of photos. I felt outrage and despair. My affection and esteem for the judge and his family was shaken, my respect for the dean and the police chief was crippled, everything seemed utterly lemurian. My hand trembled as I held the picture of the girl and the dog, and I pushed all the photographs away.

Then I went and opened my private locker. I removed the rag covering the scrub bucket and took out a bottle of kirsch which I keep there. I drank a big slug out of the bottle and put it back in its place, locked the door of the locker. The liquor gave me back some of my hard-won equanimity, the

balance which it's taken me so many years to acquire. Then I
went rapidly through all the pictures, around twenty of them
in a rather large format. The judge's degradation I couldn't
look at. The next one showed the dean and a girl, barely
beyond puberty, whom he was biting in the breast while he
carefully deflowered her with a large thick middle finger.
They were all of the same sort. Director Kuhnert was mostly
pictured with boys and girls simultaneously, the judge several
times in an unmentionable fashion. Ambassador Leonhardt's
activities were such that I don't want to talk about them. I felt
perplexed and uncertain, not knowing what a Servant of
Justice ought to do with such a find. It involved my superior
and a number of persons who were socially above me, and it
would certainly be most proper to ignore it. Actually the
whole thing would have been a private matter and perfectly
in order if these pictures hadn't interfered with the judge's
daily work in such a catastrophic way, if they hadn't already
made him unfit to pronounce judgment. Poor Polynari's sentence was spectacularly bestial. And the current case would
doubtless end just as horribly if I didn't take action regarding
the signs of decadence which had appeared. It didn't improve
matters that the police chief as well was probably gilding his
office hours with exactly the same kind of pictures. As a representative of the prosecution he would certainly never take
action against his old friend on the bench.

By myself I couldn't possibly be a match for such oppo-
nents if I wanted to try to stop the photographing and the cir-
culation of the pictures.

I decided to wait with the whole thing and think it over
first. Meanwhile I removed the pictures from the protocol
and locked the locker carefully. I considered having another
slug of kirsch from my bottle, but didn't feel like it. This
evening I wanted red wine from Tuscany. The inn would be
open for two more hours before it got to be *Polizeistunde* and
the guests would have to go home. I wanted to ask the bell
ringer what I should do next.

On the way to the inn I met the dean, who was out walking his huge great Dane. They were an imposing pair. The divine was over six feet tall, with soft white skin, powerfully built and muscular, and about sixty years old. He greeted me smiling, with great friendliness and majesty. The evening air from the mountains was clear and fresh, with a touch of the coming winter in it. Altogether it's been a wonderful autumn, long and sunny, endlessly clear and bright. It reminds me of the autumn my father died. That too consisted of just such an endless chain of sun-filled, southern days, with ever more red and yellowed leaves in the flaming treetops under a silk-bright sky. That whole autumn was like the wonderful peace and cheerfulness that he himself showed during the last days of his life.

It's turned into a beautiful fall this year, with golden fields above the lowlands and with air so clear that the stone gray mountain giants seem small and near, instead of enormous and faraway, because all the details in them are so unbelievably plain. But it won't be long before winter comes now; and three, four, or five times every winter we have foehn days, with tropical air and a burning Alpine sun, with premature births—with heart attacks and cerebral hemorrhages, a couple of bloody acts of violence and a number of serious traffic accidents; along with a servant murder or two, preceded by rape.

There will be several foehn days before I'm finished with this book.

I walked through the cool dark autumn night and finally arrived at my beloved inn "Zum Henker." Inside the room it was dark and smoky, full of good, decent citizens of the town.

From St. Anne's church both the bell ringer and the sexton were there. They were playing cards and were drunk, which disappointed me because there could hardly be any organized conversation under such circumstances.

But I sat down at the table and ordered a bottle of wine. The desire to talk was gone, and I drank the aromatic, grape-fragrant wine hurriedly and in large gulps. The sexton drinks cider, and that says a lot about him. Cider has terrible effects when drunk in such great quantities. It's made of apples, and it doesn't get quite so strong as wine, but contains about ten percent alcohol. People here in Schwarzbubenland drink it literally by the bucket, there are two-gallon men and three- and four-gallon men. A consumption of around ten quarts a day, or more, always seems to lead to catastrophic acts of violence. At least they count on it, and the principality's judicial archives are full of court cases indicating this. A big cider-drinker sooner or later has his typical outbursts, often reminiscent of the states which the foehn can provoke. In general both of them resemble the Malayan concept *amok*, and reveal, even in usually peaceful and good-tempered people, an almost unbelievable bloodthirstiness. In this valley the mildest running amok is usually done by cider drinkers in their earliest outbursts of rage. Later they get more dangerous, as the attacks continue to recur at regular intervals—if the person in question keeps up his heavy consumption of cider. If he switches to wine or kirsch the attacks cease. But it seldom happens that a cider drinker can get used to anything else.

The reason is that cider has a different effect from any other kind of intoxicant. It acts to deaden the nerves to an unusual degree, and already after one quart your body feels indescribably good—you feel a great peace, an endless repose which glides in over you and puts your soul in an incredibly peaceful mood, at peace with the world; whatever nerves you still have become smooth and relaxed, they no longer stand bristling like barbed wire outside your skin. Then if you get into the habit of drinking cider from morning till night over several years, you can easily get up to a consumption of three to five gallons a day; and sooner or later the deadened nerves rebel, the cider doesn't work anymore—and the attack of rage comes from a tormented animal, unexpected and headlong as an avalanche from the mountains. And because of their numbed condition cider drinkers usually seem so good-humored and peaceable, which makes the lightning outbursts seem all the more surprising. Very often cider is drunk secretly and on the sly, because it's regarded as a vulgar, ridiculous, and plebeian form of drunkenness—besides, everybody knows that it's dangerous.

I sat silently at the table drinking red wine. Beside it I had two large slices of the fresh, coarse bread which is so common here, and some cut-up slices of smoked horse meat, all served on a spacious wooden platter with a little raw onion. It's one of the best evening snacks I know of, provided that you gulp lots of wine with it. I chewed and drank, looking at the sexton, who had gotten his cider served in a large stone jug with a glass beside it. He is a man of something over my own age, with a pale face and large, prominent features. I mused a bit over how far he'd come in the mysteries of cider intoxication, and from there went on to think of my points of contact with it—from the courtroom.

For instance, there was the trial of the kind, good-hearted butcher Ratznick, a master at making garlic sausage and one of the most faithful members of the church choir, with his beautiful warm bass. A large, powerful man behind his mustache and under his bowler hat, a good husband and father, a good-natured person, and an excellent shot, member of the Heiligenberg Rifle Corps for thirty years. One day he closes his shop before lunch, draws the Venetian blinds—whereupon with a knife and a meat axe he butchers and quarters his beloved wife, his dear daughter, and his honest, hardworking shop woman. He put his whole professional knowledge and all of his pious soul into the work; and when the police came, all three were perfectly cleaned and flayed and hung up behind the Venetian blinds, on those big hooks.

Nobody had known that for years he'd calmed and consoled himself from a barrel of cider which sat out in one of the cold rooms, and which everybody thought contained salt. The court couldn't do anything but find the good fellow guilty, but he was sentenced in the mildest possible fashion, and for manslaughter. Now once again he's out working, has his shop going, a new wife and a new shop woman. He drinks his cider as before, working behind the counter and humming, always with a cheery word for staff and customers.

He's again a member of the rifle corps and once more sings in the choir.

Or for example forester Haase, who killed all of his numerous family plus the servant girl with an axe. He kept his cider in the woodshed, but he hanged himself in prison when his head had cleared and he understood what he'd done. Each reacts in his own way.

The red wine did me good. It had the light, fruity taste which a red wine from the Tuscan region should have, and was full-bodied and rich. By the time I was halfway through the second bottle, I was in a really lyrical mood and could take a different view of the experience with the judge's unsavory pictures. I began to listen to what the bell ringer and the sexton were talking about, and to be amused by the conversation.

The bell ringer went on:

"I remember," he said, "from my incarnation as a rabbi in Galicia—and I mention this in connection with *La Storia della Bestialitá*—a special pogrom. The brave cossacks, those damned hunchbacked bastards and pederasts, the cossacks, they held a pogrom, an orgy of Christian joy, against my congregation and my people. Those dirty Christian mongrels crucified a village in my parish—like the true Russians they were, they nailed the population of the village to the house walls, they brought out tools—this was just before Passover—and the villagers: men, women and children, old folks, sick people and infants, little children at their mothers' breast—they were all nailed to the house walls, and they hung there crucified side by side on all the houses down the line, it was Passover, so they did it in memory of the Savior's resurrection and the first Christian Easter, and being good Russians they drank vodka instead of altar wine, but they ate roast lamb as if they'd been believers themselves and not goyim. When everybody was nailed fast, they circumcised the men once again, but far more thoroughly than before, in that all penises were removed at the root, and after that they set the village on fire, so that the crucified were burned alive. I'm thinking of your lifework about our friends, the little bears. You can learn something here, because a pogrom is always a revolutionary act, it's carried out ritually and by ideologists, so as to overthrow the existing order and change the world. Of course you can do like Lichtenberg and call it *"Experimentalpolitik,"* but in that case the whole history of the world is experimental politics—and in Spain it wasn't us but the fascists who were the insurgents, it was the fascists who made a revolution, and because the revolution was fascist, it was therefore recognized as a legal basis for Franco's regime by all the big powers, and all the little lapdogs like Switzerland, Sweden, Denmark, Holland, Norway, Finland, et cetera, all the states which today refuse to recognize, say, China or my fatherland, they recognized the regimes in Spain, Germany, and Italy one after the other, because the United States and England wanted it. Now I'll sing a little song for you, as we sang it in Spain in those days. But before I sing it, I'll tell what happened afterwards. As a rabbi I gathered together the remnants of my congregation and left Holy Russia and headed west. This is centuries ago, of course, but in fact we found refuge in Germany, among the goyim. To get in, though, we had to get new papers, which gave us names which could be pronounced by the people we were coming to. So we all ended up with names like Silbermann and Goldstein and Schalom, and Lord knows what. Some of the congregation received totally absurd and idiotic names like Schweinebraten and Sauerkraut, owing to the sharp-witted officials' Teutonic humor—names which the members of my congregation didn't know what meant. If they'd given us ordinary names, much would have looked different later on."

In his strong, warm baritone he began to sing his *canciones de las Brigadas Internacionales.* He leaned back, red-faced above his bushy beard, holding the liquor bottle in his hand like a red flag, and sang so that the whole inn became still. Everybody listened to him, as they'd done hundreds of times before, every time the bell ringer was drunk enough to believe that he was in Spain, and to forget that that was thirty years

ago. People in this valley and town are lemurian, they don't
sing. Between verses he drank now and then from the bottle.

Vier noble Generale, vier noble Generale
Mamata mia!
hab'n uns verraten, hab'n uns verraten.
Und die Faschisten-Staaten
schickten auch prompt soldaten.

As I walked through the town the moon shone down on
the empty streets and with its dark shadows redrew all the
houses and corners, squares and streets into a picture in black
and white—and above the rooftops the mountain giants arose
modeled in the same way, plastic and grotesque like enormous horns. I walked rapidly, with the pack of photographs
under my arm, and little by little the heavens again began to
bleed. Blood collected in the vault of the sky and ran down
toward the horizon in all directions, it reached the mountaintops and trickled over the glaciers and down along the
mountainsides, then turned into brooks which disappeared in
clefts and gorges, and collected down in the valleys into
larger streams which would soon come flowing into the city
and through the streets, following the gutters and disappear-
ing into the blessed sewers which swallow all.

I was a small child the first time I saw the sky bleed, and I've
often seen it since—in the days when I lived in the jungle, the
days of my long journey, before I became the way I am now.

I came home and put the pictures away—not with the
material for my work, but out in the toilet, high up under the
ceiling between the old-fashioned tank and the wall.
Something had broken into my usual, balanced work day and
made me uneasy again, my rhinoceros hide was destroyed,
my isolation broken.

I brought out two bottles of red wine and set them beside
the bed so that they'd be easy to get hold of if I couldn't
sleep. Then I undressed and went to bed, scared and restless
as a child.

I thought about how I'd staked everything on achieving one single thing: to be at peace with the world! Through many years I'd sought out injustice in order to inure myself to it. That was the whole secret in my plan: to tolerate unfreedom and injustice. My calm is destroyed, and the sky bleeds. I have a gray beard. An aging Servant of Justice should be tranquil of mind and at peace with the world. With a quiet heart.

No, I'm not at peace with the world. My heart hasn't become any calmer.

Tonight I looked at myself in the mirror again, I studied my mirror image with the same perseverance and interest as a vain woman, and partly with the same satisfaction and pleasure. But it's something else which consoles me, something entirely different that I wait and hope for. I watch with longing for signs of age, for anything which shows that I'm becoming an old man. Every white straw in my beard gratifies me, every gray hair makes me happy. Every wrinkle is a consolation.

When I stand naked, the signs are clear. The sunken, flat seat muscles are visible now. And the chest muscles have something hanging, old-man-like about them.

But there's still too much left. In particular the neck and shoulders and arms are round and powerful, and the dark, shiny, violet-brown skin, colored by wine and sun, is encircled by a beard and hair that's still black at a distance of a few paces. I look like a black, bushy dog.

This man in the mirror I've never been intimate with.

All this apparently robust flesh, which wouldn't be able to stand French electro-torture, but would writhe and toss and become my enemy, betray me immediately. This flesh turns against me continually. The man in the mirror has always turned against me, and is entirely unknown and alien to me. The deep voice isn't my own, but my father's. This stout man in the mirror, virile and brown and bearded, he's still strong enough to come forth from the grave, to arise from the dead on the third day. But he has no freedom. He isn't a person, he's first and foremost a sex, more closely related to the naked and passionate fat bald man with the walrus mustache in the judge's obscene pictures—than, for example, to the Virgin Mary in Rosenhain. And this flesh one must bear.

It's no wonder that I rejoice over every white straw in my beard, for he's the one who must decline so that I may come into being. One day he'll be completely white-haired, stooping and stiff. That will be my hour!

Now if I could only remember my name! Then I could find out who I was, who I am. Maybe remember how I happened to become a Servant of Justice in this Alpine valley. Somewhere or other far down inside of me it must be buried, in the dark holes and crevices between the disjointed fragments and half-formed pictures which live in my memory, far down in my youth, in my childhood, in my lost and forgotten genesis.

I've turned out the light, but the moonlight seeps through the open window into the room, and the whitewashed walls around me are visible. The walls are bleeding slightly; here and there, drop by drop, the blood drips out and runs down in thin stripes. It draws patterns on the plaster.

Today I stole the judge's pictures. It's a long while since the last time I stole. And the bell ringer sang so beautifully tonight, the sad and heroic songs from Spain which bear witness to the prewar era's all too sentimental, all too emotional hope. Why should that intrude upon me now? I had put my stake on being at peace with the world, on being among those dead to the world, and now maybe I'll come to see that I've built on an illusion, on quicksand.

I lie here and remember my life.

THREE

It was during Stockholm's black-haired period. Lemurs, eschatologists, and scholastics from many lands had gathered and
set their stamp on this city, otherwise blond as a summer night.
If I could manage to remember those years in Stockholm, I'd
be well on the way to knowing what my name is.

It was a thoroughly lemurian time. Along Sweden's
boundaries the storm raged against the cliffs. The little bears
had declared a state of emergency for all people in all countries, and had agreed to kill each other's women and children;
and generally speaking they achieved good results—above all
in the area of children. Scarcely any previous battle actions
have led to the destruction of so many and such varied and
grateful children. One has to admit that during the years
between 1939 and 1945 the dispatch of little and bigger chil
dren reached a high point both in scope and in technical
beauty. It's almost impossible to say how many children of
both sexes were done away with, because no detailed statistics on the subject exist. At least not publicly.

On the other hand statistics do exist on almost everything
else, thoroughly and accurately researched and calculated.
For example on the durability of children's shoes, the significance of bee-keeping for the Swiss balance of trade, etc., etc.
People have also undertaken rather precise calculations of
how many Russians, Englishmen, Poles, Hebrews, Yugoslavs,
and little bears in general were dispatched during these
years—but one misses a scientifically reliable work on chil-

dren. This may be because nobody's especially interested, and of course the surviving able-bodied children themselves couldn't set up a central bureau of statistics to determine how many children were liquidated between '39 and '45—quite simply because they were children, and hence incapable of performing complicated statistical calculations. Consequently this tempting problem remained unsolved, while people were figuring out that ca. 20 million died in Russia, ca. 5-6 million in the gas chambers, etc. Of course it's possible that the U.N.'s secret files contain clear figures and precise data on the number of children killed—and that the U.N. leadership doesn't wish to publish the figures for humane and moral reasons—e.g. so as not to scare children living today, or so that present-day children won't lose their trust in adults. But in any case I myself, even though I've read and examined thousands of files and documents, have never seen any scientifically reliable statistical or graphic representations of child mortality during those years.

I only know that they kept right on dying without any special protest, and that a great many children were very good at dying.

As I said, it was a lemurian time, and it was here in Sweden that my own journey in the land of Chaos began to pick up speed. So we were gathered in Stockholm as refugees from every land, and many of us were rather nervous. I had no real awareness of death and was consequently a bear among bears, with insects and filth in my fur, and pretty intent on eating my fill. However: man does not live by dialectics alone.

I met Otto that last wartime winter in Stockholm; it was so cold that the ice was almost solid over the strait to Denmark that year. I lived in a really remarkable house. I mean the house was only remarkable seen from the inside, and probably only on the third floor, where we lived. It was an ordinary brick house from before the turn of the century, adorned with stucco and plaster cakes and whipped cream under the eaves, but in its way it had a certain humanity. After all, both the plaster garlands and the reliefs were once put there in all good faith for the purpose of beautifying the house, to lift it above pure utility; the rooms were large and high-ceilinged and had high windows with crosses in them. The house had certain conveniences, among them an old-fashioned elevator, set in a kind of shaft of iron bars and thick steel netting—an elevator of the sort one so often sees in Stockholm, no doubt of the Ericsson Brothers' renowned manufacture. It's strange; no other city in the world—not even Paris—has so many old elevators as the capital of Sweden. One may be tempted to regard it as a sign of underdevelopment, but the opposite is the case: Stockholm simply had elevators installed earlier than other cities, and the firm Ericsson Brothers, which installed them, provided the city with electrical components of indestructible quality. Ericsson elevators were built to last forever, they function just as well today as then, and they'll go on working as long as there are still rainbows in the sky, and as long as the country doesn't get involved in the Third World War. Well, we had one of those Ericsson Brothers elevators in our house. It rattled and cried when it moved, it crashed like a bomb hitting when it arrived at a floor, it sounded like a panzer attack when it started. It sobbed when it was standing still. But it ran, and it's still running, provided that the house is standing.

The house had both spaciousness and a certain comfort—something which I, as an old revolutionary and anarcho-individualist, know how to appreciate. It was a marvelously well-ordered world which found expression in that house, full of decency and meaning, a patriarchal and Marxist atmosphere from the days when two times two was four and not yet anywhere near seven. I liked that house much better than the nesting boxes being built for our grateful subjects today. But I am, or was, an old-fashioned man. Today, strictly speaking, I no longer like houses at all.

What made our house something outside the ordinary was the inhabitants, or to be exact: the inhabitants of the *third* floor. We were all emigrants, we each had our own room in the large apartment and shared the toilet, kitchen, and bath. Aside from a couple of *émigrés sexuels*, we were political refugees from all over our beloved Europe, from the old monarchies and republics which had now been so swiftly transformed into police states, which of course they'd always been at bottom. We were one Norwegian, one Czech, two from Austria, one sexual refugee from the free Hansa city of Hamburg, one Pole, and yet another German, but with political interests. Except for one of the Austrians, we'd all lived in the house fairly long and knew each other pretty well. We celebrated Christmas and birthdays together, consoled each other when we were suffering from homesickness or received word that relatives had been shot, flogged to death or gassed in the rest homes for the dissenting and the black-haired. The Austrian who had come to the house last was also the one who moved again first, and he became the cause of a certain change in our life. Namely, in his place moved in a new and unknown person.

It was Otto.

What's become of the rest of us today? We're scattered over the globe by the winds, like subway tickets at Stureplan station—blown around between the corners of the earth, from Palestine to Canada to Hong Kong.

Otto was an Estonian, small and blond, not much to notice and not very talkative by nature. At first none of us came into closer contact with him, we only met him on the stairs or in the entryway. Our common house language was of course German, and Otto spoke it badly—without the eschatologist's feel for cases and subjunctives, but in return with an amazingly strong Estonian accent. He had rowed across the Baltic Sea in an open boat along with a couple of other young men, and had registered as a refugee. None of us knew any more about him than just that, and we refrained from asking whether he'd fled from the heroic Germans or the heroic Russians. It didn't make that much difference: he didn't invite questions, and nothing would have happened if we hadn't chanced to hear that Otto was an SS man. Suddenly we'd all heard it, we whispered together and quizzed each other, but nobody had any factual information and nobody could even account for how the rumor had started, much less say whether it was true.

I don't know of anything which could have had a more inflammatory effect on a family of refugees from the Teutons' appetite for life than to find out—and at this juncture—that they were probably living in the same apartment with an SS man, even sharing the john and the bathtub with him, with little Otto representing the very backbone of the Teutons' only true form of society. It was a nightmare for us all, we who had felt and seen the Alemannic tribes' activities at first hand. After a few days we held a house meeting about what steps we should take to put an end to a situation which was unendurable unto sleeplessness for us all. Although none of us was an advocate of violence, it was unthinkable to keep an SS man in the house. On the other hand it would be terrible if we were to expose an innocent person to such a vile suspicion. We agreed that we should ask him straight out about his political vita. Despite the fact that I was the youngest of all, I was delegated to talk to him.

What Otto lived on or otherwise did in Stockholm I don't know, but he went out regularly in the morning in a gray coat and gray hat, and he came back in the afternoon just as gray as when he'd left. Often with a briefcase under his arm and usually with a few things he'd bought for his little ménage: a bit of bread, marmalade, tea. There was something incredibly unassuming about the whole man.

The next afternoon I knocked on his door. He had a big, light room with two tall windows.

"Come in," he said.

When I opened the door I saw him at a table right beside the window, sitting straight up and down, without eating, without reading, without doing anything. He just sat, completely still, straight up and down. It seemed as if he'd been sitting like that for a long time. For years. He looked at me with his light, somewhat watery gray-blue eyes. His face was pale and moist, his skin dull. Then he got up and greeted me, but without smiling.

I felt uncomfortable, and the situation was painful. To cut the unpleasantness short, I came straight to the point and asked him without any preamble if it were true that he had been a member of the Waffen SS. To my great surprise he answered without the least sign of emotion or discomfort that yes, he had—as if it were the most natural thing in the world. He'd fought in Russia, but had escaped with no more than a couple of slight wounds. He stood while he talked.

"Is it really true?" I said, staring at him. My Estonian brother human looked less devilish than ever.

"Yes," he answered, "do you like to see the mark?"

"From the wounds?"

"No," he shook his head; "the tattoo."

"Are you tattooed?"

"Oh yes," he answered briskly, almost cheerfully, while a faint and fleeting smile glided over the aging baby face. "Everybody in the SS has got his blood type tattooed inside on his upper arm."

He rolled up his sleeve to the shoulder and showed me. There were a couple of blue lines on a pale and flabby upper arm; I'd never seen that mark before. I felt faint, unreal, and a bit sick, standing so near and staring right onto the skin of the mortal enemy himself. Then I noticed that he was proud of showing off the mark; his front teeth were just visible through a faint smile. That made me even more numb and speechless; in the same apartment, wall to wall with him, were living people who'd had friends and relatives, comrades and kindred spirits killed and maimed by the murder organization he stood here being proud of belonging to.

I looked at him while he rolled his sleeve down again. The shirt, the sleeveless pullover, the pants, everything was gray on him, like a uniform.

Then he sat down again, pointed to a chair and said, as if he were giving me a valuable gift:

"Be seated. You may well sit here awhile."

I was so taken aback that I sat down, staring at him mutely. Otto affected me like a surrealistic picture. He belonged to the most hated, most criminal organization in the world, and besides to an army which stood on the verge of inevitable defeat, but he was perfectly calm. This was at a time when the city's newspapers were chock full of information about Nazi atrocities. Even the old king in his palace had understood that Germany now lay like a mortally wounded, crippled, and still dangerous carnivore, rolling in its own and others' blood, in its last violent convulsions. And Sweden's foreign policy had changed direction; all those things that the refugees had known for years were now there to be read in the papers. Every single day ought to have reminded Otto of how the land lay. Instead he looked trustingly at me with big, open, and completely guiltless eyes, with an expression of perfect candor. What he said seemed so bewildering to me that I remember it word for word today, over twenty years later:

"The Russians do not recognize the faith."

From politeness I was unable to ask him how the SS stood with respect to the faith. Besides, I was suddenly struck by the full consequences of his not knowing any other languages than his mother tongue and a little German; of Swedish he understood not a word, and he got all his information either from the Germanic legation or from his own countrymen. In the streets of Stockholm he walked between the notice boards of the newspapers as if they had been in Chinese. He was like a fish on land, just as dumb and just as ignorant of what was going on around him. I was sure that he wasn't putting me on.

"Was that why you fought with the SS against the Russians?"

"No," he said in a faint voice; "we fought against Russia all together. All decent people did it."

"Why?"

He went on talking, calm and explanatory:

"It was natural. The Germans helped us, from the time they freed the country from the Bolsheviks we have stood on the German side. It was a case of honor."

"Freed?"

"Yes, you really do not know that? They saved us and freed us from the Bolshevik murderers."

"Excuse me," I said, trying to wake up out of something which felt like a dream: "I thought that they occupied and ravished Estonia just like they took other countries, Poland and..."

He smiled. He almost laughed, then he shook his head.

"No, no, no, no," he replied, "the *Germans* were not like that. The *Germans* do not that kind of thing, they are good and civilized people. They freed us, they chased away the murderers and let us have our government again. Oh, we welcomed them with flowers and flags and music and singing when they came and helped us. We had feasts for them and hung flowers and ribbons on their uniforms.... You do not know that Estonia was conquered and crushed and put down by the devils, the damned Communists from Moscow and their helpers from the party in Estonia? When the Bolsheviks took Poland, they took our country a while after. They only came right into the country and made themselves the masters, they decided all things, because their country is big and strong and has a very big army, but our country is little and poor and has not many tanks and cannons and planes."

"Was it a hard occupation?"

"Very hard. The Bolsheviks killed many, many thousand people of the ones who were from good family and have worked in politics and the public life in the country, and the others—the ones who had property—they took and arrested them and sent hundred thousands away, deported them to Siberia. In masses they were shot or deported right away, and so the Russians put communists into all the positions, they set up a big secret police and put in informers, and people were hanged in public. In the schools the children must learn Russian, and the churches were closed.... It was much, much blood that flowed. The whole country—all was only blood."

He sat still, looking straight ahead, completely expressionless.

"We've heard very little about this," I said in order to break the silence.

"I could tell much, I could sit many hours and tell about it," continued Otto. "The Russians and our own Bolsheviks didn't want to recognize the faith. All the police became Bolshevik and Russian, and they arrested people day and night. In the middle of the night often. They never came back, and they were tortured terribly. It was very terrible to live in Estonia then."

"That was in 1940?"

"The same year that the Bolsheviks took Latvia and Lithuania and many other countries farther south. I do not remember what year."

"Did you lose relatives or friends yourself?"

"Oh yes, yes. Everyone lost someone. They took my father and two uncles who were small tradesmen and a cousin. They were taken at night, because they were clever and hard-working people and had property. Those were very terrible times. They took many, many people in the night, and they were gone for always."

"And then the Germans came?"

"Yes, the Germans came at last! They were fine people, they were like God's angels when they came and chased the Russians away to hell.... They all ran, they jumped like hares when they saw the German helmets.... We laughed and sang and danced in the streets...and all the Bolsheviks and Russians tried to run away. But we caught many from the police and the party and their spies and informers."

"What did you do with the Communists?"

He looked at me, and the dull gray-blue eyes came alive, a sort of glow came into them, and he lifted his hands. Then he laughed aloud.

"Them we took as prisoners," he said, looking almost happy: "We chased them through the streets and through gates and back yards, we followed them upstairs and grabbed them in the attics and cellars. The Bolsheviks had many helpers and police spies and a mass of Jews who have sympathized with them. So we took all the Jews and Bolsheviks and informers and policemen and hung them in the streets and everywhere, some of them we hung up with the feet, and where it was too many we shot them, after they dug their own graves, with children and wives, so that nobody could survive them and take revenge after…. Some got a very ugly death, I remember a fat Communist who was raised up with his sex organs, with his balls, and he screamed terribly, but then he fell down, and then I saw that it all was torn off, because he was so fat and heavy. Many Communists were raised up the same way, but I only saw one fall down. We took all of them, every single one who has helped the Bolsheviks or showed them sympathy, and all the Jews…. All are dead now, hundred thousands, none is alive."

"So then you joined the SS?"

"All decent and patriotic men did it. The Germans saved us and freed us, and it would be a terrible shame if we did not help them against the Bolsheviks in return. And they were our only friends. All young and healthy men went into the SS and fought in Russia to be at the last victory over world Bolshevism and the Antichrist."

"You were there the whole time?"

"Yes, both in the advance and the retreat. And besides, we in the SS had a special job with liquidation and many big executions of hundreds and thousands of people. We must do it, because we were the hardest and because we were trained to do it, so that we could execute hundreds and still stay decent people. I was along the whole time, as well as I could."

"Were there many hard battles?"

"Yes, many. It was a very, very severe war. Those who do not kill first are killed themselves."

"And during the retreat you came back to Estonia?"

"Yes, it happened so. I was in Estonia, and then came the Russians. They were very angry at us, much wilder than the first time. When they came back, they killed all who have helped the Germans, and many others too, who were only reported. They will certainly kill all. They took all who have got their property back and put them in the prison, and they closed the churches and the schools and the university, and they chased people in the streets."

"How did you escape?"

"In a rowboat together with three other soldiers. We left right away, at night. And we came to Sweden."

"Do you hear anything from Estonia?"

"Now and then have come a few refugees over the sea, and they say that now the Russians want to take everybody who didn't make resistance when the Germans came. Almost all will be arrested, because all hate the others and denounce the others as friends of the Germans. The Russians think that all who have survived have helped the Germans.... Only those who report somebody can survive themselves."

"They can't exterminate everybody?"

"They will either be killed or deported. Most of them will certainly come to Siberia, but nobody knows who will die and who will be deported. People say it is best to die."

"But the people will be almost wiped out?"

"No. It will be some left. We reckon that it is about a third part of the population who remains. They are the informers."

Otto was very calm as he talked, and he looked straight at me with his light, colorless eyes. Almost the whole time he sat just as he had when I entered: straight up and down.

"It is worse now than anytime at home. It is certainly the most terrible time the country has had, say the people."

"Now the war's coming to an end," I said; "and then it'll be better than it is now."

"Yes," he said. He paused, then he narrowed his eyes slightly and looked at me confidingly: "I may well tell this to you, even if it is a secret only we in the SS know about: It is not so long left till the last victory. The secret weapon is almost ready to use now. It is a new kind of bomb, a bomb which contains not ordinary explosives, but something which is a thousand or a million times stronger—I do not know exactly—but now it will be used soon. It will be used one such bomb on Moscow, one on London, and one on New York, and only one will be enough to destroy each of these cities. Then they must surrender, and we have won the last victory. The secret weapon will be used on the Führer's birthday, the twentieth of April. Then we are going to kill all the Bolsheviks in the world. But it is only we in the SS who have heard exactly about this.

"We are several people here in Stockholm. When we meet we talk about what happens in Estonia. All the time we talk only about that."

The same evening I presented the results of the conversation to the others in the house, and we decided not to do anything to get rid of Otto, but to just let him stay there and avoid talking with him. We continued to say hello to him in the hall or in our old elevator.

All the same it wasn't more than a few weeks after this conversation before Otto's room stood empty again. He hadn't said goodbye to anybody before he left. He had just gone.

The last news I had of Otto was an item I saw in the paper awhile later. He and two other Estonians had been drowned while trying to cross the ice to Denmark. Some Swedish fishermen had seen them and tried to come to their rescue, but in vain. The three refugees had their papers on them as they headed in the opposite direction from the usual stream of refugees. There was no difficulty identifying them.

Otto was on the way to Denmark to join the Germans and take part in the last battle against the Bolshevik murderers, who where now advancing on Germany herself. It was his plan to delay them as long as possible, until the Führer's birthday, when victory was a fact.

In this way Otto won the war against the whole world.

❖ ❖ ❖

I'm sitting here today, and I've eaten my supper; my graying beard is wet and shiny with olive oil and lemon juice. I work as a Servant of Justice under a prince, *il principe* Michael of Heiligenberg, who knows the secrets of the underworld and outer space. I'm sitting in the mountain air, remembering my youth. If I'm going to be of any use, this is the last moment.

I can't be fooled any more: A life spent in lies can't be saved by anything but more lies. Besides, I know too much, I've seen too much: and I don't *want* to see any more, don't *want* to know any more. I know everything and would rather just sleep and drink as consolation and escape. That's our best chance of fleeing from this latrine of a planet.

But in Heiligenberg we don't do that, not under Prince Michael's regime. For us there's no probation, no dismissing the charges.

Oh Lord, this ghastly fear of saying or writing the truth! A lie can be corrected, it can be retracted, lied away—it isn't final. The truth is definitive, a poison like opium and cocaine. Once tell the truth and there'll be no way back, no more contact, conviviality, community with people. It's one thing to live in a mountain valley, a completely different thing to go over the passes, 7000, 10,000 foot up...into the starry sky. Away from the inn, the liquor, and the sexton....

My excuse, my defense, my last bastion is that I don't know the truth, and therefore can't say it. But that doesn't help, the public prosecutor has said; if the accused knew the truth, he still wouldn't dare to utter it. He can be convicted on this, and all his unsaid words will be used against him. Every word he doesn't say will be entered in the record.

At the same time, of course, I *do* know the truth, I just don't dare to look at it. The prosecuting attorney of Heiligenberg is right. Of course I'm acquainted with the truth—after my Meeting with the Leopard. It's original sin and that alone which holds me back. I know that I have to tell about my wanderings in the mines. I would rather escape, for it's not only unpleasant, it's also very difficult to express oneself correctly and clearly and coherently.

My stay in Stockholm I haven't mentioned. I seized the first
opportunity to talk about something else...the refugee Otto.

✧ ✧ ✧

When I arrived in Sweden, the craving for fat was the most
important thing. The happiness of drinking all the olive oil out of
a can of Portuguese sardines is something I'll never manage to
recapture. Of course it was strange to go to the Sturebadet and be
washed and fixed up by female attendants, stark naked as from
the hand of God. But the olive oil was more important. All in all
I'd come to a remarkable country, far more alien than Guinea or
Santo Domingo. Sweden is a mixture of Russia and America.

Stockholm, the first time I came there, seemed more oriental
and more Russian than Moscow did when I came there many
years later. It was due in part to all the cupolas and onion-
shaped church towers with spires which the city was full of, but
there was also something else—a breath, a whiff, an odor of
brackish water and flat land, of great expanses—no mountains
between oneself and the Urals. Was that my first meeting with
the Baltic? The first feeling that to the east lay the Hungarian-
Mongolian regions, Finland, and Estonia...the realization that
Leningrad was the nearest large city? Over there—to the east—
lay the front, the eternal front, where the Teutons' wild horde
was engaged in massacring the population of Leningrad. I don't
know, but Stockholm was a milk-colored, Baltic, North Russian
city. The sea water wasn't really salty, and at that time I was
coming from the North Sea, the Atlantic Ocean, and the Arctic
Ocean.

No, when I arrived in Stockholm back then—109 years
ago—I was in the East for the first time in my life. When I later
came to Naples, I was a native there from the first minute; in
Stockholm I was a stranger for several years. The light, the air,
and the opening to the east: Oysters were no longer called
østers, but ostron, strawberries weren't jordbær, but smultron—it
was as exotic as northern, flat Siberia, covered with fairytale
plants—with lingon, maskros, and näckros.... I also know of oth-

ers who felt it that way. Austrians, Germans, and God knows who...we were on the tundra in open, wealthy, beautiful Stockholm. I walked around in the parks and streets, along boulevards and over bridges, in Gamla Stan...sat on the stone steps down at Strömmen. Stockholm is the city of my youth. It's in Stockholm that I lived those decisive years. Therefore I'm by greater right a Stockholmer to this day than many who live there now. Stockholm was the city of my youth, the place where my awareness first began to sprout—as when a kitten begins to get eyes for the first time, small, narrow slits out toward the daylight and the world. It was there it began. Stockholm gave me my youthful playgrounds, my youthful city, my....

Oh Lord, I notice how much it hurts to touch on that, how painful it is to finger the rims round the holes in my memory...the large sores which have been eaten away, there where I don't remember. It hurts so much that I feel only one need: to throw away the goosequill and break off the whole record, not to add any more to the books, let the protocols be.... What is it that can have happened to me in Stoccolmia? I have only to think of it, and there's something in me which refuses, which turns away and doesn't want.

If I know the little bears—and hence myself—aright, it must have been a degradation, some unheard-of humiliation. More than anything the little bears hate to think of the times when they were humiliated, made small and ridiculous. For the little bears are convinced that they're all—bear by bear—significant, proud, free, and great creations, to be taken seriously by the sun and the moon and the mountains and the sea. The stars shall bow down to us.

It must have been a humiliation, deep and permanent, lasting for years. All the symptoms point to it. And it was still at the beginning of the great wandering in the land of Chaos, long before the solar eclipse and the leopard. I was very thin-skinned about humiliation in those days. Well, so I don't want to remember what happened in Stockholm...I don't want to remember it and wouldn't tell the truth if I did remember.

Ever since I could breathe, ever since I could drink milk from a cup, I've been trained and schooled to lie, to despise and hate everything which partakes of truth. From the cradle on, in kindergarten, in primary school, elementary school, in high school and ever since, I've been taught that to speak the truth is either stupid or immoral—or both. Is it possible that this instruction in falsehood—in being another than who I am—in talking like another, thinking, acting, believing like another—is it possible that this schooling reached a climax here, in the city of my youth...?

I have a college education in falsehood. Trained, trimmed, polished, and thoroughly drilled in lying—practiced as an acrobat in the avoidance of reality. I began to understand this *nel mezzo del camin' di nostra vita*, with the leopard by my side. Not everything, no—as far as I remember it's only fragments, but the fragments are jotted down in the San Praiano papers. And I don't have them at hand.

If I can find the Praiano papers, I'll record them here, just as I wrote them down ten years ago.

All this became clear to me during the violent, regular attacks of rage which were so common those first years—a rage which was directed against everything and nothing and against myself, so powerful and so senseless that it was probably called forth by some earlier, indescribable humiliation—a humiliation which must have lasted for years in order to store up such a reaction.

There can be no doubt that lying is the deepest pathogenic force. Falsehood's first and nearest, most immediately visible task is to hide the truth about ourselves from ourselves.

Taking into account the anxiety I feel about touching the time in Stockholm, and the hate and rage I felt during my attacks of sickness in the leopard years, I will propose the working hypothesis that the humiliation to which I in one way or another—or in many ways—was exposed, must have consisted in the fact that, *against my profoundest better knowledge,* I accepted and submitted to the education in lying—that I conceded that falsehood was truth and truth was falsehood—that I acknowledged that it was moral to be someone other than oneself, that it was immoral to be the person one is. It's conceivable that in those days I finally *consented* to let other people's conscience be transplanted to me—that I acknowledged that it was stupid, evil and immoral to speak the truth; and that for the eternal in me—entelechy, as Goethe would have said—this was such a spiritual abasement and humiliation that the loss of memory has closed itself mercifully around the shame.

This, to acknowledge that it's evil, criminal, stupid and harmful to speak the truth—in other words, to agree that one must offer one's *sacrificium intellectualis*, sacrifice one's own personal intellectual life to live another's, or *the* others' life instead, to establish the others' conscience as one's own—I know well what this sin is called, and that it's a sin for which there is no forgiveness. *The Sin against the Holy Spirit* is unforgivable, because it denies the meaning of earth and of the starry heavens: individuation—coming into being.

It's understandable that one refuses to remember the circumstances which led one to commit such a sin.

I perceive that I—or something in my consciousness—would rather die than remember what happened in Stockholm.

To talk about Stockholm is like digging with a fork in a wound; all that exists of flesh and nerves protests against it.

✧ ✧ ✧

"Listen!" he said: *"Herr konstnären* shall have a very cheap room, an incredibly cheap room. Provided that you can use it. That is, it isn't a room in the usual sense, but a walled-off corner in the hallway, and the partition is only a Spanish wall that doesn't go all the way up to the ceiling. But there's a bed and a washstand inside, and no one can see through the wall."

He showed me the corner, and it was very usable, but open to the corridor the last few feet under the ceiling. There was a little mirror on the washstand, and a jug and a chamber pot.

"It costs ten kroner," he said.

I became anxious:

"A day?"

"A week."

The corner became my home for a long time, and with the help of a chair to sit on and the little mirror on the washstand I painted many self-portraits there. That was the only thing my atelier was good for. In all the time I lived there my landlord was just as friendly and just as polite, and I was never called anything but *"Herr konstnären."* His wife, who was just as fat as he, also treated me with respect and with motherly kindness.

In all I lived a year in my hall corner in Clara.

Clara was also the newspaper district at that time. That seems like a bad omen for me, who was later to consume so much printer's ink. But I didn't suspect that.

The first few hours of that first day I spent in getting some money, buying working materials and finding myself a usable lodging. When I left the hotel a little later, it was already evening. It was getting dark, and I went out into a city which—after the blackouts in my original fatherland—was the greatest of all miracles: a lighted city—with burning streetlights, illuminated windows, and flashing neon signs!

I walked through the artificially lit streets. The day had been a success. I hadn't eaten since I came to the city. And I continued on my way past cinemas, shops, restaurants. I had a plan.

The city gleamed with light, while the twilight grew thicker and thicker; it was blue, and slowly it turned to black. The streets were full of well-dressed people, the cars were shiny, the restaurant menus hung by the doorways, and well-fed doormen stood outside in reddish-brown uniforms. I knew exactly what I wanted; I'd set aside money for it, and now and then I asked people the way. I distinctly recall that only then—so late in the evening—did I buy my first cigarettes in Stockholm: a pack of thin, round cigarettes with long and bad-tasting cardboard mouthpieces on them. They were rationed and tasted like paper, without a suggestion of tobacco. They represented the war. But if you had the money, you could also buy real cigarettes, made abroad and not by the state tobacco monopoly—cigarettes which tasted of tobacco, from England or from my homeland, which in those days made cigarettes which tasted of tobacco. I lit my first thin Swedish cigarette, half of it hollow cardboard. Even today, twenty-five years later, I remember exactly how it tasted and smelled. It was made in the same way as a Russian *papyros*; one half of thin paper with tobacco inside—the other half an empty tube of cardboard.

It had a slight taste and made your nose burn a little, but bore no resemblance either to Virginia tobacco, or to Turkish or Egyptian tobacco—it wasn't Balkan tobacco and it wasn't Maryland tobacco. It was quite simply welfare-state tobacco, without face or features: *standard* tobacco. It didn't satisfy the tobacco hunger even if you smoked it continuously. You could smoke ninety cigarettes a day.

I continued through the city, traversing the main streets. A few more times I asked people the way, then I was there: before the lighted, gleaming entrance. I looked at myself in the mirror.

How did *I* look back then? Who was I?

According to an old passport I was five feet nine inches tall. So I've grown since then. Of course I was very dark, and since I weighed a little over 130 pounds, I must have been very thin—with a long, bent nose.

That night after my first meal in Stockholm I slept peacefully in my bed back home in the hall corner. Now and then I'd awake a little when somebody came and went, but after a few nights in my cubicle I was never again disturbed by the traffic in the hall, even if it was at times both lively and loud. If the full and complete truth must be told, then the house, "The Star," wasn't a hotel at all in the usual sense. Nor was it a youth hostel. In reality I lived that whole year in the corridor of a brothel.

This is a peculiarity of my life; a remarkable circumstance which has always pursued me, almost all over the world, in an endless series of cities: everywhere I've ended up staying in brothels. But the Clara district near the church was the only time I lived in the hall, and the only time I lived a whole year in the same house. When you come right down to it, "The Star" was one of the coziest brothels I've lived in.

The last time I traveled over to the south side of the mountains and down to Milan, I stayed at a brothel only a bottle's throw from our beloved Piccolo Teatro. The preceptor, choirboy and icon painter Leporello laughed like a madman when I told him that I was staying in the neighborhood whorehouse. Anyway, it was an unusually clean and pretty house, and all the girls were wearing chamois skin, which was the fashion that fall.

Meanwhile, on my second day in Stockholm I left my corner in the brothel corridor around nine-thirty, went to the nearest newsstand and bought all the morning papers. Then I went to a little basement café and ordered my coffee with two *bullar*.

One of the first things the occupation forces had done in the fatherland I'd left was (for good reasons) to abolish all public information, and after a few days the Norwegian papers came to sound so much alike that from day to day and from composing room to composing room they might have been run off from the same typesetting. Germany was incessantly winning on all fronts.

It was bewildering to sit in my quiet, cheap, half-dark beer cellar with a whole pile of uncensored newspapers. From that morning I was a newspaper reader, and have been one ever since. In a way I began my records that morning; not consciously and systematically, but on another, more unconscious basis I began to store up material—not least for what has since taken form in *The History of Bestiality*.

The newspapers contained a complete summary of the little bears' war and its status on all fronts. In that humble café the uncensored newspapers were a wealth of facts and human freedom. At least it resembled freedom, it smelled of wildfowl. The papers contained news from my fatherland, where the Germans, true to custom, had carried out new executions—not so many as in Poland or Yugoslavia, but in their way enough. It struck me again how the Germans always act on behalf of world moral order when they mutilate or kill someone. This time they'd shot three or four people who hadn't understood the times and didn't think the world should be ruled by the Krupp family or AG Farbenindustrie. But the uncannily simple mechanism of the power struggle wasn't clear to me back then; I didn't understand that the politics of the whole century finally revolved around the business community's untrammeled right to rule mankind unrestrictedly and arbitrarily as they saw fit.

The same morning I went to the Royal College of Art to ask if I could work there. The director welcomed me like a long-lost son; he asked me how the trip over the border had been, and how I was getting along in the city. I registered at the academy and got to meet my professor, who was just as friendly and hospitable as the director. The same day I went to the city's largest library and got my library card in order.

From then on I drew croquis or painted from life a few hours each day at the Royal Academy, sat in the library, went out and painted or lay at home in my brothel corridor and read or slept. Aside from the daily newspaper-reading and my half-conscious storing up of material for later records, I broke every conceivable contact with the world. In the middle of the whorehouse I led an undisturbedly monastic life, I built up a wall which first began to show cracks fifteen years later—and which still today, up here in Heiligenberg, hasn't been fully and completely torn down.

The cracks in the wall are recorded in the Praiano papers and will be entered here, if I find them.

✧ ✧ ✧

Naturally I suffer from my sick, aching, and perforated memory, my accursed, destroyed recall: And I know it! I know it: *Everyone complains of his poor memory, but no one complains of his poor understanding!*—All the same it's true: in this great sea of darkness and oblivion there are islands of awareness and reality; something under the sea binds them together. My whole memory is like a spoiled, torn-up fishnet—as if the net had caught too big a fish.

Is it possible that the sickness begins here? That I can get hold of some of the threads during this time in Stockholm? Naturally it goes much further back, but there's no law that says you can't grasp the threads in the middle, there where you can see them. If I dare judge by the degree of resistance, discomfort and pain at the touch—then I'm indubitably on the trail here of this strange, unknown man I must have been; and I'm on the trail of how I must have committed the Sin Against the Holy Spirit.

There's something else which strikes me as important from these years—somewhat later, to be sure: it was back in the house where I lived that time, where Otto, the heroic representative of his heroic people, visited us and left behind some shreds of his life, as a little bear and as an individual! Of course there were several of us in the house, as I've already mentioned. Besides Otto and our Germanic *emigré sexuel* from Hamburg, Dr. Rosenbaum also lived there—a descendant, in fact, of the congregation which in a previous incarnation our friend the bell ringer up here in Heiligenberg led from Galicia and into Germania, where they subsequently laid the groundwork for the culture.

She was a doctor and her name and title were: Dr. med. Maria Rosenbaum.

She was considerably older than I, by at least twenty or twenty-five years, and for innumerable years she'd been a member of The Great Party which lives in the Kremlin. Since the early thirties, after the bears had come to power in Germania, she had been living in Stockholm. Her two brothers and her husband had emigrated to Russia even earlier. It is here her story begins.

She treated the rest of us with the German intellectuals'
megalomaniacal arrogance, which is already grafted onto
them in school and which bursts into full bloom in company
with their wretched, stunted little Teutonic doctor's degree.
Intellectual Teutons have this arrogance in common with
their officer brothers, but if possible to an even higher degree.
Our good old brother Lichtenberg, who knew them, says that
his university-educated countrymen learn to turn up their
noses before they learn to blow them.

Maria Rosenbaum lived without any blood relatives in
Stockholm, because practically all of her nearest had gone to
Moscow more than ten years before. I forgot to mention that
one of her brothers had taken along his wife—Dr.
Rosenbaum's sister-in-law, that is—to the Great Land. All the
Rosenbaums were *doctores*, except for the sister in law;
brother number one was a doctor in chemistry, number two
in physics, and Maria's husband was a Ph.D. in engineering,
with a specialty in locomotive-building, if I don't remember it
wrong. She had pictures of all of them. All four—the brothers,
the husband, and the sister-in-law, as well as Maria herself—
were members of the Great Party, passionate antifascists and
absolutely loyal Communists for whom every tittle in the
great law of Karl the Colossal was above any doubt or criticism. They were all mighty dialecticians and pure in heart.

Maria Rosenbaum was also pure. She had come via
Stockholm about ten years before I met her, in order to join
her relatives in Moscow as a next step. Because of internal
political developments in Moscow she never got a visa, and
hence remained sitting and waiting in Stockholm for an indef-
inite time, i.e. twenty years.

Dr. Maria and I met often in the hall or the communal
kitchen in the house, but we weren't intimate
acquaintances—I greeted her politely every time we ran into
each other, and she responded with an absent nod. Even
after more than a year in the same apartment we were still
saying "*Sie*" to each other. The acquaintance remained dis-

tant, not least because she wore thick glasses and had difficulty recognizing me on the street—and sometimes also in
the corridor in the house. Her arrogance lay on the same
plane as that of an ordinary SS officer on an inspection tour,
but had received an extra impetus from the fact that in addition to all her other merits she was also an academically edu-
cated *woman.* She despised me openly and permanently for a
number of valid reasons: a) because I was a *man*, b) because
I didn't have a *doctorate*, c) because I wasn't in the *Party,* and
d) because I was a *Scandinavian* and not a German. This contempt applied to all the inhabitants of the house—except the
sodomite from Hamburg.

One day when I came home she was standing and crying
her eyes out in the kitchen. Her glasses were befogged and
her face red and wet with tears. She was leaning helplessly
against the wall. For a moment I was completely confused,
then I took her arm and asked what was the matter. She
didn't answer, but took hold of my jacket, will-less as a little
child, while she went on crying.

She leaned on me for support, and I carefully led her
across the hall and into her own room, where she collapsed
into low sobbing. She sat down at the table and leaned forward, took off her glasses and let the tears flow down onto the
tablecloth. I looked around. On the table and the sofa the
day's papers were spread out. There were both morning and
afternoon papers, so altogether there were a great many. She
seemed to break loose as she leaned over the table, weeping
ever more heedlessly and uncontrollably.

This was at a time when the knell had rung for Germany.
Day and night the bombing squadrons from the west went in
over Germany's rich and blood-soaked fields, over cities,
cathedrals, prisons, castles, and factories. The land lay under
a rain of steel, phosphorus, and fire. It was being broken into
pieces, into shreds, crushed, mutilated, and killed, bit by bit.

The whole day's harvest of newspapers was filled with
enormous headlines about the bombings. Cities were transformed into burning, flaming mountains of crushed houses.

Maria had opened up all the papers at the biggest headlines and laid them out around her in the room.

She was sobbing more loudly now, at the top of her voice, like a child who has hit himself hard and must be tended to. There was something completely helpless and hopeless about the way she was crying. Then with a remarkably stiff and unnatural movement she slid from the chair and down onto the floor, where she lay and went on sobbing.

I looked at her, and once again I became aware of how people in a very strong state of emotion can behave theatrically, so that it seems unreal as if played by a bad actor. Even with the dying one can observe the same thing—that the very moment of death seems acted, counterfeit. The very second when the look ceases to be a look, when it *breaks contact*, has something of this. And many women have the same thing in their face and eyes during the act of implantation, when the moment arrives. It doesn't seem genuine either. As she lay on the floor in mountingly violent, unbridled convulsions of weeping, Maria too had something bogus about her, which reminded me simultaneously of death and of propagation. Anyone who has observed a real outbreak of an anxiety neurosis or of full-blown hysteria has seen the same thing, it's as if another being inside the person—an inner double—takes complete control of the muscles and nerves and makes a mechanical copy of a human being—stiff and false.

I quickly cleared the newspapers off the sofa, threw them on the table and picked her up and laid her on the sofa. I don't remember exactly how it went from there, but in any case I fetched some water and a washcloth and after a while she was in condition to talk between the crying fits—which lasted all afternoon and late into the evening, when she took some sleeping pills and quieted down.

But before it got that far, I knew the whole story.

The first things she said, or rather managed to sob out, were of course about Germany and the bombings there. She cursed England and America for the child murders and the mass obliteration of the civilian population, and I refrained from objecting that the Germans themselves had started it over London, not even mentioning Warsaw or Rotterdam in the first phase of the war. She spoke softly and incoherently and named names of people and cities in Germany, street names and places she had lived. She cried again. Then she raised her head and said:

"We're losing the war this time too!" And that same second the tears came like a waterfall, while she mumbled indistinct words which I could only partly put together into sentences and pictures. It was obvious that she thought Germany would be crushed and destroyed forever, that the English would keep it from rising again, that Germania would never again be a great power, but divided up into sixty-four small states so that the envious Englishmen could rule the earth, grab all the money in the world and destroy the German culture. She repeated the words:

"We're losing the war this time too, and they've sacrificed so much to win.... They're losing it...losing!"

I knew instinctively that what she was saying was certainly not her own true opinion, but something which literally oozed out of her whole heritage, from her blood and skin and even the language she spoke. But the reality, the concrete situation itself, was that here she lay, a Communist and a Jew, convulsed with weeping because Hitler's empire was collapsing before our eyes.

"They're being murdered and burned," she said. "And here I am, a doctor, far away, I can't help them, I'm not doing my duty to my country."

She looked at me wide-eyed and continued:

"They'll never forgive us for being away from Germany during these years, and now in defeat.... We should have been there."

It was obvious that she felt like a traitor. I said:

"You had no choice. You were chased out—of course you had to emigrate."

She didn't answer that, but put her hands over her face and wept again.

"It'll be different soon," I said in order to calm her. "After this is over, you can go back to your country...there will be an entirely new Germany. You can work to build a socially decent and humane Germany, which can finally come into its own and show what it really has to give...."

She cried louder, in long, almost animal-like gasps. I wanted to go on:

"The war will soon be over now.... And you and your husband can return, just such people as your brothers and your...."

"No!" she cried sharply. The sobs ended: "No, not them."

"Why not them?" I asked carefully.

"No!" she said decidedly: "They're traitors!"

"You don't mean that, Doctor Rosenbaum. They aren't traitors, of course they all had to flee from the Nazis, just like you did.... They didn't do it willingly, and it wasn't any treachery against Germany."

She looked at me, and when she spoke the words were distinct.

"Not against Germany. It's far worse...much, much worse...."

She looked at me meaningfully, searchingly. She wasn't crying anymore.

"Excuse me," I said, "but I don't understand. Then your brothers and your husband haven't betrayed anybody?"

I thought she had gotten confused and no longer knew what she was saying. Then the tears came again, this time more quietly, merely streaming. Her voice was clear and distinct, but dull.

"They are traitors to the Party. Didn't you know that?"

I was completely dumbfounded, I felt the room revolve silently around me. For a moment I had the impression that I myself was in the process of losing my reason.

"What's that you're saying?" I said uncertainly.

"They're traitors, all of them. All four. My husband, both my brothers and my sister-in-law. They've betrayed the proletariat...they've betrayed the Revolution and the human race."

I must have looked incredulous, and said:

"That I can't believe."

"Oh yes," she said, while the tears flowed more strongly: "It's been proved. They came as spies to the Soviet Union, spies for...Hitler and...and the United States, they were bribed, they were paid to do espionage and sabotage in Soviet industry...."

She began to cry hard again, she covered her face.

"Surely that's not possible."

Between sobs she became almost angry:

"It's true!" she said: "They've confessed, all four of them, that they collaborated with foreigners...they've been in jail for years...."

Her voice disappeared in a new and violent fit of weeping. For awhile she sobbed freely. Then she said a little more:

"It's wholly certain that they are guilty. The court had the proofs. My eldest brother and my husband have even been handed over to the Gestapo in Germany. He's in a camp."

She saw no contradiction in the fact that the Gestapo too had put him in a concentration camp.

"He was found guilty in Moscow," she said. "My younger brother is dead, and my sister-in-law is in Karaganda."

"But if your husband and your one brother are in a Gestapo concentration camp, then they certainly can't have been guilty of treachery toward the Party," I said in a vague attempt to cling to reason.

She looked up, and through her tears shone a wholly clear and alert, conscious look:

"There can be talk of a certain degree of subjective innocence, but objectively they were guilty."

She obviously felt this to be an annihilating, rational argument, and she raised her head—almost in triumph.

"If it's a question of such charges as sabotage and espionage for a foreign power, there's no difference between subjective and objective guilt," I said.

In some way or other I thought it would console her to prove their innocence. In reality it would have been the opposite of a consolation; she wanted proofs that *they* were guilty and the court just. She was on her high horse at once, she curled her upper lip in an arrogant, scornful smile—while the tears went on running from her eyes. It was clear that I was a Scandinavian and an idiot.

"You have to understand," she said, talking down to me, "that the court in Moscow does not convict without reason! It is wholly certain that they were traitors—quite simply because the court doesn't *make* mistakes. They were guilty, and I would have convicted them myself, for betraying the people and the Party...."

"To life imprisonment, to Karaganda or to being handed over to the Gestapo?"

"Yes," she said, and a spasm of strange cruelty crossed her face, almost a smile: "They were traitors to the people."

Then she put her face in her hands again, drew up her knees and sobbed loudly. For a long time we didn't speak, and she went on crying. It was my idea that she should take a sedative. She had some on hand and was conscious enough to take the pills. After awhile she became calmer, and before midnight she was asleep.

Naturally all this wasn't new to me. Such things happened daily.

Ever since the pact between the Soviet Union and the Third Reich the Russians had delivered German Jews and Communists to Teutonia's executioners, hundreds and thousands, nobody really knows how many. It came as a natural consequence of the developments in the Soviet Republics and the great Moscow Trials. When you come right down to it, human life has never counted much with little bears who have managed to gain power over other little bears. They're themselves and always will be, and only an imbecile can be surprised by it.

What filled me after Dr. Rosenbaum's day of weeping was not indignation over the little bears' wickedness, I was sufficiently familiar with that, but I felt a strong hatred towards Maria herself—because I hated this need for subjection, for genuflection and intellectual abasement. I already hated it then, which means that at that time I already had an inkling of my own sickness: when one hates intellectual submission so violently, then of course that's because it's a picture of one's own subjection. The process was underway.

The next day Dr. Rosenbaum was her old self. She hardly recognized me through her glasses, and she was as arrogant as a Teutonic general with a riding whip in his hand. In addition she had a sharp, contemptuous smile for me as well.

A short time afterwards the papers had a new story which filled all the front pages: one of the strangest sex murders in Swedish criminal history. It was a man who had killed a woman by sticking a broomstick up through her belly, straight through her entrails and all the way up to her throat.

After that the war news continued from day to day.

The Praiano Papers

I've found the Praiano papers just as I wrote them down ten years ago:

I've always known that this town existed; an all-red, very old town of brick. I saw it in my dreams when I was still a child, and now I recognize it as a memory from those dreams; it comes to meet me out of something otherwise far-away, dark and forgotten. It's a part of the darkness which surrounded me in the nursery after the light was turned out—it must be an important part of me, the fact that I've always known about it, that I've so often carried its image with me out of sleep. Nobody had told me about it, but I knew it.

Like many other medieval towns it lies on a height, on a small mountain. And it's small, you can walk through and around it in something over half an hour. The town is unkempt and decayed, it's dirty and poor, has one main street and only some few towers. The city-hall tower, which is by no means in good repair, has a bell and stands at the end of the main street, closing it off. All the stones in the town are rounded with age, the way pieces of glass get from lying in water for a long time, in a river or at the beach. Everything here is as if it had stood undisturbed for six hundred years, as if no one had been here since the time when a great plague or sickness passed through the streets and houses.

The tower is square, not so very high, but red like everything else in the town. This red color strikes me as extremely important; that's how it always was here in my dream.

From the plain there are three roads going up to the town, all very steep; one is for vehicles, the other two are for foot-passengers, or perhaps a donkey cart if the load isn't too heavy. There's refuse everywhere, bottle shards, paper, chestnut and lemon peelings. It isn't a pretty town. But everything is age-old, everything is in earnest, and the town's interior is a red, closed world, a red stone world where even the streets are paved with brick.

I've been here for two days now, and I know that it's not only in dreams and as a child that I've seen a picture of the town before this; I've also seen it in a waking state, or more precisely in a state which is more than waking. In this state one's body feels as if it were packed into something soft and warm, something infinitely yielding, pulsing and life-giving. All pain ceases. And the space around me seems filled with a mild, friendly substantiality, something which recalls milk, but airier and more spiritual—and which has to do with childhood. I've often seen knights, swift mailed knights chasing away over the crest of a hill, when I felt like this. A long series of black, lightning-swift knights with contours very clear and sharp, they're like cutouts, dark against a light background. It isn't a picture seen in a dream, but it's seen with the same eyes one uses in dreams.

What eyes are those?

In dreams you see pictures. Your ordinary eyes lie closed in a dark room, not functioning, and they aren't affected from the outside. All the same you see pictures. What eyes do you see the dream-pictures with? I think this is a very important question.

With these eyes which one uses in sleep I've seen, both asleep and awake, the town to which I now have come. Why did I know about it as a child? Why have I always known it? What does it have to do with the darkness in the nursery, when the light has been turned out and my parents have said good night?

The day before yesterday, when I came to this town, I saw a cat. He was quite young, not grown yet, and very thin. He was sick. He had lost the hair on his tail and hindquarters, and something was hanging out of him behind. He didn't move like a cat at all; he walked stiffly and slowly with his legs far apart, as if he were wound up, going mechanically. Or else this kitten crawled the way a crab walks on land, sideways and in jerks. He meowed with every step he took and lifted his paws carefully. I looked him in the eyes, and he looked at me with a question. It was clear that he didn't understand what was tormenting him; perhaps he thought that something had got its teeth into his rear. Then he went his way, sideways, meowing, stiff-legged. Such a cat can have a remarkable gaze. And he lives in this town. But the streets are so empty, they consist only of brick, and there's nothing to eat in them.

I couldn't get the cat out of my thoughts all day. It also bothered me that he was a kitten, and that perhaps he had nothing to eat. It's often like that with cats in this country, that they're sick and slow-moving. In a fishing town along the coast further north I gave food to a cat who had only three and a half legs. This cat wasn't yet full-grown either, and his neck was thin as a pencil. He had never been able to learn to walk on three legs, and at every step he took he tried to set down the half, the cut-off foreleg—and every time the stump came near the ground he quickly pulled it up again, as if he had burned himself. But at the very next step he repeated this and put the foreleg down again, while the hind leg on the same side was trying to leave the ground and move forward—purely and simply as a reflex—and again he drew back the destroyed leg as soon as it touched the ground. It all was like clockwork, he *had* to set the sick leg down whether he wanted to or not. This gave him a strange jerky way of limping, so that this cat wasn't very agile and cat-like to look at either. All the same he was easier to get out of my thoughts than the little cat which lives in this town, although this one has four legs. It's as if he's walking on broken glass. He lives in a world where all is pain.

Yesterday I walked around the town, but I didn't see the

kitten. I'm very glad, because I don't know what I should do with him. Should I give him food, or should I shoot him? Most of my baggage is sitting packed up in another town. So to shoot him I'd have to go down to the lower town and buy a pistol; I've seen guns in the store windows there, and they're not at all expensive. But then it's conceivable that there may be someone who owns the kitten—and besides, it would make an awful bang here between the stone walls. It bothers me that I don't know what I should do with the cat who lives in these streets. Only in the South can streets in a small town be so dead; they're cold, a bit dusty and without a trace of green life. They're like the house walls with their few and small windows. Six or seven hundred years ago they put the windows on the first floor very high up. And the red stone houses in this town are remarkably tall.

I've got a room to live in, and it's cheap. No tourists ever come here, despite the fact that this town has preserved the Middle Ages better than other towns. Here there's no hotel, and no bar with a glass-topped counter and a radio, and so people don't want to come here. But I think this is the best of all towns. And there isn't any falsehood here.

In the town wall I found a narrow gate down at the end of one of the back streets, and outside was a road which was more than usually filthy. I hadn't discovered this road before; the earth was black and moist, slippery, polluted. There was a placard nailed up on a dead tree trunk at the road's edge: *"This area is infested with . . ."* Then followed a word I don't understand, a monstrously long word containing something with *". . . ixo . . ."*

I don't know what it is, but I turned back. A terrible loneliness and a vague anxiety had come over me. Perhaps it only meant measles, but I was a bit afraid. I must have been afraid both of contagion from the difficult word, and because the road itself is so dirty and slippery, and everything is so dead there. But it's strange and somewhat pleasant to be a bit afraid. Not too afraid, of course. But this kind of faint, vague dread reminds me a great deal of childhood.

There's something rotten about everything in this town, as if it were full of contagion. The town is unimaginably still; it has closed around me like a box, and I know that my childhood is very near, and that this town has lived in me forever. I walk now in a kind of swoon, inside a dream.

It's like a shaft, a dark tunnel.

I was a little child and stood looking into all the color and all the light in the world. I had it right before my eyes and was reaching for it. Two big red hands and arms were working with the color and all the white in which it shone and glittered. It swelled and puffed up and collapsed and rose again; it lit up with colors which freed themselves from the white and mounted into the air and hovered in the sunshine. The red hands plunged down into it and lifted up something which splashed back again. The light was filled with thousands of small, glittering pearls. They were white and luminous and yellow and blue and violet and all the colors in the world, and they weighed nothing and were light as the air. It made me very happy and I laughed at the light.

That is my first memory. The first thing I remember is light and colors, and not until long afterwards did I understand that I must have been standing beside a washtub, with my eyes just over the edge, watching the work and the soap bubbles. Perhaps they were my mother's hands washing clothes. I remember feeling a wonderful safety and happiness at the sight of the bubbles sparkling in the sunshine. This must have been a reflection of a yet earlier memory, from something long, long before this. Before everything. But I can't remember farther back than that. I was probably about two years old at the time. This is a very pleasant memory which I often think about. I have no very clear picture of myself when I was that age.

Later I blew bubbles of soapy water up into the sunshine with a clay pipe, and that was also lovely, but still it wasn't the same.

I also have a memory of sitting in the grass, and the grass is higher than I am. And I have the impression that I'm wearing some kind of white pajama suit. There must have been flowers and insects around me, and I was very happy. I turned over on my stomach with happiness and yelled loudly. Nearby was a large white wall, an enormous barn and a high mountain. Some gigantic boys sprang up the mountain wall and slid back down the face of the cliff in wooden shoes, as if they had been on skis. I've since sought out the place where my parents lived that summer, and I recognized it. Everything was right, except that the great flowery meadow I had been sitting in was a grassy slope ten or twelve feet broad, lying between a fisherman's very small house and a tiny little barn. The mountain was a rock, something over a yard high. I was always fond of sunshine, and still am.

It's very difficult to remember one's childhood, especially for me, because there's something wrong with my memory. Someone, God or life or whatever—has torn great pieces out of it as out of a sheet or a blanket. There are terrible holes, a sort of wound in my memory; and these holes, which the Lord or something else has torn out, are to be found just anywhere—sometimes things disappear which happened only a few days ago, sometimes I notice that I've lost things from several years back.

It's most uncomfortable to come into the neighborhood of such a hole. One morning I woke up and couldn't remember where I'd been the afternoon and evening before. I hadn't been drunk. Luckily I managed to press it forth from my memory, but the picture of the previous day still remained fuzzy and dim. I felt rather sick until I remembered it, and was terribly anxious. These losses of memory are generally related to the fact that something is torn to pieces inside me, not only in my head, but in my whole body. But then when I suddenly remember or recall something which was forgotten, then I become somewhat happier and feel that I'm well.

Again I've walked around the town without running into the cat, but I'm thankful that I escaped meeting him. I'm rather afraid of that meeting. To tell the truth the thought torments me dreadfully. He's probably undernourished like so many cats in this country, but I also wonder what disease he has. And how much it hurts. Science has now worked out a way to measure sensations of pain, just like distance and weight and loudness. Thus: a 1-pain pressure, a 2-pain pressure, a 3-pain pressure, and so on— something like 1 atmosphere's pressure, etc., and then with the unit *dolore*, like 1 kw., 2 kw. I wonder how many *dolores* the cat feels, how many I feel myself, how many I *could* stand. But on the other hand I can't find it proper to think that it will do to stay sitting inside for a cat's sake, so therefore I went out and walked around in the streets as if nothing were amiss. There is never a bird to be seen in these streets, but I did cast a glance into the cabinetmaker's shop with the old frescoes on the walls. The door was open and the cabinetmaker was a little old man who sat there in his hat and winter coat, working. He was narrow across the back and very stoop-shouldered, sitting there in his workshop, and I thought how in a few years I myself would be an old man sitting in this way that only old men can sit: immovably sunken down into oneself, with a thin neck and blue veins on one's hands, occupied with something external, a thing or a task. His back under the worn black winter coat was turned toward the door where I was standing, and he didn't hear that I had stopped to look in. He had a wine bottle and a bit of white bread on a stool beside him, and once in the middle of his work he reached for the bread. Then I went my way, but with this strange feeling of having stood and looked at him. I came back to the gate in the old town wall and stopped and looked at the sign with the long disease-word, which I don't understand.

Now I screwed up my courage and walked past the sign and forced myself to go a ways down the road, which was sticky and dirty and full of garbage from the kitchens on this side of town. The whole time I had this feeling that even to

read the word on the sign was contagious, and that it was
courting disease to walk there.

There's a barbed-wire fence here, and the trees have no
leaves because it's winter. There's nothing but rotten leaves,
decaying lemon rinds, and then the mighty red-black stone
walls of the houses and the town wall looking out at me. The
wind is cold and piercing outside the wall, and the steep slope
from the city down to the plain of olive trees has a sickly
ashen color. The place is strewn with bones, fish scraps, veg-
etable parings, and rotten fruit rinds. You feel as if you're in
an old-fashioned hospital here on this side of the town wall
with all the dirty, worn-out things which people have thrown
away, out the windows or through the narrow gate. The
houses are built right up from the wall here on the damp, raw
north side.

Has *la bella Italia* always been the same poor, sick, filthy
garbage can? I thought about what kind of contagion it is that
this area is infested with, and then I walked back through the
gate and up along the red main street.

All this porphyry is cleansed, sterilized by the noon sun
and the night frost. Dry cold dust drifts into the corners and
along the house walls. Everything is red and made of stone.
The sky is whitish blue. There's also a library here. It's closed
and locked, with an iron-studded door and with lattice windows set high up in the wall. The lattice is made of heavy,
coarse, lovely wrought iron and sits in front of the window. I
think the whole thing is a special library about the town saint.
He's supposed to be very holy and very famous; I've heard
the name before. The town contains much more than you'd
think at first glance, and in one of the halls in the old cloister,
a room now converted into a repair shop for mechanical
things—on the street side there are some very lovely frescoes
on the walls. Since there aren't any cars in the town, they
mostly do bicycle repairs in there, and occasional smithing
jobs for the families. By the door there's a sewing machine
waiting to be fixed. It's been standing there for days. The
mechanic is a pale man in his fifties, and he nodded at me

when he saw me standing in the doorway. I nodded back. All
the bicycles in this town are very old. There were bicycle
parts on the floor and a couple of rubber hoses hanging on
the wall, on a hook driven right into the fresco painting.

In this red-brown town all the people are dressed in black.
The men may sometimes wear dark brown or gray-black, but
the women are always entirely in black. So the town is red-
brown and black, and the sky whitish-blue. There aren't any
other colors. Red houses. Black people.

As a child I bicycled a lot.

And I often stopped in at a bicycle repair shop, one particular shop, with oil on the floor and rubber hoses on the walls.
Everything is black inside a shop like that, if it's old enough.
Inside they had a German shepherd which lay by the door,
and which I was afraid of. Finally he bit me straight through
my jacket, sweater, shirt, and undershirt. It was late autumn,
or winter, just as it is here now—dry and snowless—and I still
have the scars on the inside of my left upper arm, right by my
armpit. Looking at them today I catch a glimpse of my own
face in the mirror, and see that it's changed again. It's gotten
younger and belongs to another time. I've also gotten thinner.

When the dog bit me it didn't hurt, but I could feel that I
was bleeding under the cloth. And I remember the sound of
the chomp when he opened his mouth and snapped his jaws
together; it was like when you pull a pole up out of a bog.
Nobody could understand what had gotten into that old dog
who had never bitten anybody before, and I was ashamed. I
tried to hide the bite when I got home, but I'd gotten blood on
my clothes, and besides it was running out of my sleeve at the
wrist, so I was discovered. Today I looked at the scar, and it
looks smaller now; just a sort of whorl of irregular white spots,
which nonetheless hang together in a sort of dynamic image
or ornament. I wonder why my face has changed now again.

It's quite right that the town is red. But I was wrong the
first few days when I thought it was built of brick. It's actually

made of a porphyry. Old buildings of brick eventually
become black with age, but this town has retained its clear
color. I said that the town had closed itself around me like a
box, and it has. There's nobody here that I can talk with. I
only know the language imperfectly—not to mention the
beastly dialect—and it's typical that I'm ashamed to ask anybody to explain to me what the long, difficult disease-word on
the sign outside the town wall means. I have only memories
and small day-to-day experiences to hold onto. I'm dying to
know what kind of sickness the word stands for, but I can't
bear to ask anyone.

It's quiet to be alone.

I live in a cell here, and I'm not clear whether it's in a
cloister or a brothel, but I have a very good room, with a
stove. It's of red porphyry like everything else. There are no
pictures in the cell except one, which shows the town saint—a
chromolithograph or whatever; he's standing with a heart in
his hands, and the heart is impaled on a sort of long, unpleasant hatpin. But you see pictures of saints in the bordellos too.
Then I have a bed, two chairs with wicker seats and a desk in
front of the high-up window—which is set far into the wall,
more than two feet into the masonry. The walls are red, the
floor is red, there are beams under the ceiling. Everything,
except for these beams, is of red stone. From the window I
look out on the roofs of the town—all of billowing, curling red
roofing tile, and behind them a strip of dull, earth-green landscape. The fact that the window sits rather high up in the wall
gives the room a closed, confined peace. On the desk there's
a half-gallon bottle of vermouth and in the window stands my
grappa. It's a fine place to work. No sound. No voices. Only
myself to listen to.

The condition can't be described. I walk in blood to over
my ankles, I wade in blood. Actually that's the whole story.
There's blood running from all the walls, and it collects on
the street, in the gutter, or it just flows along the sidewalk. It
can reach to my knees now and then. Yes, I know very well

what this is. The light is turned off. I'm in complete, coal-black cellar darkness, imprisoned in black color. It's a well-known phenomenon. I even know both the popular and the professional medical designations for it—a man of *my* experience and *my* reading! But that doesn't help much beyond just making it possible for me to say that this is sickness—I have an awareness of sickness; I can attach a name to it. It's one thing to live in a world where blood runs off the windowsills, from the mountains and the clouds—it's another to pin a little Latin name to it. In a world of pure pain, where all impressions from outside are like being touched on a part of your body where the skin is peeled off. It's a state of absolute, pitch-black darkness and pain—where one is confined under a dome which makes it impossible to perceive any other living being in the world but oneself. Nothing exists outside me—which is hell.

Not if I met the Crucified One on the street would I look up or turn to follow him. Nothing else exists but *I myself* in this world of blood and darkness.

Winter is cold in this part of the country, and we often have frost, both at night and in the morning. The great, far-away landscape is now completely dead.

Once again I'm alone with a strange man. I should talk with him and explore him, try to find out the reason. It isn't even that. I want to know *how* he is, not *why* he's like that. That's something one can never know. I've lived in the same space with him for thirty-six years, and he's become a cross for me to bear. He never answers questions. And I don't really know which of us is Christophoros. Now I shall become intimate with him. He shaves every morning and has a rather coarse beard—black, naturally. In many ways he still reminds me a bit of my father, but is utterly without his beauty and dignity. The likeness lies in his being so cut off from others, so impossible to talk with. I don't understand him at all.

On the other hand it's incredibly easy for him to associate
with people, but always without involvement. In conversations—which with the help of a polite and noncommittal
savoir vivre he's learned to avoid almost to perfection—he can
easily and quickly achieve a personal and deep-going rapport
with others, with just anybody—if he wants to, but he always
lets it drop. However, he gets into these conversations more
and more seldom. On the other hand I see him get up every
morning and shave and wash, and his color becomes warmer
from it, he turns slightly reddish-brown with soap and water.
The strange thing is that this is almost unnecessary; he's one
of the few people I've met who seems well-dressed and
soigné even if he is unshaven, has slept in his clothes, is
unwashed and has unpressed pants and unpolished shoes. He
can spend the night in the seat of his car, and the next morning go to the most expensive hotel in Europe and eat a cheap
breakfast—rolls and coffee—while the headwaiter and the
garçons bow deeply and respectfully to him, without suspecting that he goes to the toilet afterwards to wash and shave
gratis—and also to perform the necessary in clean and decent
surroundings. Although this too—aside from the
"necessary"—is absolutely not needful at all. But here, in this
red stone room, he pretends that it's very important, and he's
very well packaged in flesh and blood and bones. I see by his
heels that he wears a size eleven shoe. The same as I do. He
too weighs about 175 pounds. This flesh he got from his
father and mother. He displays an incredible seriousness in
his dealings with soap and water, towels and razor blades.

When he's finished with that, I'll sit beside him at the
breakfast table, watching as he stirs the sugar into his pale *café
au lait* and drinks a large grappa before he eats the white
bread with a scant teaspoon of bad marmalade on it. Here I
am sitting with him.

He is mute as a stone, and I think—that is to say: *I know*—
that he doesn't think either. All is stillness inside him. He
only sees. He looks at the light falling in onto the red stone
floor, and he thinks, quite simply, nothing. He just takes up

pictures into himself, and then he sits there with them, with thousands of pictures inside him, from the Arctic Ocean and Brooklyn and Africa—and for that matter from Öland in the Baltic Sea, from a summer many, many years ago. A picture of a summer and some roses. And I am beside him and must become intimate with him. But what have I to do with him? A grown, strange man about whom I know nothing. I even have my own, totally negative theory about him: it's very possible that he's a *finished* man; empty, stupid, and idiotic. He's probably a cretin, a wholly idioticized cretin, almost without a look. He's most alien when he goes around doing little things—taking the blanket off his bed, straightening it so that it lies smooth, or doing something about his clothes.

✧ ✧ ✧

There are few people in the world who know more about brothels than I do. I've lived in them for months at a time. Not because of licentiousness, but because I always live in brothels if I get a chance. By now it's even become a habit. Or if they aren't brothels in the public sense—the state-owned brothels one of course can't take up lodging in—then at least in the common bordello-hotels with rooms all the way down to fifty cents a night, as in Naples for example, or in the small hotels where streetwalkers and girls from the houses sleep and play their tunes on the phonograph, or in the slightly more expensive places where the girls from the nightclubs live. I'm used to living quietly in private brothels, I live there and get up early in the morning, always greet the receptionist most correctly before I go out for breakfast to read the papers. I live there in the houses of pleasure and read my Meister Eckhart, my Thomas à Kempis, my Dante and my Novalis or my beloved Hölderlin—and now and then also Stendhal and Swift, of course, and the footnotes of Lichtenberg. It goes without saying that they all belong to my traveling library which I always lug with me in a couple of suitcases in the car. Max Stirner, Feuerbach, the young Marx, and the Gospel of John also belong to my whorehouse reading.

As a child I was enormously fond of grinding with the coffee mill. I wanted unspeakably much to be with older people and grind on the quern.

In my grandfather's yard there was an old-fashioned pavement of round kohlrabi stones with grass growing between them. From the very earliest times I remember comparatively little about my grandparents, but on the other side of the courtyard there was a little house where there lived a childless couple, who at that time were probably a little older than I am today. To them I went often and ground coffee on their old-fashioned hand-mill of brown wood and brass. It was good to watch the coffee beans sink down little by little into the brass funnel and be crushed while I struggled with the grinding. It was like a hole in the earth or an undertow and a whirlpool in water. I drew the long, curved arm with the wooden handle round and round, and it made me happy to hear the crunchy, scraping sound inside the mill. I don't remember this exactly any more, but I have the impression that it all happened in semi-darkness. I almost remember the face of the wife in this house, mild, round, and pale, without firm features. There was peace and warmth around her, and I believe that she sometimes told me fairy tales or legends. Today I have the idea that the husband was a smith, for he had something secure and peaceful about him, as a smith sometimes has. He was quiet and kind. I was happy when I had ground a whole drawer for them and my arm had gotten tired—but at the same time I was sorry that it was over for that time. They only drank one drawer's worth.

Here in this red town, now—in one of the winter months— when it is in fact quite cold, I can observe a whole new process in myself: a growing *insensitivity* to temperature. I don't mean that this is of recent date, it goes back a year or two—no, *three* years; and it has developed in this land of stone, sun, and poverty. In a strange way I'm without feeling for frost and heat. During the winter in this town of stone it was naturally my insensitivity to cold which I noticed, since it was never uncomfortably warm except in the afternoon. On the other hand the late night hours, mornings, and forenoons were often extremely cold. I'd often been bothered by cold in earlier years, but all at once it was over. I felt right at home in a room where it was less than fifty degrees; I would put on an old brown bathrobe, a black shawl around my neck, and the thickest socks on my feet and in this get-up I could—with blue hands, which didn't bother me in the least either—sit for hours and read or just look toward the window, perhaps also write, if it had any kind of meaning. Like this, too—in the black shawl, bathrobe, and felt slippers—I would also go out on the street, down to the vintner's, and buy my two ounces of smoked ham and some bread and olives and red wine, and talk with people a bit. Then I was dressed just like everybody else in the winter months in this town, aside from the wholly black women. Likewise I've often swum in the sea in midwinter, in February and March, or in January, without the cold water of fifty, fifty-five degrees bothering me any. In the same way I was completely unperturbed in the summer by the fact that it could be a hundred or more in the shade; I went around in a dark jacket and with a hat against the dazzling light at noontime. It was like that for several years.

I enjoy this insensitivity and regard it as a sign of health.

My grandfather was a very good man. But I remember almost nothing but his beard and his rocking chair; his beard was white, but had yellowed somewhat in the course of time. He was strongly religious, I've since found out, a peaceful, good-natured man by and large—Swedish by birth; all his life he spoke a rather broken *Norwegian.* Originally his hair and beard were black as charcoal, his too, but that didn't stop him from saying to my father, when the latter was presented as a son-in-law:

"Are you Jewish, you have such black hair?"

All of them, on both sides, were black as Doberman pinschers. My grandfather I have little impression of, but my grandmother I knew better, because she lived much longer; he died when I was very small. All the same I remember sitting in his lap. Otherwise my grandmother was the one I knew best.

I must not have had much appetite at that time, because when I was staying with my grandparents she was always busy making the only nourishment I would take: white wheat-flour porridge. At that time it was a great torment for me to eat anything but that white porridge, and my grandmother understood this and made porridge for me. She'd cook white porridge morning, noon, evening, and night, if only I would eat.

"My poor boy," she said many times a day, "don't you want something to eat?"

And if I answered white porridge, she'd act just as surprised and happy every time, and she'd say that it would only take a minute. So then she'd go and put wood in the stove and make porridge. My grandfather was also enormously glad that I would eat porridge. Yes, it was a great joy for them both.

Me, I couldn't understand why my mother was embarrassed that the old people should go to so much trouble to make porridge for my sake. She suggested bread and butter, but I never had any desire for that. My grandmother said that she was glad to get up in the night and make a fire for my sake. I never got used to ordinary mealtimes.

To all the others this seemed rather remarkable, for toward her own children she was a strict and headstrong woman, and even toward her husband she was obstinate and willful. She was a farmer's daughter and descended from a petty king who was executed after a revolt against Denmark. And she was a dragon toward the servant girls, so that my grandfather often had to go out to the kitchen and console them. In lots of ways she must have resembled her ancestor—the beheaded one. During a great epidemic she even lost three children in the course of one month, but she still had four left.

I remember her only as a very old woman, but she was still very beautiful, with a narrow nose, straight back and shoulders, and a small waist. I know only good of my grandparents, but I never got around to thanking them for anything.

The memories end here.

He died when I was around four or five years old, and she lived several years longer. But when I saw her again many years later, I myself had become someone else and didn't understand her anymore.

I've seen photographs of myself from that time, mostly brown snapshots. They show a rather unhealthy little boy with bad milk teeth and with very long curls down over his shoulders. My hair was black and curly and hung way down over my shoulders. I had a big lower lip and thin legs under the long stockings.

This, that my memory is ruined, doesn't just have something evil and unpleasant about it. The tapestry which should have formed a kind of coherent web of pictures is torn to pieces, but now and then something entirely different appears in the holes. I can't say just what it is, but it's something different. The holes which are relatively new are the most uncomfortable to come near because there's a kind of paralysis, as it were, spreading out from them. I can't bear to examine them more minutely. I become faint and powerless as jelly when I try to put my fingers in the wounds to explore them. For these holes are a kind of wound. All the same I have to keep doing it. Relatively recent periods of time of up to a whole year can be covered with oblivion, and often to such a degree that I can't even say where I lived in such and such a year, or what I did. Often I get letters from people whom I no longer know who are. But I often manage to press such things out of oblivion.

I've stopped opening letters.

✧ ✧ ✧

Today I met the cat while I was out walking, and I ran away, but he saw me. He was very sick and moved with difficulty. He meowed after me and I saw his eyes, small, coal-black, and shiny, and he understood nothing of his sickness. He just opened his little pink mouth and meowed. I think he has lost more hair since last time. But his teeth are white and sharp. He walks in small jerks like an old man and lifts his paws and looks around and meows. A cat should be pure movement, it should be a gleam and an explosion when it springs. This cat isn't like that, although he's young.

❖ ❖ ❖

I do know something about animals. A couple of months ago, in one of the large cities where I go sometimes, I saw a chimpanzee. I always go to zoos when I have a chance. This was an adult male of almost 150 pounds, and about ten years old. He sat in the corner of the cage, with his left shoulder against the bars. Outside the bars there was plate glass—he lived in a hermetically sealed, climatically regulated cage. But I saw him from a distance of eight inches, I could see every single wrinkle, and he sat motionless for nearly half an hour.

Despite his being more than twenty pounds lighter than I, he seemed colossally large. The face and hands were the most interesting thing about him.

It has always been inconceivable to me that some people can find apes comical. This one was so old, so endlessly age-old. How is it possible that so much age can take form in flesh and blood in the course of ten years? How can there be room for all this *time* in an animal so young? It's clear that what I saw was the frightful age of the species, not of the individual but of the simian race itself. Certainly we too carry with us an age which isn't our own and personal, but belongs to the species. This ape was all chimpanzees and not just the one, he was an endlessness of generations.

His red hands were more than twice as big as mine, but the thumb seemed small and weak compared to the other fingers. The remarkable thing about the hands was that they were simultaneously working hands, huge and coarse—and also refined, strangely degenerate, noble hands, like those of an old lord. I've seen old noblemen who had such hands, all too long and thin and bony, and so old, so wrinkled. The ape's nails were long and oval and curved down around the fingertips. The color of the hands was red and dark, but with a blue ingredient, so that they seemed violet—as if they were very old, and frozen. The index finger was as thick as three of my fingers, and bluish-red. I have never seen such hands as on this chimpanzee. Likewise his wrist and forearms were of a preternatural size and power, covered with thick, black strands of hair.

The animal sat with his shoulder against the bars and with his arm bent at the elbow and wrist—like Michelangelo's David, so that the fingertips and knuckles touched his shoulder again. His face was like that of an old prisoner, but there was something mechanical about the eyes, something shiny and black and speechless, something *swift*. His look was both deep and shallow at the same time. His eye was black and still, and both the sky and the bars of the cage were mirrored in it. I've often seen this look in animals, but in this ape there was something special going on. His eye had nothing of the shy and airy quality that a horse's eye has, and nothing sentimental and personal like a dog's eye. The chimpanzee's look was immeasurably old, and entirely without feeling; he was like a mountain in his eyes. They were so age-old, so black, they had nothing to ask about. A colossal memory lived in him, as in the night. The ape had an enormous night inside him. He was like sleep itself, and still it was this which was the wakeful thing about his eyes. It was something like this which looked out at me. And beside this blank look: the sunken, stunted nose, the enormous lips and all the wrinkles. There was also a mysterious contempt in his look.

And I felt guilty toward the ape, as if I'd been caught practicing racial discrimination. It's impossible to say exactly what this guilt consists of.

While I stood looking into his eyes, an older man came over to us, with hat and stick—and the chimpanzee lifted his

hand slowly; solemnly, almost ritually he took his lower lip
between his fingertips and bent it down, drew it far down
over his chin. With full consciousness he displayed the red,
silky-soft, obscene mucous membrane on the inside of his lip,
on his gums and around the remarkably large, yellow teeth.
He showed us his oral cavity and remained sitting like that,
but with the same black, mute eyes. The man beside me
laughed—a delighted, virgin laughter. He appeared to be a
sound and healthy man, in his mid-sixties. He was hardly stig-
matized, and there's small probability that the Holy Spirit had
made any special descent on him. In contrast to the chimpanzee he was created in God's image.

I started reading the placard beside the cage, where I
found the ape's data and biography. I have difficulty understanding that he's ten years old; if it had said nine thousand
years, that would have seemed more likely—for he has, as I
said, a supernatural age. The pyramids are dwarfed beside
him. This ape could have sat like an enormous mountain and
seen everything from the Creation on, from before Noah and
the Fall, before Adam and Eve. But he was born in Europe
ten years ago, and I compare the enormous old man in the
cage with a slender little ten-year-old boy or girl, I hold his
huge wrinkled hand beside the supple, plantlike little hand of
a ten-year-old child. The placard relates that this ape lives in
the same cage with a slightly older female, but the female has
seen him as an infant, watched him grow up, and therefore
won't recognize him as a man. He lives in celibacy because of
her viewpoint. But he's the biggest chimpanzee in Europe.

The man standing in front of the cage has gotten out a
bag of sandwiches which he eats from, and the ape is watching him, still holding his lower lip inverted down over his
chin. He is certainly no image of Buddha. He has so much of
flesh and bones, and his forehead is so inconceivably low
above the black eyes and furrowed all over with wrinkles.
Likewise the area around the eyes is nothing but wrinkles, the
skin is loose like an old person's. Then the ape moves, turns a
bit and makes a remarkably indecent movement down

toward his sex, which is stirring. And I see that his sex isn't old, it's the only youthful thing about him, plantlike and very young. Now the ape sits facing us, and all at once I see him completely: the ape consists of sex, hands, and eyes. That doesn't make his frightful age any less, and the expression in his eyes is unchanged.

Now and then I leave this red town I live in and travel into the famous old cities nearby to see how the medieval painters portrayed angels. The biggest and oldest angels are painted with six pairs of wings, with the wings forming a circle around them. Such angels look like wheels of flame. In all the pictures of Saint Francis's stigmatization the angels look like that: with six pairs of wings, and with rays of fire and gold going out from the angels and over to Francis, evoking the nail holes in his hands and feet, the wounds from the crown of thorns and the stab of the spear in his side. Saint Francis himself has carefully described the vision which accompanied the stigmatization. It wasn't a question of ordinary angels in his case, but of cherubim or seraphim and maybe also thrones, in other words the very highest hierarchic triad. But otherwise Dionysius the Areopagite has doubtless provided the most comprehensive systematic representation of the angel world, more or less what Linnaeus did for the world of flowers many centuries later. The painters in late Antiquity and throughout the Middle Ages adhered strictly to Dionysius's textbook in angelology and gave every single specimen precisely the number of feathers and wings befitting its rank and age. The biggest angels have a frightful age, they're almost eternal.

I love pictures of angels and I've driven back and forth all over this country to look up famous or outstanding angels, whether in mosaic or fresco. Some of the loveliest ones I've found in illuminated manuscripts. I've been to Ravenna several times because of certain angels.

In Florence they closed the brothels while I was staying there studying angels. Only the state-owned ones, of course;

that is to say the controlled and well-ordered houses, where you stood or sat in line and waited as at a polyclinic. They really were a kind of love clinic, these renowned and hygienic places from that time. And the hygiene wasn't there at the expense of the human quality in the atmosphere. After these pleasant places were banned the girls had to go out and walk the streets, where they became dependent on pimps and certain hotel owners, and where they didn't have cheap medicines and free medical care. All the girls I know think that it's all a great step backward in welfare—they no longer get regular vacations or vacation expenses and pensions as they did back then.

Here in Florence my alcoholism has sprung out in full bloom. I obviously suffer from every known form of alcohol neurosis; I'm both a false and a true dipsomaniac, I drink periodically and every day, I'm a mealtime drinker, habitual drinker, and closet drinker, and in addition an occasional drinker and a social drinker, but I also like to drink alone. It's especially when the darkness appears at full strength that I drink in this manner—around the clock and everything I have on hand. In the morning I have a couple of glasses before I go to breakfast—but they aren't the first of the day: I usually wake up at four or five o'clock—and of course I have the red-wine bottle standing open right by the bed, so that it's easy to find. However, I know very well that depression and alcohol mutually aggravate each other, and when the darkness has reached bottom and becomes a full-blown night, a pure imprisonment underground, or turns into what I've mentioned: when I wade in blood and pain at every step I take, whether I'm walking on the street or in a museum, or driving somewhere or standing at a bar—when hell has broken loose in earnest, then I stop drinking, or almost. Instead I go to the *farmacia* and buy sedatives; you can get lovely cheap sleeping pills and tranquilizers in this country, and without a prescription. When I've bought the means to deaden myself, I go up to my hotel room and lie down. I then stay in the room, for the most part in bed, for two or three days, taking more sleeping pills every time I wake up. I usually wake myself up by crying, and then I take a handful of pills and belt the whole thing down with a glass or two of red wine. After a few days like this it seems as if the depression has "burnt itself out." I feel like a human being again, and go out and eat well and drink wine with the meal. Then several weeks can pass in which the depression stays within the bounds of the tolerable, until I notice that I'm building up to a few days' new madness. One of the first sure signs is that I've suddenly gotten so drunk that I end up lying on the street or on the floor in a *bottigliera*. This repeats itself several times, and then comes the darkness at full strength, followed by sleeping pills and three days in the hotel room. After that, the whole thing over again. I'm fully aware that I shouldn't be at large, but safely stashed away in an institution. On the other hand I have the strange certainty that if only I manage to live through this alone, it will turn to blessings and health. Sometimes I wonder whether I've met the angel—and I know that he won't get away until he has blessed me.

I also know that he who hasn't experienced a full depression alone and over a long period of time—he is a child. Such a state is like meeting something from outside, a carnivore, a wild beast which tears the flesh from your bones. Dante's image—the leopard—is wholly exact and true; I suspect that he met it here in Florence, a city which is excellently suited for lasting depressions.

And the same goes for all old cities where one can be completely alone. Naples, Marseilles, and Paris are also splendid cities for this purpose.

Although the best of all is perhaps my old red town with the cat and the long sickness-word in *"ixo."*

By and large I travel around. In the car I have paper and clothes and the books I need. Often when I load the car to head for a new town I have no idea where I want to go, or where I'll end up spending the night. Many nights I just lie drunk in the driver's seat and sleep. One time I stayed in Milan for several days, right beside the Cathedral. It was

magnificent to look at in the gray light of morning, at a time
when only I and the street sweepers were up. I would sit on
the running board with a roll and a bottle of wine for breakfast, looking out over the square at the building. That was last
year, I think. In late autumn, and with gray weather the
whole time. One day a street sweeper stopped beside me. He
didn't speak. He looked at the bottle I was drinking from.

It was a half-gallon *bottiglia*, not the round *fiasco* which is
so common. I held it out to him without saying anything,
since I had food in my mouth. He tipped his head back and
drank long from the bottle. He was toothless, ragged, and
dirty, but he wore his scarf and his sixpenny cap with as
much freedom and confidence as if he had been of the House
of Colonna. He took the bottle from his mouth and wiped his
mustache with the back of his hand. I gestured to him that he
could drink more. He nodded, but first took a couple of deep
breaths. Then he put the bottle to his mouth again and drank
long and deeply from it.

He smiled as he gave me back the bottle, then he took his
broom and went on with his work. In two draughts he had
drunk over a pint of wine.

Afterwards I headed south. I stayed overnight in old cities
and drank at the cheapest *bottiglieri*, just as I always do. I only
want to see old things around me; everything which has a
past seems warm and dark and does me good. Sometimes I
find towns which seem much older than the well-known
tourist cities, and far more isolated and confined. It's as if the
old, dark, closed-off architecture heals something of what has
gone to pieces in me.

This whole culture is 4000 years of stone and sunshine.
There's also a lot of blood and iron in it; it's a cruel and
harsh culture, but without falsehood. Why is it that cruelty
calls forth laughter? Those who founded this culture, that of
the Renaissance, were all men who laughed at atrocities. The
whole of our new world, our modern culture, was born in
Tuscany; the whole of precise, empirical art and the whole of
exact science—it all comes from the stone cities of Tuscany.

And the Tuscans were feared for their laughter. The Florentines were envious and malicious, but witty. They were great observers, cool and detached—they taught the world to distinguish between arbitrariness and law. Aretino laughed himself to death when he met his sister in a brothel, he was one of the few people in world history who notoriously died laughing.

This summer I came upon a fisherman in one of the small towns. He was sitting on the wharf, skinning a ray which he had caught. I stopped to watch him. The ray was alive. He cut the thick skin up into strips, and peeled the strips off one by one, slowly and with great force, because they were so firmly attached to the fish. It jumped up and down on the stone pier in its half-flayed condition. When he noticed that I'd stopped, he looked up and laughed heartily. It was clear that he was amused by the fish which couldn't die.

But this laughter is the reason why the Tuscans invented science and the clear Tuscan drawing in their cool paintings; laughter means distance. Conversely: where laughter is absent, madness begins. Every time I've had a chance to observe an outbreak of psychosis or a first-rate clinical anxiety neurosis the signal has been given in the absence of humor the moment one takes the world with complete seriousness one is potentially insane. The whole art of learning to live means holding fast to laughter; without laughter the world is a torture chamber, a dark place where dark things will happen to us, a horror show filled with bloody deeds of violence.

The ups and downs of my own case give me the opportunity to observe the transition with hairlike precision, I can capture almost the very second when I slip over the boundary—including the fact that laughter ends, that distance is gone; I unwittingly become identical with myself, a condition which is total unfreedom. But the fact that I do observe the transition to pure sickness—that, of course, is what keeps me out of the madhouse where, clinically speaking, I belong. The classic moments are those when a crying jag goes over into laughter, and then I'm on the other side of the line again, and have preserved laughter and reason.

Naturally I brood quite a bit about which main lie is the reason for my sickness. To think about it is to rummage in a chaos of a thousand lies, with the hope of finding exactly the one which has been the source of the disease. But if my tendency to find anesthesia in alcohol is an important symptom of where the shoe pinches, then this basic lie must have come at an early point in my life, for the need for anesthesia had already shown itself clearly by the time I was fourteen or fifteen. How early can one work one's way into a life-lie?—It is related of Leonardo da Vinci that he had a laughter which was so beautiful that those who had heard it could never again forget it.

❖ ❖ ❖

Now and then the world and reality lose all coherence and become in the higher sense non-figurative. Phenomena turn into loose, free-standing pictures. I force myself to write down something every day, to continue with the records. In the middle of this I eat; I eat two dinners every day. After especially powerful depressions my appetite becomes uncontrollable. I can eat three or four helpings.

A few weeks ago I ate supper in Florence with my friend Alberto and his wife; during the evening I came into contact with one of the current problems in this melancholy Italy. The country has been suffering in recent years from epidemics of suicide, and in particular a certain type of suicide, practiced by people who are quite young, more precisely by intellectual young men, often under twenty. The suicides always occur in the same way, by a resolute leap out of a window from the seventh or eighth floor. They've become so common that there's a slang expression for it; people don't say "suicide" but just *"a la fenestra."* One simply goes to the window.

The result of this migration to the window is, however, anything but simple, and a fall from the eighth floor entails an almost unimaginable mess on the stone pavement or asphalt; to begin with, of course, the earthly remains must practically be gathered up with a putty knife and a sponge, and then the place has to be hosed down and washed thoroughly with soap besides. People splash dreadfully.

On this evening Alberto and his wife and I got together to have a really good meal. They were both a little late, and she looked pale. The restaurant has one of the best kitchens in Florence.

She surprised me by drinking two glasses of neat whisky before dinner.

Alberto looked up from the newspaper which he was hurriedly leafing through.

I got the impression that something had happened and asked what it was.

"Well," answered Alberto, absently patting her hand, "Paolo has gone *a la fenestra*. Just as we were going out the door. Not more than fifteen minutes ago."

He buried himself in the newspaper again.

Paolo was the son of their neighbor, right across the hall on the same floor. A likable boy of about seventeen. He was a student.

There is nothing I'm so afraid of as the next attack of depression, yet I know that it's coming. But not exactly when. Still, there's a certain regularity and rhythm in it. Anyway it certainly happens very rarely that physical illnesses, for example, even very painful ones, lead to suicide. Almost all *a la fenestra* cases happen during depressions—often in the end phase when the patient becomes active again but his power of resistance is worn out and used up.

So I write a little almost every day but it doesn't help much, because I carefully avoid writing a single word which has anything to do with the truth.

❖ ❖ ❖

Of course there's quite a bit of suspense in seeing how long

such a thing will last and how one will personally meet it in
the end. Besides, one hasn't learned to tell the truth. In ancient
Persia young men were brought up with three goals in view,
they were supposed to learn to ride, to shoot with a bow, to
tell the truth. We don't learn anything, except that it's important to assure ourselves of a comfortable life—such a fairy-tale
lie in itself that it is surely pathogenic. One feels it particularly
here in this region, which is full of past and seriousness and
meaning. The women are dressed in black in this red town,
and not without reason. Things have happened here.

It will be exciting to see whether I'm suffering from a
sickness unto death or a sickness unto life. If one ever gets
over it, does one come out of it as a healthy man or as a spiritual invalid?

One of my friends, who runs a charming little madhouse
in Switzerland, says that if one manages to get through it by
oneself it will "lead to a significant increase in one's depth of
experiencing." That sounds delicious.

That reminds me of a dream I had recently: I was lying on
an operating table, and the neurosurgeon was bending over
me with an electric scalpel, while he described the imminent
operation to the students: The top of the skull would be
opened, and a square of about four by four inches would be
removed, something like the top of a coconut—"so that it will
be possible for the patient to breathe that way too."

Otherwise my mornings in Florence pass for the most part
in a pleasant and proper way; I get out of bed in my bordello
and if my fingers aren't trembling too much, I shave. Down at
the corner I have a cup or two of coffee mixed with a shot of
anise liqueur, and after that I usually go to the cathedral by
Giotto's campanile to look at the Pietà there. From the bordello to the Pietà is only a few steps, and it stands there all
alone, in a room by itself—open toward the main church, to
be sure, but quiet and isolated. It's one of the finest Pietàs
there is, and perhaps Michelangelo's best. In the morning I
have it all to myself, completely undisturbed—the room
around it is cool and shady, with a gentle light. There are

benches along the walls in the room, so that you can sit and observe the group from one angle after another. The heavy white marble block has a strange life in the shadows and the half-light. The Crucified One lacks a leg, but it's almost impossible to notice it because the composition of the figures is such that you don't miss the leg. I wouldn't have seen it myself if I hadn't accidentally discovered the surface of the break.

All the same it's not certain that this is my favorite of Michelangelo's Pietàs. I'd probably rate the Pietà in the Accademia even higher than this one. That's the Pietà where the legs are small and weak as after an attack of polio, and where the shoulders, arms, and rib cage are as heavy and muscular as those of a blacksmith. The arms are longer and considerably thicker than the legs and one hand is twice as large as the other, the whole block of stone quivers with pain—and I think it must be the best Pietà which has ever been made. At least I rate it far above the one in Rome, and I also like it better than the tall, thin one in Milan. But the Accademia is quite a ways from my inn, and anyway the cathedral is almost always open, and in the morning it's wonderfully still inside.

A few months ago there was a state-run brothel right around the corner here, easily recognizable by a series of sandblasted nymphs in the frosted plate glass on the entrance door. One afternoon I was walking past and heard a frightful commotion from above. I grew curious and went in. On the first floor I checked my hat and coat and paid the small checkroom fee before going up. Upstairs, in the big reception hall, things looked funny. The madam sat in her throne-like place looking out over the hall, which was full of soldiers. The atmosphere was different from usual: a great excitement reigned, the soldiers were yelling, and a couple of the girls were yelling too, furious and indignant. When the madam saw me she greeted me with friendly politeness as always, but she was obviously embarrassed about the situation in this otherwise so quiet and peaceful establishment. I didn't immediately understand what the soldiers and the girls were howling about.

But at regular intervals the madam's voice sounded, clear and distinct. She repeated the same words time after time, like a church bell:

"No, no, no, *signori!*" she said. *"Non è vero. La signorina* is not *ubriacca.* . . . The girl wasn't inebriated, she was tired and sick, but not drunk."

The girls sided with their madam and defended their sister's honor: she was a girl who almost never drank, or anyway never more than a very little. But the soldiers stuck to their story; she had smelt strongly of wine, and she had been swaying—she had been so drunk that she couldn't do her job. There was awful shouting and yelling, but the situation wasn't serious in the least, it was simply a question of principle, an almost academic discussion. Down on the street it sounded like a mass murder.

Meanwhile the soldiers sat waiting their turn, and one by one, with a bow and an "Excuse me," left the company for a few minutes. The rhythm of the house was undisturbed.

At this place I would now and then visit my friend Bruna, always bringing along a bag of candy or a little chocolate as a personal thing in addition to the fee. Bruna always saved the chocolate, and if the weather was warm she put it in a little box outside her window so that it wouldn't get sticky or melt.

Bruna was a sweet and clever girl, and she doubtless gave the chocolate to her brother's children when she visited them out in the country on Sundays. But when the brothels were closed in the name of socialism and morality, things went downhill for her terribly—she ended in the street up by the railroad station, completely exploited by her pimp and her landlords, so that private enterprise saw better times. She was hardly allowed to keep more than ten percent of her earnings, and that was of course too little. She became diseased as well.

Then I often walk way over to another part of the city in order to look at Cimabue's *Crucifixion*—the great crucifix which dominates the whole room. Naturally I'm also taken with Giotto's crucifixions, as with crucifixions in general. In the same place there's also an outstanding collection of angels; Simone in particular has a couple of splendid examples there, among others an outstanding Annunciation. But as I said, when it comes to angels I like the Middle Ages better than the Renaissance, because of the Middle Ages' far greater dogmatic insight into angelology.

My favorites are the ones with six pairs of wings and a complete halo, from the crown to the soles of the feet and outside the wings.

But the Holy Spirit is just represented as a dove, something which was possible before the Renaissance, in a pre-empirical time when the Spirit hadn't descended into matter to learn about causal thinking. Nobody today would represent the Spirit as a dove or a lamb.

For neither the lamb nor the dove can laugh the Florentine laughter, which is after all a prerequisite for carrying out experiments and adventures with matter. The dove would never have discovered nature's eerie secret: that at bottom all matter is explosive. We eat our sandwiches, pursue our love lives, are born and die on the lid of a powder keg journeying in the cosmos. I realize that the word "powder" is rather dated.

Furthermore the cosmos itself is located in the middle of a gigantic explosion, with the galaxies fleeing from each other at a speed considerably greater than that of light. The whole thing yields a splendid picture of our situation in the cosmos and our momentary glimmer of consciousness, with the morals, norms, and standards we have conceived during the explosion.

Still it's important to live in the dull-green Tuscan landscape, and I saw it early one fall morning a few months ago from the balcony outside my hotel room in a small Tuscan town: the fog lay over the gray-green hills with their vineyards and olive trees, but down close to the ground, so that all the hilltops rose above the fog like still wave-crests; on some of them were towered cities, and above them all the sky was thin and blue-white. The landscape didn't really resemble Tuscan painting at all; it was Japanese.

But it was here that it began. This is Europe's heart. Here they painted the most beautiful madonnas, here they cut up and dissected the first corpses, they broke with theology and angelology and wrote down the first observations which were subsequently to lead us out into great, empty freedom.

Last year I awoke one Good Friday morning in a small mountain town: in an old stone room which looked out on the narrow, cobbled main street. I went down to the bar, and while I was standing in the doorway with my cup of coffee, the whole crucifixion of Christ came walking toward me. It was a long, long procession. They were all dressed in black, and they all had black executioners' hoods drawn over their heads, with only small holes for their eyes. All the black-clad executioner-folk carried long, heavy, ancient wooden crosses. They were singing. They sang with deep voices, some dreadful monotonous tune. They were barefoot as they walked over the centuries-old pavement. The huge dark-gray wooden crosses and the black hoods haunted me for a long time afterwards. It was an evil dream, arisen from the earth's interior—from the absolute, fearful darkness which has created us.

In contrast, Cimabue's crucifixions shine like gold.

Also metallic are Dante's topographical communications from hell, where he relates—and this corresponds to the teaching of the Church—that in Inferno there's an especially gruesome pool of mud and sulfur reserved for those who have fallen into the vice of melancholy:

Fitti nel limo dicon: Tristi fummo
Nel aer dolce, che dal sol s'allegra
Portando dentro accidioso fummo:
Or ci attristiam nella belletta negra.

We were despondent in the mild air which rejoices in the sun! And for this we shall atone in the nether world. Can Dante possibly be unaware that with this slimy, muddy pool of blood and shit he is giving an exact description of the punishment for melancholy here and now? No, it isn't possible, he must have known that the very despondency, the melancholy or depression itself, is a *substance*—rotting, viscous, stinking matter mixed with blood, which one wades in up to one's knees. In the same way *time* is also a substance, viscous and heavy-flowing.

Of Leonardo we know that he laughed this bubbling laughter of gold, which was the Florentine laughter in the deepest sense. Yet Leonardo was not a happy man, and his laughter had nothing to do with happiness.

Dante also had this laughter.

For no conscious person can live without this ability to laugh at cripples, disease, and suffering. To laugh at maltreated animals and children, to laugh at everything. Without the Florentine laughter one goes mad. So we should laugh in the mild air which rejoices in the sun, *nel aer dolce. . . .* Without laughter you sit fast in the pool of excrement, and you will slowly go into decomposition, into autolysis, you will fall apart, and yourself turn into living excrement. Dante and Leonardo knew how to meet a world of blood and stone and iron—Tuscany.

"The deeper the feeling," said Leonardo, "the greater the pain."

One may object that this is neither very deep nor very original, but one must admit that the observation is sober and realistic. His spirit was Tuscan. All the great masters from Tuscany's ateliers took their sketchbooks along when they went to watch the public executions.

When the air gets colder I head south, to the ancient regions of this land—one can exchange the Renaissance for Antiquity. You can go to the museum in Naples and look at pornographic sculptures. One of the most amusing is the girl having intercourse with the goat. The expressions on both their faces. Or the large silver bowl which is borne on the necks of four naked young boys, each with his huge, erect member—and the same jubilant, playful, irrepressibly laughter-loving smile on their faces. It's executed in heavy silver and with the most minute craftsmanship.

The tradition involving boys has lasted for a long time in these antique regions around Naples, at least four thousand years.

Just take the story of little Giovanni! I've rented an apartment for a couple of months in a small tourist and fishing town down at the coast, right on the ocean. To be exact, that is, it's a tourist town in the summer and a fishing town in the winter. I have a terrace looking out on the beach here, only a few yards from the water line, and I can hear the surf day and night. A few foreigners live here in the winter because of the climate.

All who come to our little town fall in love with it. And that's highly natural, because it's so pretty and whitewashed, and because the climate here is perhaps the most pleasant on the whole Mediterranean. The winter is mild and without much rain, so that even in January the men can sit in their shirtsleeves and drink at the restaurants along the beach, and you live with the windows open night and day and can breathe in the air from Africa even at the coldest time. On the other hand the summers aren't so hot as you might fear, for the ocean always sends a cool breath up through the streets, a faint breeze which is just enough to keep the heat from being oppressive or fatiguing. Then the town itself is one of the prettiest and most pleasant that you can imagine: in color it's either white or pink and light blue, the houses are often rather Moorish in style, with cupolas and curved arches; the town has almost no regular streets, but only narrow alleys, stairs, and arcades; and almost everywhere there are small, sparkling white piazzas with cool and pleasant bars. Yes, they lie so thick that you don't have to go more than ten steps between every glass. The wine is uncommonly good on this sunny coast, fruity and refreshing, with a faint acrid taste. The town is terribly steep, as if a child had painted it on the sheer mountainside—and faces straight south. Then there are a number of small, cozy *trattorias*, where you can eat mussel soup and squid and clams and *scampi* and delicious fresh fish from the neighboring towns— the fishermen in this town don't fish much anymore since the tourists came. Instead they rent out their boats all day, while they themselves sit on the beach and have their pictures taken. But the town is still regarded as a fishing town in the winter.

Until last year there was a lovely luxury brothel here too.

Ever since the tourists came here some years ago everyone who lives in this favored little town has become enormously happy and content, for no one is poor or hungry anymore. According to native sources it is definitely by God's personal directive that all the foreigners come here every year; in the old days people had enough of both care and trouble, and almost nobody was dressed as well as even the poorest are today. Now both boys and adults earn so much in the tourist season that they can go strolling on the beach all winter, and many of them also get unemployment compensation during the time the hotels are closed. All the people here are on the whole pleasant to each other and use a civilized tone in their daily relations. And they clearly have fun on the beach in the off-months. The male youth of the town play soccer and roughhouse or play cards and pitch pennies all day, and now and then have joking conversations with the foreigners who have become so fond of this idyllic town from Antiquity—it's so old that it actually has something in the direction of temple ruins up in one of the marketplaces—that they've settled here for good, or at any rate for a year or two. They're always nice to the boys here, and the boys often bring them flowers or a few oranges from their gardens at home—which they find touching. The boys on the beach feel a strong affinity for foreign men, and rejoice that more and more of them are coming here. Many of the foreigners have distinctive customs, and the ephebes can do them a service in just half an hour, and be paid very well for it.

For the grown fishermen too the stream of tourists has been real luck from heaven, but in their case it's mostly the visiting ladies who are interested. Many of the fishermen never need work again, but get everything in gifts from nice foreign ladies. All the same the men—probably from old habit—stay down on the beach, painting and fixing up their boats. Perhaps it's countless generations of seamen's or fishermen's blood which demand the proximity of the ocean. Of course they sometimes do a little fishing to pass the time. The old people tell how in the old days the fishermen had to go out to sea both when it was raining and when there were waves, and in those days of course they were sometimes drowned at sea. But nowadays almost nothing ever happens here which is sad or in any way distressing.

The only time in several years that anything tiresome happened was the thing with little Giovanni. In this region every other boy is called Giovanni, and if you see a flock of boys and call Giovanni, half the flock come running, thinking they'll get some small change. This particular Giovanni finished school three years ago, and he was the prettiest boy in the class—and that's saying no little down here, where Africa is a neighboring land and there have been Arabian settlements for centuries. Both the boys and the girls can be amazingly beautiful. The place is swarming with people with Arab blood in their veins, and they're slimmer and often lighter than the usual round, swarthy South Italian type. Giovanni is a very sweet and nice boy, and he's certainly one of the prettiest boys on the beach—even if he's still a bit thin and pale after what happened a while ago.

Giovanni would rather have been a waiter right from the beginning, and that's easy to understand—in the first place because being a waiter carries a prominent social status—most mothers are proud if one of their sons can become a waiter; and in the second place because it entails getting unemployment compensation while the hotels are closed for some of the winter months. But anyway it didn't work out like that for Giovanni. His parents were serious people who wanted him to learn a trade, so they apprenticed him to a barber. After he began at the master barber's he was naturally seen more rarely down on the beach where the other boys hang out during the winter, because of course the barber had to stay open the year round, and not just in the summer as most of the hotels and many of the restaurants do. Giovanni's parents specifically wanted him to have a job which lasted the whole year.

The barber he began with is a very nice and pleasant man who is the best friend of many of the foreigners, both the ones who live here and those who come here regularly in the summer. He is often with them in the evenings. He plays a first-rate tambourine besides, and can sing a lot of the old Arabic songs from the region. He was unusually nice to little Giovanni and paid him right from the beginning, even though the apprentice was only fourteen years old.

It was after Giovanni had been apprenticed to him for a few months that his parents first noticed that there was something wrong with the boy, for he was thin and listless and had stopped eating almost entirely—although fourteen year olds usually have an excellent appetite. He almost completely stopped playing soccer, too, when he was down on the beach in his free time.

For awhile they gave him pills and cakes and medicines and drops to build up his strength, but nothing helped, and finally they took him to the doctor, *dottore* Moratto.

Giovanni himself has since told all over town exactly what the doctor did to him: he examined him several times and in every possible place, but couldn't figure out what was wrong—even though it was clear that the boy was sick. Finally he gave him some new pills with iron, and said that he must get to bed early and try to eat more. But Giovanni, alas, didn't manage to eat noticeably more, and his parents sent him back to the doctor several more times, without Dr. Moratto's finding anything.

Little by little Giovanni became very ill and developed a pain in his belly too. His parents took him to a larger town nearby, to a doctor who is very well-known, but neither could this renowned physician make anything out of Giovanni's illness. He just took his fee and prescribed some more tonics.

Giovanni had severe pains in his belly, and now looked miserable; so his parents took him to Dr. Moratto again, but the doctor still didn't manage to discover Giovanni's illness.

People rarely saw anything of Giovanni during this time, for when he wasn't at work he was outside very little and could hardly do anything at all—neither run nor play soccer nor anything whatsoever. When the barber had closed his shop the boy went straight home and rarely came out anymore in the evening.

It wasn't until a few days later that *dottore* Moratto chanced to come into the barber shop to get a haircut, and noticed that it was Giovanni who was tying the big towel around his neck. So he asked him how long he'd been an apprentice there.

Afterwards Dr. Moratto went to Giovanni's parents and asked them to send the boy up to him next day during the siesta, but this time alone. He'd just thought of something, he said, and would like to examine him again.

When Giovanni came up, the doctor examined him in a couple of very private places, and then asked him in detail about the master barber. Thus did Dr. Moratto manage to find out what kind of disease Giovanni had caught. It had first occurred to him when he saw him at the barber's—for the thing was that Dr. Moratto also had the master as a patient.

Giovanni's father was furious with the barber and threatened to take his pocket knife and shave him with uncommon thoroughness in a very different place from where the master barber was wont to shave his customers. But then the barber said that he would make good all the doctors' bills and pay damages to the family besides, and then the father stopped being angry, and they went out and drank a couple of aperitifs together before supper.

Giovanni, however, was ailing for a long time with the disease, because he had got it both fore and aft, and it had gone up and taken hold several places in his belly. Afterwards Giovanni got permission from home to be a waiter, so now he's once again at the beach while the others are playing. And thus the story had a happy ending.

People in the tourist and hotel trade say that there have

always been a number of gallant diseases in this town, but *dottore* Moratto claims that they came with the tourists. He is a communist.

While this story shows love from its more clinical side, the next episode shows it more from—well, probably from the comical side. It's possibly comic, and in any case not the least bit sad.

Some time back there lived an American writer in our pretty little town. He was—measured by the standard of the Holy Spirit—absolutely no Dante, but he wrote for American magazines and was paid in dollars, which made him a kind of multimillionaire and tycoon of industry in a town like this—at any rate outside the tourist season. As noted, he was a man who could pay for things, and that was his misfortune, if it makes sense to talk about misfortune in connection with Americans. His checks for dollars led people to see him more as an object than as a fellow human being with a soul, made of flesh and blood.

One of the families in the town had a daughter named Maria, she was over twelve years old and definitely *immaculata* and *virgo intacta*. This had been ascertained by the virgin Maria's grandmother, a nimble-fingered, toothless, and black-clad lady from the hard old days when surgical examinations of this kind were very common. As noted, Maria was a virgin, and Maria's father knew the American writer and his wallet. The father dropped a few words about his daughter's condition, and our friend from the prairie got the message. They haggled for awhile, and agreed that the *americano* would get to deflower little virgin Maria for a cash payment of twenty thousand lire, in other words about thirty dollars. Strictly speaking it was a high price, but the girl was pretty, a mere child to look at: slender and brown and supple. With the money the father bought himself a white summer suit.

The day arrived, and in accordance with the bargain the writer came and was admitted to the virgin's chamber. The girl lay undressed, waiting, and everything went according to plan, except that the whole thing was a trap. When the defloration had been accomplished, the door to the bridal chamber was charged from without, and the invited witnesses to the rape of the minor were supposed to stream in. The object, of course, was to blackmail the American, and had been all the time. That's an old tradition in these parts.

But our man from the U.S.A. must have quick as lightning detected a snake in the grass, and there was a crash as the clothes cupboard was overturned in front of the door. Afterwards an even more violent crash was heard, and the American disappeared in a wink, lightly clad but without leaving evidence behind, through the closed window. The *virgo* was no longer *intacta*, and the father sat there with the white suit as his only profit.

The whole town laughed about it for several days. Soon the family was laughing about it too. But everybody would have laughed even better if the affair had been a success.

Of course it's lucky for the town that it can make money from the natural riches of the coast and of the children—as one knows if one is at all familiar with the conditions in this part of the country and southward. The poverty down here is no longer *ein großer Glanz von Innen,* but a sick, black, stinking sore. Outside the tourist districts nobody would pay more than fifty cents for a maidenhead. The thirty dollars from the American was still an unusually good price, but it shows how absurdly high the market is just in this town. To comprehend the standard in the South, one must know about the traffic in children which is still going on even as far north as Naples, where both urbanization and the housing shortage drive prices sky-high. The price for a fairly usable child in good condition—reckoned at the international rate of exchange—stands at about $1200. This price level has remained fairly stable ever since the war, i.e. for almost ten years. The unusual stability of the child market suggests that conditions are in equilibrium.

Today there are a significant number of Italian children being exported to the Arab countries and to India, where white girls and boys are sought after and bring a much higher price on the market than African children—who are usually dark, somewhere between brown and black in color. In India the children are used in brothels, while those in the Arab states are sold to the oil sheiks' harems, paid for with good dollars from the United States. The oil-dripping, dollar-paid democratic heads of state are members of the UN—and that, at any rate, is a consolation. Ethiopia is thought to be the most important point of assembly for slave transports of this kind. It isn't far away.

Parents are very fond of their children here, and another reason they sell them is because they think the children will be adopted and be better off than they would have been at home.

Here in this clean white town, where there is so much falsehood and where the boys first get gonorrhoea in their bad lies at the age of fourteen, we don't have this problem of child sales—at least not in any other sense than that specifically pertaining to the right of sexual access. That the price of a maidenhead can reach the dizzy sum of thirty dollars is a guarantee for human rights.

So I've rented myself a house with a terrace facing the beach here in this little whitewashed lie of a petty welfare state, and I'm sitting on the terrace with a wicker bottle between my legs, attired in the only clothes one needs to wear in the winter here: sandals, khakis, and a short-sleeved shirt. The winter morning is as clear as if there were no air in the world, only pure absolute space. It's cool, but the sun is burning and the sea is a sharp blue, drawn against the sky as with an iron ruler. There's a bitter taste in the hard blue color, as in ink or in Prussian blue, and something puckers in my mouth when I look at it. I experience color as much with my organs of taste and smell as with my eyes. *Time* lies around me like a fluid, a kind of slime.

I've had three black days again, and for the most part stayed indoors, much of the time in bed—with tablets from the *farmacia* and with bottles of red wine on the floor in front of the nightstand.

It's clear that the depression isn't a force or a power within myself, but something which meets me from the outside: a substance or perhaps in reality a being, something which resembles a carnivore—it's like a strange, spectral being which is just on the brink of taking form in flesh and blood. And I feel it that way when I'm alone with it. I could almost call it "him." He's sitting there when I wake up, and I know that I'm not alone. There's another living being in the room.

Shortly before this three days' isolation in my house I noticed that it was on the stairs, and I spent a couple of days in Naples. I drove north in the car, left it in an attended parking lot, and walked down to the harbor. Afterwards I went out to Pozzuoli, which is more Neapolitan than Naples itself. I had my back trouser pockets full of 10,000-lire notes. Under the conditions here a large sum. Nobody here would be able to see that I'm a foreigner; I had on a pair of old brown pants, a black sweater and outside that a dark brown jacket of the shiny leather that truck drivers wear. My face and neck are so brown from wine and sunshine, and my hair is so black, that people who ask where I come from believe me when I say that I'm an African. Besides I was unshaven that day, which didn't make me any blonder. In Pozzuoli I began to drink.

Down by the docks I found a *trattoria* surpassing everything I've hitherto seen for poverty and filth. The furniture was nailed together out of crating, and old newspapers were tacked down onto the table tops. These newspapers were all that had been done to beautify the place, which also had a gate opening out onto the fruit rinds and garbage in the street, and one lone window which was small and high up. It was clearly an old cellar which had earlier been used for storage.

I ordered a slice of roast ox meat, cheese, apples, and a quart can of wine, and asked to have the wine right away, so that I could get half of it into me before the food was ready.

I belted down two or three beer glasses of the acrid red wine at once and began to feel better. At the side table sat three other men drinking in the same way I was, glass after glass, but without eating. All three were stamped with deep misery, but were talking together and laughing now and then. One of them was big and very dark, with sharp features and thick eyebrows. He was missing some of his upper teeth, and had a strange expression in his face, a mixture of goodness and hardness.

When I'd eaten the apple as a conclusion to the meal, I got a new quart can and went over and asked if I could join them. They immediately made room for me. This was the upbeat to a three-day binge.

As soon as I spoke they heard that I was a foreigner, and began to complain about the conditions in Italy, especially in the South. They were also very friendly and praised me because I could say anything in their language at all. We drank in a way which was surprising to me in this country: each man in turn ordered a can of wine which he paid for on his own check. Then we drank it up together. I, however, was not permitted to order more, because I was their guest. I said I had lots of money, but that didn't help. The three were occasional workers on the docks here, but had also done fishing now and then. Two of them had been to sea. They were scandalized by the Christian Democrats' government, which they regarded purely as an instrument of the church and of the rich; it wasn't doing anything to improve conditions, and old and sick people were still sleeping on the streets at night, as if there had just been a war or a natural catastrophe. It was a camouflaged continuation of fascism, but without any of the latter's good points.

"What do you think of Mussolini?" I said.

The big man across from me grabbed my hand and pulled my arm straight across the table, all the way over to himself. Then he kissed me on the wrist, over the pulse.

"*That's* what we think of Mussolini," he said.

They were agreed that only Mussolini and the Communists cared about poor people—and back then, in the days of Fascism, a fisherman who lost his rig in bad weather got compensation from the state, and so could buy himself a new one. Today a fisherman in that situation was a finished man, it was most unlikely that he could earn enough for new gear. He had to take on occasional jobs for others, and would never earn more than a dollar or so a day—just enough to keep his family alive. They talked about this in a gloomy but dispassionate way, without any yammering. We drank steadily, chewing on some olives which lay in a wrapping of newspaper.

After awhile we got drunk, and went to a bar. I stood at the counter and brought out some bills to pay with, but the big man took them out of my hand and shoved them down in my pocket again. *He* was doing the inviting. The rest of these days I remember only in glimpses. I remember the brothel room where I spent the night, both from the night and from the morning. The sheets were literally black as dirt. The next night I was better off; I slept on the beach, right down by the sea under a boat. There must also have been a third night of which I have no pictures in my memory. I don't remember anything about it.

One evening I'd gotten away from the others, and was walking alone down a street which lay right by the sea, with a yard-high wall on the outside, and with great blocks of stone and cement outside that, as a breakwater. I had regained consciousness while walking on the sidewalk, and was suddenly clear and awake.

Coming toward me was a young, black-clad woman holding a little girl by the hand. I stepped over toward the wall to let them by. They stopped. The girl must have been seven or eight years old. The woman spoke to me and asked if she could do me a service. I was automatically about to say the usual "Another time, *signorina*," but then I saw her face. It was fair and thin. The whole black-clad form was tiny and seemed so young that you couldn't tell whether the little girl was her sister or her daughter. It *could* just barely have been her daughter, if she'd had her very early.

"Where shall we go?" I said.

"There," she said, pointing over the wall, down on the cement blocks.

"And the girl?"

"She'll come with us."

We jumped over the wall, and the girl squatted on the
ground beside us. She watched us alertly. The mother—or the
big sister—lay down and quickly pulled up her black dress.
She had nothing underneath. She lay like that for a moment.
The minute I came near her she slung her arms and legs
around me with such force that she nearly squeezed the
breath out of me. She began to whimper in drawn-out sobs.
The whole time the girl was sitting and watching us.
Afterwards I lit a cigarette and gave the grown one a couple
of bills, which she stuck in her pocket quickly and indifferently. She seemed not to notice how much she got and didn't
ask for more. But the little one stretched out her hand, and I
gave her a couple of coins. Now I noticed that we'd been
lucky when we chose the spot; right beside me lay a big heap
of human excrement. We could easily have happened to lie
down in the middle of it.

The big one lay still, breathing heavily, and I wondered
why she had the little one with her—whether it was to have
some kind of protection, or whether it was simply because
she couldn't leave her alone in the evening. The grown one
lay on my right, between me and the girl. On the other side I
had the pile of excrement.

When we were standing on the sidewalk again, the little girl
extended her hand and thanked me for the money. She curt-
seyed. I observed that both were well-dressed, and as I left them
I thought about the violence in that embrace and how the
grown one had been practically unconscious. I got a vague feeling that the money played no particular role, and that perhaps it
was only used as a pretext. At any rate she had shown a much
greater interest in the act than in the money I had slipped her.

When I turned a few minutes later and looked back, they
were standing a bit further away and talking with a new man,
while they held hands. Then he accompanied them along the
sidewalk, off toward the place we had been. Both girls had
something gracious and refined about them.

I crossed the street and went into a bar.

Inside I met my friends again, and after a while the memory was gone. Those three days are almost pure darkness.

When I gradually awoke the next day, I knew that a worse darkness was coming and that I had to get home to my apartment in the little whitewashed town. In both back pockets I still had the rolls of large bills. They were untouched, I'd been a guest the whole time.

Now I'm sitting on the terrace in the sharp morning air and the sunshine, in sandals, thin pants, and a shirt. I'm washed and shaved. I know that I have to get away from here, up to the red stone town where I have something to do.

Over this sunny coast crackling with color there lies an appalling melancholy; that is falsehood's peculiarity and nature.

❖ ❖ ❖

I'm again in the red stone town, my infected region with the long, threatening disease-word in *"ixo."* There are only old people here, almost always dressed in black. Of course the town isn't particularly old, the present buildings can hardly go back more than six or seven hundred years, but on the other hand it hasn't changed since then. And the donkey at the town gate was standing there when Dante rode by. The architecture is hard, severe as iron, and wholly medieval. Since the town is situated on a hilltop, it must have been able to withstand a siege when the gates were closed. The plain around it stretches far out in gray-green waves, which mount into crests toward the horizon. On a couple of them there are other towered cities.

It's possible that I've found a lasting place here. Among the red stone houses in or within the walls there are a couple which are vacant. One of them even has a tower, and that's what I'd like. It certainly wouldn't be expensive to live here, even if one had to buy the house.

Here I have important cities nearby, I can go to Pisa now

and then and look at the tower where the prince was shut up without food along with his two sons, and where the old one finally ate the princes, his children. I can go into Florence and look at the Palazzo Vecchio; or to Siena and go to the cathedral library to see the illuminated books with pictures of angels and evangelists and saints, or to the museum to see the old Siena masters whose paintings were almost icons.

Above all I can stay here and walk on the black, moist road outside the wall on the north side, where the sign about the disease and the danger of contagion has been put up, and where the garbage is thrown out. Or on the naked, hard streets which don't have a blade of grass.

There is someone who sings here, a woman's voice which can be heard through the open windows. I don't know who it is, and the voice sounds young, but I haven't seen any young people in this town. They move away. This voice sings one particular song, and I remember some of the words, it's a love song:

O, questo ardente dolore
questo sole di fuoco
questo tormento d'amore. . . .

The melody is wild, and the song comes from the South, where the earth is of hot iron and the sky of glowing copper, where gonorrhea is inborn and syphilis a children's disease acquired on a privy or in a bed or in a back yard. . . . *O, questo tormento d'amore . . . .* I have no idea who is singing, although I know a lady in the town who isn't old yet. I've met her at the vintner's now and then. Love has two sides—the clinical-surgical and the metaphysical. The fact that people have the ambition to unite them entails *questo ardento dolore*, this sun of fire. . . . The images come from the South.

It's cold in the town. The wind is blowing and I wear a heavy winter coat. The cabinetmaker is sitting as usual in his workshop with his collar turned up and his back toward the door, with his heel of bread and his wine bottle beside him.

I met the cat today. Now he can hardly move. Hunchbacked and with stiff legs he creeps around as if he had splinters of glass in his paws. He's slimy around the mouth, and has lost even more hair behind. Large parts of his body are naked and a swinish mess hangs out of him under his tail. He's so gaunt now that no one would think it possible. He's been without food for weeks.

He looked at me today, but he didn't have a gaze anymore. In his eyes he looked like the old pictures of St. Sebastian with sixty arrows through his body. No one could tell by looking at the cat that with his upturned face he is looking into the kingdom of heaven, in onto all the hierarchies of angels which were named by the great Dionysius.

I really don't know what I should do; to give him food would only mean prolonging his agony, and I didn't get the pistol.

Lemuria

One

As I work at copying the records from that time, my beard is turning white.

Nevertheless I've kept my peace of mind. I'm tranquil, clear-sighted, and free. It's evident that a process has now been set in motion and will continue. My great friend in Heaven, the choirmaster Rainer Maria, has touched on this in his cantata *Buddha in der Glorie*, which begins with the unambiguous words:

Mitte aller Mitten, Kern der Kerne

and ends with the lines:

denn ganz oben werden deine Sonnen
voll und glühend umgedreht.
Doch in dir ist schon begonnen,
was die Sonnen übersteht.

There is no doubt that it's this stage which has been ushered in: the formation of a nucleus, the coming into being of the one, microscopic first point of real and absolute existence, the first transfigured substance which shall outlive the suns; the first matter to be transubstantiated into the stuff of the spirit, to become eternal, because an illusion has been transmuted into reality and the act of creation has been accomplished. In my Father's house are many mansions, and a thousand ways lead to each. Likewise in me is begun that which shall outlive the suns and the stars: . . . . *was die Sonnen übersteht.*

Winter is coming now. There's a cold wind from the enormous mountains above the valley, the air becomes clearer and clearer. In the morning there's often snow in the highlands, but it melts in the course of the day; so that already by noontime the layer of snow has turned into fine, openwork lace, and at last only a few white threads and strips remain. Except, of course, on the lofty peaks. They lie in eternal snow. For thousands of years the snow has lain on the mountaintops. The evenings are getting dark earlier.

The winters are good here. They're full of stillness, clarity and peace. They're like old age, like the winter I at last feel in myself, a chilly, frozen calm—a feeling and an insight that all things are equivalent. A fly wakes up and buzzes against the pane, a sheep gets lost in the mountains, a shoelace breaks. . . . Yes, I have my hard-won calm and peace of mind. My heart is quiet.

One day I'll begin to remember forward.

I'll begin to remember myself as an old, old man, a white-haired, stiff-legged, and stoop-shouldered man, sitting on a bench looking out over this gray stone valley, the green pastures, the gray stone fences, the gray, blue, and black mountains. I've met myself thus several times; every time I remember forward I meet the old man.

Yes, the wind from the Alpine passes goes like a draft through the streets, making my coat flap. I have to hold onto my hat. Soon there will be frost. Soon it will snow. Happy the one who has a room!

While I was longing for winter I walked down to the inn. I was in equilibrium, but melancholy—perhaps just a bit sad, as one can get after a long working day, a tiredness as it appears in a man of my age. Tiredness. There was a thought going through me after these two things: the attempt to remember my youth and the time up north—and then reading through

the Praiano Papers. It has made me sad. Not despairing, not
beside myself, no. A thought went through me, this: I am
now forty-six, the ninth of last month I had a birthday—and I
know too much, I really don't want to see any more, I've seen
enough. I know everything. Everything and nothing. I long
for the old, dim, black, alcohol-charred inn, for the aged
wooden furniture, for the ancient bar, not altogether clean.
The innkeeper. The guests, *die Schwarzbuben,* black from sun
and wind and alcohol. Horse meat smoked black is what they
look like. We live in a city, but we're peasants. All the people
here are peasants. They can't get used to city life—or, more
precisely: city life can't get used to them. The town can't
absorb them. They'll never turn into city folk, not if they live
here for generations. On the contrary: they turn the town into
countryside, just as our great neighboring nation of sun-
burned winegrowers and millers and ploughmen, the French,
have transformed their great city Paris into a Gallic landscape, into nature for the second time. All those I meet in the
tavern Zum Henker are, and will remain, peasants. Dark
brown, charred by sun and kirsch and wind. I am also a peasant, I too. We are the last to have roamed the pastures and
the woods and the mountaintops.

I mentioned that these people know something about
killing princes. It's true: these heavy, bearded, brown, and
patriarchal wine- and schnapps drinkers are revolutionaries,
democrats. They've beheaded emperors, kings, and generals
with scythes and axes. They take them out in the fields and
kill them when they get too power-mad. Of course they
sometimes tortured them first, but for the most part they
chopped off their heads just as matter-of-factly as they reaped
wheat in the fall.

But, Lord Jesus, here in the inn we meet the elite of the
people! The others, there's something wrong with them.
Among other things they're losing the power of speech, they
can no longer articulate words, they're on the way back to a
stage where they can no longer pronounce words distinctly,
can't use a subjunctive, can't form a sentence. Soon they'll no

longer be able to read. In a few decades they won't be able to do anything but gurgle, make some kind of sounds which are abbreviations of whole sentences. They'll have thirty different grunts—one grunt for each of the thirty sentences they need to grow up, get married, go to the polls, have children, and die. They'll get by splendidly with thirty different sentences, these will cover all situations in life.

We peasants, patriarchs, revolutionaries, we don't accept them—that far our democracy doesn't go.

When I got to the inn, both the bell ringer and the sexton were already sitting at our table. The bell ringer was a bit gloomy, but the sexton was sober and in a shining humor. He was eating poularde, drinking red wine, and talking about literature:

"I've gotten a letter from Moscow," he said. "From my friend Ilya Pessarovich Pissovsky. He has survived all regimes, and is now putting the finishing touch on the galleys of the third volume of his collected self-criticisms."

I ordered my supper: smoked horse meat, black bread, onions, and red wine. The sexton was eating his juicy poularde, roasted on a spit; he ate so that fat, gravy, juice, and wine ran down from the corners of his mouth and remained hanging in his beard, which was wet and shiny. Between chomps he said:

"Ilya Pessarovich wrote at least ten new self-criticisms for every new direction in the Party line, and hence today is able to publish his collected writings. At the end of the twenties he wrote a revolutionary novel, but since then it's been only self-criticisms. He's also been a ghostwriter for the bigger Party people, and has written dazzling self-criticisms for them, of which they subsequently made public use. He is today in the tiresome situation—after so many self-criticisms of himself and others—of no longer remembering his name, it's only the editor's secretary at *Pravda* and the proofreader at *Izvestia* who remember that his name is Pessarovich, that is Ilya P. Pissovsky. Anyway he confided to me a long time ago that his name was a matter of crushing indifference to him.

Meanwhile he has now received a special medal from the government in appreciation of the fact that in forty years he has performed the most and fastest complete about-faces in the Soviet Union. He can turn on a two-kopeck piece, in a quarter of a second. At the moment he's a liberal, but not without reservations. Ilya is not a man who goes too far."

He went back to eating his chicken, but drooled forth a couple of words:

"Shall I tell Ilya hello from you when I write him?"

"You can ask your friend Pessarovich to kiss himself in his gonorrhea-infested rectum," said the bell ringer: "Destroyer of the people's liberty! Intellectual pederast—political faggot—literary asshole for the Establishment! He has betrayed freedom."

The sexton wiped the gravy and fat from his beard and the corners of his mouth with a large white napkin. With his black, Frankish beard he looked like a combination of Émile Zola and Paul Cézanne. He grinned, showing the bad teeth behind his beard, then he said:

"Freedom? Three billion two-legged friends in full freedom?"

Today I'm happy—completely happy—because I died twenty years ago; and then I'm happy because I die every day. Every day—by eleven o'clock—I've died twice over. There's a tiny bit of freedom in this: that I die twice. There's a tiny bit of freedom in this: that I've become irrelevant to myself. When I had turned thirty I abandoned all hope and began as a naturalist.

After eleven o'clock I'm finished dying for the day.

I sat there without listening to him.

My own thoughts had become all too strong and vivid. Wine bottle number two was almost empty, and it left a faint and lyrical giddiness in my head. There was a soft halo of alcohol around my temples, and the thought was very concise: Freedom is not having any standard outside one's own consciousness, but bearing all responsibility oneself. Freedom means that one can never again receive help. Joseph Conrad

says this in *Typhoon*: The loneliness of command is that there
is no help from anyone in heaven or on earth. I've experienced that, in one single, decisive moment: no one could help
me, I had to do everything myself, without aid or advice from
anyone. It was an enormous loneliness, a moment of total
loneliness between the stars and the earth. I understand today
that this was my first experience of the moment of freedom,
and that I didn't dare to seize it. It was a moment of recognition. From that second I could have continued alone—in freedom. Freedom is that you must choose for yourself every second—and that no one in heaven or on earth can help you
with anything.

❖ ❖ ❖

"And behold!" said the sexton. "And behold, when he
woke up in the morning, after sleeping off the drunk, he had
become a holy man. It strikes me that all my friends are holy
men. My friends are holy men because each carries his own
little truth under his cloak. I would even regard it as entirely
possible that we three in this valley are a collective reincarna-
tion of the Three Kings.

"Listen," continued the sexton. "*I'm* telling you this.
According to tradition it's all right to joke about your own
wounds. But when someone—like *me*—has an 'I' which is no
longer personal, and which includes not only my own experiences, but also those of my friends, my fellow humans—and
above all: the experiences of *enemies*—then my 'I' becomes far
more than I am myself, and consequently I'm also allowed to
joke about *others*' wounds, because they are mine. . . . Is this
too difficult for you?"

He continued eating: after the chicken there now came
cheese, and after that fruit; moist, juicy, ripe fruits which he
washed down with white wine.

"As you know," he continued, with a peach in his mouth,
"I'm by nature and upbringing both a moralist and a democ-
rat, but now, at a mature age, I must confess that there isn't

any democracy in the World of the Spirit. I have—as a steward of psalm books and keeper of baptismal records—gone into my privy chamber and promised God that I shall never again write a decent word."

"I'm listening," said the bell ringer, "and there's only one consolation in it all; it won't last forever."

We looked at each other, and then, as if on command, we lifted our glasses simultaneously: the sexton his white wine, the bell ringer his kirsch, and I my red, cheerful, lyrical, purple-colored, full-bodied Tuscan wine. We emptied our glasses.

I'm not searching for a lost identity. Quite the contrary. I suffer from an excess of identity, from an ego which is as solid and massive as a boulder. How did all this prodigious identity arise, what substance is it made of, how did this existence get its massiveness?

Certainly in its very concreteness it has much to do with the records which I've been keeping intentionally for about fifteen years now. This incontrovertible material against the little bears forms much of the basis for my identity: the knowledge of the irrefutable evidence which I've gathered for my prosecution of our two-legged friends has hardened and solidified my ego into an unusual degree of density.

The daily papers and the current news were my reading during the journey in Stockholm, but—since I myself was fluid and without identity, as unconscious as protoplasm—so likewise was my relation to the data and the records. This material was recorded only in my unconscious; though a period of nearly ten years it was floating and amorphous.

It was only when I definitively laid aside the brushes and gave up Bible illustrations that my labor of years began: the attempt to form an archive of this material which is now developing into *The History of Bestiality*—collected and written down with an ever higher degree of consciousness and an ever more massive identity.

As for the awful degradation which must have come upon
me in Stockholm, and which led me to spend so many years in
spiritual amoebahood: something must have scared me away
from my real task at this time—to begin, on my own, to record
the documents which were to be the main evidence in the
coming prosecution of the bears. For this was a court case
which I must have known about ever since childhood: I've
actually had a premonition of this coming trial as long as I
have existed. I was in enemy territory from the very beginning.

Because of my lack of courage and of independence, I
deferred to the little bears for years and years, and as time
went by this submission became a disease.

The thing was that already in Stockholm I knew *enough*: I
had seen the decisive proofs and the signs in the sky long
before. The question was clear: Is it I who am mad, or is it the
world? I knew the right answer, but I didn't dare to utter it: It
is the world which is mad! Instead I bowed and said: The
world is right: *I* am mad—thus making myself the World's
accomplice in the Sin against the Holy Spirit. For many years
I concealed my terrible deed behind the mask of modesty
and humility.

For years this veil of falsehood likewise accumulated on
the records; the lie had become a disease, the crime had
become constitutional.

Is there any possibility of setting it right? Twenty-five
years have been lied away.

The years in Stockholm are so insubstantial that they're
almost impossible to press out of my memory. When I touch
on them I feel only a numb and distant pain, a discomfort
which feels as if it were coming from an organ in my belly, a
sick liver, a poisoned gall bladder. They're a kind of excrement in the memory, feces which have lain there until
they've putrefied. I was actually aware back then that nothing in the existing world was useful: all thoughts were mad,
even my childhood had already shown me a sick, poisoned,
and useless world.

The horoscope at the moment of my birth—in red
October, between world wars and revolutions—shows that
Venus stood in Lepus, the Sign of the Hare, under Michael's
Sword, which augured long journeys and that I would often
sleep alone. At my birth the stars Astarte and Moloch stood
in Aspis, which foretold revolutions and wars, bayonets and
blood, burnt cities and fleeing mothers, as well as long trains
of refugees who would fill the roads in many lands. The planets Shiva and Baal stood in Carnifex, presaging a time of slavery and prison, with millions in captivity, surrounded by endless barbed wire. The planets Uranus and Pluto entered into
conjunction in Pardus, and slowly proceeded on their way—
as agents of the heavy elements uranium and plutonium—
through Lupus and into the constellation Arachne, where
they brought to pass cities leveled to the ground and charred
bodies by the hundreds of thousands.

From my childhood in a peaceful little city in my former
homeland I have a remarkable memory of a traveling waxwork. This waxwork contained precise representations of
deformed people, of self-inflicted maladies in progressive
stages of decay and deformity—and finally the most important thing: a splendid selection of true copies of the
Inquisition's instruments of torture, along with precisely realized human figures in wax—persons who had been subjected
to treatment with these same instruments.

We paid a few øre for a child's ticket to the collection.

The diseased figures, also done in wax and in natural colors, mainly showed inflamed, dripping, and swollen sex
organs, or half-eaten, rotting organs with large, bloody,
inflamed sores. The human body and substance under aggra-
vated conditions. We loved to go there and look; we sold
empty bottles and begged two-øre pieces from the grownups
in order to get in one more time and one more time.

What made the strongest impression was probably the
ecclesiastical instruments of torture. You could study a
thumbscrew close up, and also a splendidly realized model of

a hand which had been under treatment with the apparatus, a bloody and formless lump of flesh which, after the slow crushing of the knuckles, looked entirely different from an ordinary hand. There was also a hand with all the nails drawn out. A "Spanish boot" has left a permanent impression: it was nothing but a very large boot of iron, into which they set the prisoner's leg—whereupon the boot was filled with boiling pitch. A boiled leg was also depicted. The waxwork further contained a rack and a woman with arms and legs pulled out of joint. It was all done in lovely vivid colors, which I still remember well: golden skin, dark blood, bluish and violet marks of crushing and strangulation. It was Goya's world which was shown in this tent, dark and vast, with a clear and meaningful imagery. I must have been about eight when I understood that I had come to an earth where the inhabitants followed strange customs and practices, in a kind of great and endless ritual. At that time I probably accepted in part that the world was like that, but it left traces in my dreams, which were often troubled.

❖ ❖ ❖

I spent the years in Stockholm drawing and painting—or looking at pictures. The National Gallery in Stockholm I know very well from that time, but I was also often outdoors painting pictures. I took part in exhibitions, and I sold a landscape to the Götaverken Shipyard, I remember. I drew a lot of croquis, and became rather good at drawing. Both the paintings and the drawings were executed with a strict and conscientious naturalism. But all the same I think my greatest joy in the work was the sight of the colors on the palette, the way they looked when they were just mixed at random, layer upon layer. Of course I should have painted like that on canvas as well; completely nonfigurative and pure and free. But I didn't dare to do it; I would have felt it as a mockery and a blasphemy against the world, as an impudence and a fraud.

In fact during this time I retreated entirely into my sketching and my pictures, into drawing nudes, painting landscapes—or into the art galleries. In my life since then, and long after I myself stopped painting, I've still gone a great deal to galleries, in all cities and in every land. And it's probable that the painting and the study of pictures at that time prevented me from keeping records, for I remember clearly that the desire to record things would sometimes become almost irresistibly strong.

I also traveled outside the city of Stockholm to paint—one summer I was at Lake Vänern, and another summer on the island of Öland. In both places I painted diligently.

It's strange that the same way I reacted to the desire to paint consciously on the canvas just as freely as I was doing unconsciously on the palette—by rejecting the thought as irresponsible and frivolous—that's exactly the attitude I took toward the thought of beginning to record things: it was arrogant and blasphemous. I felt both things as immoral. I have never met a record keeper or a Servant of Justice with such terrible inhibitions of a moral sort as I had. Every day I had to fight against these inhibitions—and yet in fourteen years I completed fourteen protocols. They all carry traces of this, both in the choice of the subjects to be recorded and in the very way that the texts are entered—with extreme care and thought, full of deadly fear of being immoral or imprecise.

The paintings were clear, straightforward, and without any attempt at deceit; but they suffered from a caution in their execution which hindered any compelling personal expression. Today it's rather remarkable to think that I walked around Stockholm painting flower pots, apples, and landscapes while the whole world was aboil around me: it was revealing itself with terrible clarity as the combination of latrine and torture chamber it is. And my own inner pictures of the world were also an apocalypse; I knew very well that the world was a crematorium.

But I didn't dare to say it.

During this time London, Hamburg, Stuttgart were smashed. Dresden was leveled to the point that the people could be poured right out into the sewers, where there were any sewers left. Stalingrad was wiped out, villages and ghettoes massacred. Of the painters in the galleries I buried myself especially in Ernst Josephson, who is one of the greatest painters the world has seen. Theresienstadt was emptied, and the crematoria were full. Stockholm also had a significant Rembrandt collection, and several first-rate Matisses and Cézannes. In Teutonia they were completing the experiments with vivisection and frost research and transplants on humans. Aside from the painting I occupied myself almost solely with metaphysics. My interest in angels dates from that time; I became conversant with the structure and order of the angel hierarchy, along with the Egyptian mysteries of the sun. One day I came out onto the street in Stockholm, and saw that all the flagpoles were decorated with my own country's flag. It confused me for a brief moment, but when I'd gotten hold of the day's papers I saw that the war was over.

Only Japan was still putting up resistance against the rest of the world.

Technically the world had made progress in these last years. But my own life in Stockholm wasn't particularly affected by this. I was also greatly interested in Byzantine painting that summer. In August came the great change.

The planets Uranus and Pluto stood in conjunction in the Sign of the Black Widow, and I decided that it no longer concerned me what the little bears did to each other.

In my defense it should be said that several years passed before we got correct information about what had happened— no damaging communications escaped from Japan in the first few years. But the truth is also that nothing whatever happened inside me. The truth is also that the American censorship was effective. The truth is also that we were tired, tired as people get after wars—we were so tired of it that we quite simply performed the necessary on what happened in Japan.

As a Servant of Justice I would like to repeat this and emphasize that I simply didn't care to hear anything about it.

There now reigned complete peace, not least in those two cities.

Meanwhile the deed was accomplished, and many people understood that from now on the little bears had altogether new and unheard-of possibilities for harming each other; no destruction was any longer impossible; the Moment of Freedom had arrived.

During the time in Stockholm I had met with much friendliness. The people in Sweden are liberal and open-handed. They're a generous people: all during the war and afterwards they helped the losers and the refugees, the incarcerated and the persecuted, the cold and hungry. That is true.

For my own part the sojourn in Stockholm was over. I packed up my hurdy gurdy and four books and headed for Lemuria. For long years now I was traveling around.

I once had a dream which lived in me for many years, because it had the terrible force, this overpowering reality which dreams can have, and which is far, far stronger than the usual reality. It had a manifold intensity.

I was standing up in the gallery in a prison, on a floor of steel grating, looking down on the prisoners gathered on the cement floor down in the huge prison hall. The dream was in sharp images, with red and blue and black colors. Everybody inside the prison was yelling. They yelled and yelled. They yelled with a thousand voices in great, horrible rhythms . . . over and over again . . . an endless mighty surging howl of hate and vengeance. The whole enormous prison shook with their howls, and I felt the shrieking like ice in my heart. On the stairs and down in the hall prison officials and guards huddled together in groups, white with fear. The hall was immensely high, and the steel galleries shook. Prisoners were running all over in wild excitement, they were dressed in rags or insane carnival costumes, with scarves and caps in loud colors . . . and while they ran in long lines they repeated the howls, ever more rhythmical, ever more violent, ever more senseless, they filled corridors and stairways, and the bellowing began to resemble a kind of tom-tom song. I felt dread more and more like a hand around my chest, around my heart, around my throat. I knew that I was a visitor in the prison, and that the rebellion was about to break out now. The groups of guards and functionaries huddled together, lost and in mortal dread on the floor below. More and more the awful measured howls took on the form of a wild song, and the running through corridors and on the stairways began to resemble a kind of dance. The song acquired a text in the form of disjointed words and a ringing, wild, rhythmic laughter. From above I saw that the flock of guards knew that they were about to die . . . while the prisoners streamed dancing and howling through the main corridor toward the great steel gates. They swelled to thousands, pressing together, singing the song in a booming violent groan which was repeated again and again, a hoarse and terrible bellow of a thousand throats, a long "ah . . . ah . . . ah . . ." which rose to a sudden "aaahh!" with indescribable power. From the ceiling hung ropes with big sharp fishhooks on them, and one by one the guards and the functionaries were hoisted into the air with the hooks in their mouths. A couple of feet swung past me, naked, bleeding from the heels. . . . The song had a few words which were steadily repeated between the groaning rhythmic bellows: "Congratulations this lovely day . . . !" And then a new thundering "aaahh!" I understood that the rebellion was total now, and that something terrible was about to happen, something nameless and dreadful—slowly and with violent exertions, while they used the bellowing as a kind of chanty, a wild jungle-like incantation which redoubled their powers. The sound and the howls filled everything, and the bloody, tortured guards hung by their mouths like awful wriggling pendulums in the great steel hall. Their faces were very distinct, and blood was running out of their eyes and from the corners of their mouths around the hooks. New roars and howls filled this enormous house of iron and stone, and the steel gates were burst asunder as the walls cracked open. When the first ones came out of the building I was among them, and I felt as if a great hand were squeezing my heart with full strength. We streamed out into the streets, filling them—thousands of prisoners singing the words and howling: ". . . ah . . . ah . . . ah," an endless slow plaintive groan, and then the violent yell of everybody at once: "aaahh! . . . aaahh! . . . aaahh!" and then the idiotic, meaningless text: "Congratulations this lovely day!" I was paralyzed with dread as one can only be in dreams, it was a sick and powerless dread. The people streamed out of the prison, and they all had the same sinister expression on their faces, a sort of cold threatening grin, as if they knew what was going to happen, and that it would be worse than anybody thought. Many of them were running after each other in long lines, howling that song of theirs. They were clad in strange gypsy-like costumes, or in rags.

The city resounded with their bellows: the long ". . . ah . . . ah . . . ah . . ." and the violent ". . . aaahh!" from everybody at once.

The dread gripping the city was indescribable, people fled as before the plague, as before imminent death. Around me the prisoners were streaming in freedom, and it was unclear what they were going to do with me. Utterly sick with dread I began running along with the others, I had only one thought in my head: to get away, away. . . . As I ran, knowing that I had pursuers behind me, I saw a little boy who had been left behind. He was standing and crying; no one was looking after him or thinking of him. With a violent effort I overcame my deadly fear and stopped. I took him by the hand and walked on with him. He stopped crying. I knew at once that his name was Ivan, and the city around us was beautiful, it had broad streets and red brick buildings surrounded by parks, ivy, and tall poplars with dark juicy leaves. The air was clear and autumnal, the sky showed that it was afternoon by a faint reddish cast in the air. The prisoners, still dancing and yelling, ran through the streets, past us and onward. I walked peacefully, holding Ivan by the hand.

He looked up at me and smiled, and the dread around my heart vanished. Instead I knew peace and security.

Right afterwards I woke up.

This dream I had many years after the Stockholm period, but I know that the city, the lovely, large, open city, was Stockholm. The city of my youth. But there were long journeys and many years between the city and the dream: it meant a turning point and a consummation.

I'm no great interpreter of dreams, but as a Servant of Justice I know that Ivan is my own, unknown I.

And I know that if God should call me in the night, this is the name he will use. And that it isn't a nickname, the way my everyday name in this mountain city is.

This dream has recurred in other dreams for many years. The first time I dreamed about the total rebellion, this enormous chaos of an absolute revolution, was shortly after the sojourn in Stockholm. It was brief, only an introductory dream. I dreamed that I came out of my house and stood on the steps and looked over toward a woods and a large lake. Behind the lake, in a large basin, lay a city with infinities of houses, streets, and overpopulated districts. It was a swarming city, like an anthill. I couldn't see it, but knew that it was there. While I stood looking out toward the lake and the clear sky, I heard a buzz of a thousand voices, a throng of human voices, of songs and shouts and howls. It was clear that great masses of people were on the way out of the city, up toward the lake. Little by little the shouts and voices gathered into a mighty and threatening chorus of speech, an ominous threatening mutter, which gradually took form in the words: "The slums are loose!"

I went back into the house, alone.

This, however, is a miscalculation: the dream wasn't shortly after the years in Stockholm, it was at least five years later, probably six. I dreamed it just before I began to record my first protocol. It's even possible that I'd already begun on the work then. It says a great deal that I thought it was right after Stockholm, for these years which lie between Stockholm and the First Protocol have almost disappeared from consciousness. The whole thing is just a bloody stinking sore, which I can hardly bear to touch.

But I remember now that in other forms the dream was there very early. One of my earliest childhood dreams was terribly frightening: I was being pursued by a roaring mass of people, by a wild, lunatic ocean of a mob. They chased me out onto a pier, where I stood with black threatening water around me on all sides.

I know that this dream is more important that all the other things I could tell from these years in the land of Chaos and in Lemuria. And it still grips me coldly around the heart. But the dream had never been resolved prior to the prison rebellion and the meeting with Ivan.

Ivan is not my Lemurian name, but perhaps my secret night name, my astral name?

✧ ✧ ✧

Even today this makes me uneasy and disturbed. In a way I'm still as I was in my early childhood, my heart pounds and I breathe fast. Sometimes the walls would bleed. But I'm strong, and my peace of mind is like the mountain Daiblshorn which rises six thousand feet above the city here. I'm solid and heavy in bones and flesh, with an identity like a block of stone. But why don't I remember the time between Stockholm and the First Protocol?

In any case: the great red journey starts here, the years of wandering began in earnest when I left Stockholm, the city and playground of my youth. Later come the records, and now I see that all my work with the records has been—and is— an endless labor in a quarry, with no beginning and no end.

✧ ✧ ✧

One summer I lived by a coast, and every evening I set fishnets for the night. Every morning I pulled them up. I almost always got fish. The fish were often damaged, and had sometimes died in the course of the night. On the other hand there were always crabs in the net, small crabs with sharp claws, and those queer mouths under their armor, without lips or dimples, but with a kind of shell over them, and the sharp teeth which move like knives inside the mouth.

Almost none of the fish had eyes in the morning. The crabs clambered around the net from fish to fish, eating out their eyes in turn; probably the crabs looked on fish eyes as a kind of delicacy, the way we regard chicken hearts or goose liver. Often nothing else was eaten of the fish but just the eyes. Maybe a little of the intestines, but seldom any of the meat, so that the fish were always good for cooking.

All the same I could never cook these fish without getting gooseflesh when I looked into the empty, eaten-out eye sockets.

I mention this because of the equivalence of all things. When American little bears kill a few hundred thousand Japanese little bears with females and young and unborn, is this really any more shocking than when the crabs eat the eyes out of living fish in the night? Isn't that to overvalue the little bears?

Naturally I'm aware that I haven't been able to press the time in Stockholm out of oblivion and darkness; it contains thousands and thousands of external things which have vanished out through the large, blood-rimmed holes in my memory. Still, perhaps it's hardly any loss, and to a certain extent my enormous ability to forget is also due to my considerable training in leaving out essential things, through many years' work with my daily record keeping. All record keeping would be impossible if it weren't based on the ability to forget. But I remember something now:

It was in Stockholm that I first studied the drawings of Callot, Castagno, Pisanello, and del Sarto. Later at the place of execution. Their knowledge of life is extensive.

They described life on that creative and renewing, blood-soaked earth which we call Tuscany, and which is the world.

It may be that Leonardo has done the most trenchant drawings of torture, mutilation, and executions—but the other empiricists can also add a few strokes. Including some of greater beauty.

It's astonishing how much larger a place in art history bestiality occupies than, for example, obscenity. And bestiality has always been allowed in the descriptive art forms, while the inherently life-preserving and constructive lewdness, obscenity and pornography have been prosecuted.

I shall now mention Callot, because he was for many years of great significance for my spiritual health.

Callot was a Frenchman who had made a Tuscan of himself. He was by nature of a dreamy and sensitive, romantic temper, but as a child he fled from the bosom of his good, safe, deeply religious family and joined up with a group of highly crime-oriented gypsies, who supported themselves exclusively by theft, robbery, and murder. In company with this immoral, godless, plundering, and murdering band he came at the age of thirteen or fourteen to Florence in Tuscany. After a few altercations with his more orthodox-minded family, he at length received permission to stay in Florence to educate himself in engraving, sketching, and graphics. He never touched a paintbrush, but kept to the steel pin and the metal plate, on which he with never-failing conscientiousness, veracity, and clarity inscribed his observations about the small two-legged friends' way of life.

It should be mentioned that Callot was a born lyricist and nature enthusiast.

He observed the little friends, and he set their favorite pastimes into his beautiful landscapes, dreamy and yet clear.

All these men, Callot's colleagues, such as for example Leonardo and Castagno and del Sarto and the heavenly Pisanello, belonged to the usual public at the execution rites of the time; the extraordinary executions took place publicly side by side with the usual, regular executions by hanging. It's impossible for me to say who produced the loveliest drawings of exquisite sufferings and advanced methods of dying. To Andrea del Sarto—the little tailor's son—we owe a series of extremely beautiful hangings, sharply and clearly observed, lovingly and tenderly done, with a masterful control of the material. Leonardo has still provided the most incisive yet detached portrayals of the human anatomy as exposed to the hangman's operations—and the depictions go hand in hand with drawings of his famous, grotesque masks, where the individuals' bearlike character is strongly brought out, both during pleasurable experiences and under sensations of strong pain. He, like the other observers, must have spent long periods of his life at the places of execution, and he naturally brought with him to the gallows square his loud, golden laughter. Of Castagno it will only be noted here that we owe to him some outstanding depictions of men being dispatched through hanging by their feet, vivid, movingly and realistically done—not without humor. Nevertheless we owe the most beautiful line drawings to the divine Pisanello, who more than any of the others sees the matter from its graphic, its transparent aesthetic side. None of the others understood so well as Pisanello how to ignore all distracting details and focus all attention on the beauty in the long, sweeping lines in the drawn-out necks— which, because of the loosened cervical vertebrae, can be stretched out like rubber bands, up to almost half a yard. The necks are like water lilies, like long, supple plant stems with the strangely round, inflated faces like large blossoms in full bloom at the top. (I've seen a similar effect in the dead of the 1940s, especially in places where modern methods of hanging with thin rope had come into use. Still, I've never seen such beautiful necks as in Pisanello.) The graphic beauty in the simple lines between body and head give his pages a bewitchingly distinctive, almost calligraphic effect. His hand never trembled as he worked. The drawings show how at the same time he was also eating his chicken and drinking his wine.

Still—the lyricist among these great record keepers is and will remain Callot. Perhaps his Gallic blood plays a role; he was from the excellent wine districts in Alsace-Lorraine. He was born with an eye for landscape, for wind and grass and trees. And he was also the only one who gathered this material onto some few graphic sheets as the high points of his life's work. The others spread themselves over larger areas.

One of Callot's main works bears the title *Capital Punishments;* but, as has been remarked, it could also have been called *The Various Tortures.* It's an astonishing picture, because the lyrical master and romantic dreamer has gathered all his knowledge of humanity onto this one metal plate. Here all the lethal forms of torture are seen at once, as a comprehensive vision of the conservative force in society—and they're surrounded by the spectacle-loving, merry theater public which belonged to the affair. He has added to the whole a laconic commentary in the Latin tongue: *"Supplicium sceleri froenum,"* which translated means approximately: "Torture is the bridle of crime." In this one can read Callot's opinion of the system of justice.

The other engraving which I shall call to mind here has a different character, in that it is first and foremost a picture of man as landscape, between nature and trees and sky. The picture is called *The Hanging Tree,* or perhaps better: *The Hanging Oak.* It goes back to a historical incident on Tuscany's pregnant, fertile soil. The incident yielded a number of delinquents. The picture shows a large, beautiful oak tree. Above the mighty trunk there arches a glorious crown, borne by huge old branches. This whole tree is full of hanged men. I don't know what it's best to compare it with: are the people in the tree like birds filling the foliage, or like fruits borne by the tree? In any case it's a strange and mysterious picture, this age-old giant of a tree, bearing dead men on all its branches; in a way an archetypical image of life and the life forces which unceasingly bring forth more death. In the picture's mingling of enchanting, lyrical mysticism and veracious realism it never becomes overbearing as a symbol.

When I expressly say that this great poet of the graver has been of significance for my spiritual health, there's a reason for this. Callot was an observer and a singer. He died in his mid-forties, while he was still pursuing his work on the little bears. He died, however, of a stomach ailment, and he never lost his balance—his great, cool calm. He had certainly had much to upset him, but it didn't knock him endwise.

✧ ✧ ✧

In our own excellent times, many have noticed that the world to a certain degree bears the stamp of wars and acts of violence. There are people who take this hard. That's because they don't think enough about Callot's world, and about how every period has been about the same: the total picture is a bloody operating room of an executioner's workshop. Why it should—just by pure accident, *all by itself*—have become any different after the last century's technological progress, is simply a completely open and unanswered question. But from men like Callot and Pisanello we can learn to keep our minds clear and our hearts tranquil, to eat our chicken and drink our wine at the place of execution, while conversing, for instance, about the significance of the extraordinary death penalty for anatomical science, and hence for the development of medicine as a whole.

Stockholm is a city with good collections of books, sketches, and paintings. One of the pictures which has pursued me ever since, and which has been a companion through life, is Ernst Josephsson's painting *La joie de vivre*; it shows an old man's deathbed.

The whole picture is a soft, mild flicker of light and color; the white, clear afternoon light filters in through the window, dissolving all fixed objects, the bed, the bedclothes, the head and beard on the old, smiling man. Beside the old man are standing in the same all-effacing and flickering light the old wife, a little child, and a young woman. They're all smiling the same soft, contented child's smile as the old man in the bed. Beside him is a glass of wine. In the background an old French peasant cupboard, which also lies under this veil of light. The picture is heavily and thickly painted, with the colors hanging in coarse clumps—and all this weight is in Josephsson's spirit transformed into lightness, to light, to a vibrant shimmer, to a world which is no longer of earth, but of light, all the pain of sickness and decay has turned into joy in life, into *la grande joie de vivre*; the world has once again become a flowering, matter is conquered, and the old man's face, his smile—like the smiles of the others—lies, like the whole painting, between laughter and tears, lies in a double light, in a fissure between smiles and seriousness which—as the great Servant of Justice Hans E. Kinck says: "whispers of a man's soul in dissolution." Of the look, *I* would say, which sees behind reality, straight through matter which is itself in a state of dissolution. *La joie de vivre* is the most beautiful example I know of matter transformed, transubstantiated through spiritual chemistry: this is my body. . . .

This is due not only to Josephsson's syphilis, but above all to the Holy Spirit—even if syphilis too, with its power to dissolve matter, has contributed to the extremity of the vision. Syphilis and the Holy Spirit in combination have yielded the consummation.

❖ ❖ ❖

I see now that it hasn't been possible to remember more than a few glimpses from that time. This is because my whole life lies in darkness; it was unconscious and is hidden under the veils. Only today, with my enormous *existence here and now*, do I have the kind of consciousness that can be remembered.

Otherwise—this and that thread, this and that nerve ending, this and that blood vessel of significance, I've gotten hold of. Of course my life didn't begin in Stockholm, the long journey began long before that. But our brief moment of consciousness is framed by darkness; some few glimpses of light between the darkness before and the darkness after!

These glimpses are all one has to hold onto.

TWO

A highly peculiar characteristic of Lemuria, perhaps the most striking of all, is its boundless beauty. The Land of Chaos, as I know it from the floes of the polar ice cap to the equator, is just as undescribably lovely almost everywhere. The landscapes are so beautiful that they're bound to arouse suspicion; you think: there must be something underneath all this!

Of course at this time, from years of daily practice in sketching nudes, studying landscapes—and also drawings and paintings—I was trained and drilled to see beauty in nature and in people, who are really nature too, of course. Cities too are very beautiful. Good cities are also nature.

There's no doubt but that when I left Stockholm I was still alive.

Old houses are beautiful. Slum streets, whorehouses, prisons, and waterfronts are beautiful. The sea is beautiful, the mountains, the plains, the forests are beautiful. It's a remarkable earth you wake up to, you rub your eyes and look: it's all so beautiful—the clouds, fire, an empty bottle against the light or beside a lemon, all this is beautiful.

Rain is beautiful. Moss. Old paving stones. Used things. An old floor, a chair worn shiny. Sunshine is very beautiful. A lonely island group of gray-black stone in the North Atlantic. It's possible that the most beautiful thing of all is old people.

Also an orange tree and young people can be very beautiful. An old empty crate with worn trademarks and faded colored labels is a very beautiful thing. A hurdy-gurdy. A well-used breadboard. And the stones on a beach. The ocean.

I know the whole Norwegian coast. The Danish west coast. I also remember an age-old tavern in a little Italian village. Even the table we sat and drank at was of stone.

Also New York with Brooklyn is a beautiful city. I remember Charles Steer's bar, perhaps it's still there in Brooklyn, not on an avenue but on a street, I think Forty-second. It had a bar as long as a golf course. There we'd stand and drink. In the summer Charles would open the broad low window out toward the street, so that things could be served directly out to people who didn't want to come in. They just stood on the sidewalk and got their beer or their gin right out over the windowsill. A little further up the street we'd get corn—warm, yellow corn on the cob with whipped butter on it, served up from a wagon out of a huge steaming kettle. Under Charles's window our donkeyman used to sit on the sidewalk, in his undershirt and with a kerchief around his neck, with his back against the wall. He was strong and very big, and he'd just bellow a couple of words and reach up with his hand, so that the huge dirty paw became visible over the windowsill. This way he got his beer directly hand to hand, passed to him from inside by Charles Steer; then he'd smile and put the tin can to his mouth. For Europeans this was new at that time, to drink beer from a can. Inside in the long, narrow room there were also tables where you could eat a little with the gin you put away; we ate spaghetti until we looked as if we'd been rolling in tomato sauce.

Our donkeyman was also a great wine drinker. When he was tired of beer, he'd pay a few cents for a gallon of wine, a huge gallon jug, and with the enormous bottle in his lap or at his side he'd sit in his usual place on the sidewalk under Charles's window, where he'd fling good-humored obscenities after the passers-by.

For those who have the feel for it, Brooklyn is a beautiful city, dirty and raw and rather dangerous in the waterfront districts, but with a soft-colored patina like an old painting.

I remember one time we were all so drunk that the ship lay over for two extra days before we could sail. Brooklyn and New York, those two giant cities, have soul. I remember the gleam of the yellow ears of corn at night when we ate them on the street under the lights. In the daytime we unloaded sides of pork, they were frozen stiff and we took them directly out of the deep-freeze locker on board. On the pier the heat was terrible, and half-naked and dripping with sweat we went back and forth between the cold-room and the boiling asphalt. And there's nothing in the world which yells so lustily as a gang of American longshoremen. Sometimes in the evening we'd wash thoroughly, put on shirts and blue suits and go all the way up into the city Macropolis in our shiny shoes, way up onto the avenues, in an endless throng of people, yellow, black, blond, and red. I remember well the smell of Brooklyn, so many years afterwards. The people seem busy, but never really unfriendly—there was something open and hospitable about them. New York seemed like a city with big lungs, breathing deeply.

It had a wonderful sweaty loveliness and warm summer nights.

Longyearbyen on Spitsbergen was also a beautiful town, but very small. Nearby lay the mountains, full of snow; even in the summer the glaciers came down to the shoreline, so that the landscape looked as if someone had cut off the tops of the Alps, Jungfrau and the Matterhorn, and set them down right by the sea. It was all very, very beautiful. And the air was as clear as empty space, as outer space itself. At night the sun just kept going in a big circle in the sky, while we sat on the deck in heavy sweaters and drank neat alcohol out of the metal containers.

Later, heading south, we stopped at the great banks and caught huge quantities of codfish, right up from the Arctic Ocean. This Arctic Ocean is one of the most beautiful seas I have ever seen—I mean, when I stood alone on the forecastle keeping watch, and the water was blue-black and still and shiny as oil.

These white summer nights were cold.

✧ ✧ ✧

But in the black nights at Charles Steer's in Brooklyn, there the summer was warm. We'd go straight up to his place from the ship, just as we were, in our undershirts or naked to the waist. And we'd get gin and bitters on the rocks, along with crisp salty crackers. And from the dark warm night outside there was a sound of steps and laughter and now and then someone came in and now and then someone went out. When we felt like it we'd go out and the few paces down the sidewalk to the Negro who sold corn on the cob, and there was a wet yellow glitter on the round cobs. We got whipped butter around our mouths.

✧ ✧ ✧

On the North Sea, where the captain gave orders to back the engines, in half an hour we hauled in enough cod for us all, and an hour afterwards we ate it with the liver boiled in vinegar water, and with the meat lying on the platter in great curling slices like porcelain; the whole had melted butter poured over it, and was peppered cautiously. It wriggled against the palate.

Afterwards, when I'd gone ashore up by the Russian border, I went on foot through Lapland, up along the river bank to Karasjokk, over the flat terrain—wading in heather up to my waist for mile after mile. From the Lapps I got reindeer meat, smoked almost black, and ate it with cloudberries and blueberries, which grow bigger and juicier here than anywhere else on earth. I also ate great quantities of pickled salmon, again with cloudberries afterwards. The landscape was flat and barren, only here and there broken by a black mountaintop or cut up by a river. The water, clear as air, was icy when I had to ford the rivers.

I hitched a ride on a river boat a few times, going up

along the low river bank—once in company with a minister and his interpreter. I went along to a Lapp church service, where the congregation sat on the floor and rocked and mumbled in time to the great rhythms in the interpreter's grandiose translation of the minister's sermon, and in his reading of the Gospel. Several times I slept in sod huts or in small log cabins. But most often out in the heather.

For part of the summer and a long Indian summer I was up there. Mostly on the tundra, but occasionally in the scant, thin, light birch forest—where the foliage was blond and the tree trunks not much taller than a man. There weren't many mosquitoes that summer. But there was lots of sun, and I gradually got very thin from just walking and walking, and I became brown from the sun, and my hair reached almost to my shoulders. But I continued to go wherever I took a notion. Now and then I'd meet people, even if rarely. The endless expanse was immeasurably beautiful, and in particular the thin, transparent leafy forests were simply light and glitter and life.

Since then I've seen a similar thin and transparent, pale green deciduous forest again—it was outside the town of Verdun, there where the little bears had held a bit of their first world war against each other. On Verdun's battlefields all the trees are the same age, and when I came there for the first time these thousands of leafy trees were no more than somewhere between thirty and forty years old. So the whole forest was very young, it was a sort of infant of a forest, and even if it was large it still had nothing of what creates a real forest—for a forest must have age. Trees need enormous amounts of time to become real trees.

And even if the soil was rich outside Verdun, the trees couldn't grow so much faster on that account. Nature needs time to rest and catch her breath. The bushes between the trees weren't large either. For after the great battles at Verdun had been fought out, the whole area was transformed into pure mud, so that there wasn't a green leaf or blade left for miles around.

At the same time, of course, Verdun today constitutes an experiment of utmost scientific interest to forest research, in

that the soil in this region was plowed and harrowed and
turned over innumerable times, and in addition mixed with
millions of fresh corpses, boots, and on top of that thoroughly
drenched with rain and piss and blood. Only after it was all
over was a new forest planted over the hills and ridges. Slight
traces of trenches, fortifications, and old steel helmets and
weapons are still to be found—but you don't really see so
many bones. The barbed wire is almost gone. Naturally in the
course of the battles great quantities of excrement also went
down into the soil, in part evacuations from three million men
who expelled their feces in the normal or customary manner—
but also immense quantities of excrement which came out
through the mouths or purely and simply through the backs or
bellies of the combatants; in other words, intestinal content
which had been more or less fully converted to excrement,
and which naturally had great fertilizer value when mixed
with blood and other body fluids. Another question remains
unsolved, even for an otherwise optimistic biochemical science: namely, which of the combatant parties had the highest
agrarian nutrient value—the Germano-Teutons, the Anglo-
Celts, or the Gauls. Of course one is immediately tempted to
assume that the Gauls were the most valuable, inasmuch as of
all the participants in the battles, their cuisine is by far the
most fit for human consumption. But one must not forget that
at this point in War I even the Gauls were rather undernourished, and moreover this race has an inherent tendency to be
lean, graceful, and delicate. The Anglo-Celts are also in the
main sinewy, thin, often with bad teeth, even if they have nice
manners and are very brave. The Germanic combatants were
probably on the average somewhat larger in stature, also more
powerfully built, and they gain weight more easily; so that
they might have had the potential for being more valuable
compost than their English or French brethren of the same
vintage—but at this point, by reason of the ongoing blockades,
the Teutonic population and its combat forces were doubtless
the most ill-nourished in Europe. At this time the Kaiser's
army was also lean and sinewy.

Moreover one must take age into consideration: regardless of bravery, nationality, race or creed, the overwhelming majority of the departed were younger men, and therefore at an age where most of them consist almost entirely of muscles and bones and tendons and a small handful of entrails. One just doesn't get the same quantity of offal and blood out of a million twenty-year-olds as out of the same number of fifty-year-olds. The best would be material from men in their sixties. However, one should not underestimate the value of the mineral salts which in the course of time can be transmitted to the soil from remains of bones, teeth, etc.; and young men certainly have both more and better teeth, along with finer bone substance, than older men. Another thing is that the pure meat value is doubtless considerably higher per head in mature men.

If one considers what this means for agriculture, the purely mathematical result will doubtless be that officers are more valuable in a decomposed state than enlisted men. The higher the officers' rank, the older and fatter they will be. It is therefore beyond all doubt that it would be most economical to fertilize with members of the general staff. The average general would—at a quick estimate—add to the humus about 20 percent more animal matter than the average enlisted man.

If one reckons the average enlisted man's weight at 69 kg, a million defunct combatants would then yield 69,000 metric tons of high grade compost, while a corresponding million generals would furnish fully 82,000 tons of manure—to be sure not of quite the same quality, but by no means second-rate either. To this must be added rotting footgear, belts, and feces already excreted from living participants, which indeed amounted to no little in the course of the months the Verdun battles themselves were going on: in particular because of the widespread diarrhea among officers as well as enlisted men. The production of raw manure must have come to a total of around 1500 tons a day—the greater part on the side of the Allies, which had both more men and more food.

In the course of the total period of combat this would yield ca. 450,000 tons of feces together with about 120,000 tons of cadavers. Altogether one thus gets a sum of not less than 570,000 tons of corpses and excrement, in other words high-grade sewage and raw manure.

If one today observes and evaluates the thin, young, pale green leafy forest on the fields of Verdun, one may be tempted to think that the result of the organic materials added is perhaps unpromising. One must not, however, fail to take into account the enormous time a tree needs in order to grow up, compared with the time needed to shoot it away with dynamite.

There undoubtedly rests a strange, holy, and almost celestial mood over the mighty monuments which the warring states of that time have since erected over the departed. There is an atmosphere of peace and sanctuary hardly matched anywhere else in Europe.

Still I prefer the thin leafy forest, but that may be my own fault, and is probably due to my almost pathological need to occupy myself with landscape painting from different periods in the history of European art.

What I ate during my first visit to Verdun I don't remember—which in itself is noteworthy, because that's usually the only thing I remember about a place. It was probably something from Strasbourg, I hope *foie gras* or breast of goose. But I know with certainty that I drank white Alsace wine in great quantities.

The landscapes in Alsace are in their way some of the finest in Europe, and the mingling of the races has produced an unusually beautiful human type. I also like the Alsatians' temperament and their bilingual life style: they speak French on the surface and a Germanic dialect underneath. They're great winemakers. The Alsatian landscape is an ancient cultivated land, traversed by canals and rivers, green and gentle and noble. The soil is just as drenched with excrement and blood as in Flanders. The architecture has a marked individuality, and among the high points in pictorial art one must mention Matthias Grünewald's enormous *Crucifixion* and *Resurrection* on the altar at Isenheim. All in all, Alsace is marvelous. But one misses the pale green forest of Verdun.

Wholly different are the former battlefields at Chemin des Dames or at Hartmannswyler Kopp, of which I shall only discuss the latter. It lies directly west of Basel, on large hills, surrounded by a spruce forest. The landscape is Vosgian—mountains and northern forests.

The funny thing about the idyllic war cemeteries at Hartmannswyler Kopp is that there was fighting in the same place during both World Wars—something which led, strangely enough, to the corpses from the first war coming up again out of their graves during the second, because the projectiles dug up the earth to a depth of several yards.

Here—at Hartmannswyler Kopp—I remember very well what I ate: namely, a superb *truite bleu*, a delicate trout from les Vosges, boiled in lightly seasoned water with wine vinegar added, which both affects the taste very favorably and turns the skin of the trout blue. But I drank the same white Alsatian wine with the meal.

This naturally reminds me of how often I've caught and eaten trout in my former homeland, and it's possible that the trout up north there in the mountain streams at an altitude of around 3000 feet is the best trout in the world; but the trout in les Vosges is also of outstanding quality, and it was prepared with great art.

I stayed for a good while at an old inn in the vicinity of the war cemetery at Hartmannswyler Kopp—a delightful building where Napoleon Bonaparte had also spent the night, and where the walls of the house are provided with large iron rings to hitch the travelers' horses to; I stayed there partly because of the place's good cuisine, and partly because the battlefield was so near that I could always walk over there.

It's characteristic of the rows of graves at Hartmannswyler Kopp that they lie in the wonderful stillness of the forest. In the cemeteries there are still large heaps of thrown-up earth and visible craters from the impact of high explosives. Here it was, then, that the dead made their entrance anew after more than twenty years' silence and rest. Mandibles, tibiae, small bones, and pelvises rose again; even remains of uniforms had survived the hibernation.

Now these heroic corpses are happily buried for the second time, and from that standpoint all is well. Tall spruce trees grow over the undisturbed parts of the heights; in other places the forest is of course young. At the inn one can also get a splendid goat cheese from the area; it is fresh and mild, somewhat tart—and goes well with the white Alsatian wine. Of course up here one misses the big white vineyard snails which are served in garlic butter, and which are the ideal accompaniment to the wine.

There is something about this second burial which speaks to me—something, as it were, deeply democratic. The thing is that when the grenades landed twenty years later, causing the departed to awaken and arise, then they brought up vertebrae, pelvic bones, clavicles, lower jaws, and elbows in an utter jumble, so that when interment number two took place—naturally with the aid of a bulldozer—then the remains of the fallen from War I were simply shuffled together without any real system or order, they were uniformless—and thus it happened that privates, NCOs, and the relatively few officers came to rest without any difference whatever in rank and placement. Thus there is, so to speak, a kind of equality after death. After only twenty years there was an end to all difference between a colonel and a corporal, between a general and a private. Manure is manure.

There's a kind of encouragement in this, when it has so often been observed that on this side of the mass grave there is no justice, but only brute force.

From this train of thought from those days you can see how important it was for me that many years later I became a Servant of Justice, and through daily attendance in the courtroom learned to come to terms with this—by seeing daily that injustice takes—and must take—its course.

Moreover, this was at a point in time before the First Protocol, and the road which remained was long. In addition it's obvious that time and place are nonexistent, all reckoning of time is irrelevant, the whole thing is only a glimmer. Even the most intense awareness of existence *here and now* means simply that this "here" is all places, this "now" is all times.

Power, which is the sole existing principle, means only one thing: the opportunity to cause others pain.

I hadn't yet made a thorough study of how far the most powerful among the little bears can go when the stability of power is at stake. But before I come to the First Protocol I still have a couple of necessary things and journeys to describe— precisely as they can be observed through the concepts of place and time, as long as one is using these.

The time between Stockholm and the records lies in darkness. It's almost impossible to find any coherent lines or patterns in the mosaic. I was a dead man, because I was always submitting to the idea which had been forced upon me—that the world was right and I myself was wrong. Authority claims truth for its own. The law claims to be just. Power calls itself freedom—because freedom consists in perceiving necessity, which is to submit to power.

I was dying because I lived in unfreedom without knowing it, and because unfreedom is naturally more comfortable than freedom: it disperses, or even frees one from, the responsibility of having an existence. Only through the courage of despair can you grasp a handful of freedom. Freedom is not a thing you receive, it's something you *take* for yourself without asking anybody whether what you're doing is right or moral or harmful or good. And therefore, because you decide for yourself at what moment you will take freedom, every language has the expression: ". . . I *take* the liberty. . . ."

For example: I hereby take the liberty of stating my critique of the status quo, of customs, practices, methods, and above all of the underlying dogmatics and philosophy.

Matthias Grünewald, *Mathis*, has laid down his own critique of all that exists, even the laws of nature here in the neighborhood of the mass graves, right between Chemin des Dames, Sommes, Marne, Hartmannswyler Kopp, and

Verdun; he has set down his total, his absolute critique of the
whole in his great, terrible *Resurrection*, painted for the altar at
Isenheim but moved by the authorities to Alsace—which to a
greater degree than perhaps anywhere else is the region of
death. This critique of power, of death and the laws of nature
he painted in that terrible wrath which is the distinctive result
of the moment of freedom.

In all brevity I just want to add that *Mathis der Maler* was
not a human being in the usual sense.

This travel guide would set three stars by Verdun,
Hartmannswyler Kopp, and by a little town in Alsace where
the altarpiece hangs. At the same time the traveler should be
warned against excessive indulgence in the district's outstanding white wine, which excess it—by reason of its taste, its bou-
quet, and its nerve-deadening effect—unfortunately invites.

White wine has in the long run about the same effect as
cider—it rapidly calms the nerves, but then they just come
back all the more violently. The winegrowers in this district
and all along the Rhine, up to Switzerland, suffer to a greater
degree than any other viticulturists from frequent attacks of
delirium tremens, which often incapacitates them for short
periods. But they do know how to make wine.

I discovered the effect of the wine on myself when I left
Alsace and drove west, through Île de France and out to the
Atlantic coast on the western tip of Brittany. There I ate a plate
of shellfish, a selection of shrimp, small crabs, oysters, whelks,
mussels—altogether a couple dozen different animals, harmo-
niously varied in taste, form and color, they smelt of the ocean
and seaweed and algae, of stars and moonlight. For a long time
I drove around along the coasts of Normandy and Brittany; the
thing was that two of my friends from school days had fallen
here during the invasion, and I wanted to see where.

In the course of this time I became sleepless; it wasn't that
I had trouble getting to sleep, quite the contrary: after a day
spent in this way I'd immediately fall into a deep sleep, but
two or three hours later I'd wake up and be wide awake with
dread. One evening in a strange fishing village I was sitting in

an inn eating one of the specialties of the place, first a bowl of
boiled periwinkles served with white wine and with pins to
dig the cooked animals out of the shells with; they're the
same small snails which grow by the millions along the coasts
of the North Sea, and you just boil them a while in vinegar
water, with a little spice added. After this prelude came the
house's *pièce de résistance*: the great, heavy, aromatic, brown,
and undescribable crab soup.

I got into a conversation with a fisherman, and com-
plained about my increasing sleeplessness.

"I have observed that monsieur has enjoyed several
glasses of white wine with his meal," said the fisherman.
"Excuse the question: does it often happen that monsieur partakes of white wine?"

"You," I replied. "Several bottles a day."

He nodded thoughtfully, then chose his words carefully:

"Here we look upon white wine as extremely disadvanta-
geous to the nervous system. One expects that even the
strongest nerves will be disquieted by just a few glasses a day.
This form of insomnia is regarded as very characteristic of the
effect of this particular wine. The best medicine against the
disturbance would be to switch to red wine instead—one
should just remember that one mustn't drink too little of it."

I changed my diet on the spot, with immediate results.
Since then I've slept deeply and long, not least in the morning.

Of my lost friends from the earliest days of my youth I saw
nothing, not a cross nor a suggestion of an epitaph anywhere.
No monument over either of them. Just air and nothing.

These travels took place in space and time, and only
slowly did these concepts dissolve, so that things could happen outside them. Now, of course, the record keeping imper-
ceptibly began; a system began to be faintly visible. It was a
kind of encircling method. Gradually I myself stopped drawing altogether, but I continued to love landscapes and to go to
art galleries. This always glides out into the vague and indefi-
nite when I try to hold onto it; it becomes unclear and the
strands mesh together for me. There are more strands than

my consciousness can count, they're uncountable, perhaps an infinite number. Actually my whole life is something I only remember fragments of, up to the Praiano period where everything is gradually lost in darkness and oblivion.

I can't even say for sure when it was that all this remembering ended, but it feels as if one of the last things I recall was an old city with paved streets. After that everything is darkness and silence.

How I came to the city up in the mountains, to the principality where I'm a Servant of Justice, I don't know. I don't even remember how it began.

Day by day, perhaps over a period of weeks, I became conscious of myself and understood that I had my daily, regular job in Heiligenberg, and that I'd come there without realizing it. Someone must have brought me there.

But since then everything has become clearer, up to my present identity and existence. Aside from these fragments of the past, I know only that I *am* here, that I do exist. But where I came from . . . who I am . . . ?

From the time when I jotted down the Praiano papers I have those dark, sharp pictures—and then I know what this period came more and more to look like outwardly: the last part of it I drove around for three consecutive years, from town to town.

But the Praiano chapter as a whole encompasses a much larger span of time. Back then, as I've said, I had a clear awareness of sickness—and I said to myself that it wasn't the world which was like that, but my own sick and distorted consciousness which mirrored it in this way, like a fun-house mirror. If I'd known how long this condition of blood and darkness was going to last, I doubt that I would have managed to live through it. In all, it lasted fully ten years.

Afterwards came the total change, the peace, the stillness, and above all the clarity up in this Alpine valley. Equilibrium of mind. Unshakable calm in my soul.

Naturally it sometimes plagues me that I don't know how

this transition, this great transformation took place. Between the last Praiano phase and the slow, gradual awakening in the courtroom my life is for the most part massive and absolute darkness.

Between Stockholm and the First Protocol there's a period of about seven years. But the transition took place gradually and has no firm boundary. Of course I remember a lot from my life, but I have this steadily stronger feeling that *I don't remember what it's all about.*

Between the First Protocol and the beginning of the Praiano period there's a span of probably four more years.

In a way everything revolves around Teuto-Germania. That's the thorn in my flesh; Teutonia is the cross I'm nailed to.

It goes without saying that the First Protocol contains only documents about Germania. How could it be otherwise? I'm a sort of involuntary Teuton-by-adoption, the choice wasn't arbitrary—but it is involuntary, because I *had* to choose a country.

All living persons on earth are, or will be, affected by this region Teutonia, which isn't really a country at all. It created Verdun and Dachau. Teutonia has unleashed two monstrous world wars, and in Teutonia the powder is being mixed for the next one. We are at its lack of mercy.

My love for Teutonia, my Teutonic citizenship, had already come into being in Stockholm. It isn't true that love makes one blind: it makes one clear-sighted—it made me see the sickness with a high degree of clarity and certainty.

I had a dream back then.

In the dream I was climbing up a rocky slope. I had come through a huge dark forest after an endless fight with darkness, bogs and undergrowth. Gradually the forest turned into a rocky slope, into huge, rough-hewn, moss-covered blocks of stone with deep holes and ravines in between. On the slope there were also thorns and branches growing up between the massive boulders. The slope rose upward—toward something

which was lost in a boundless world of mountains and fog. I
climbed on and on, higher up on the slope, further up toward
the mountains. As I climbed it got wetter and clammier
around me, and parts of the landscape disappeared into fog.
It was misty and cold. The first damp, dirty snowflakes
appeared. I went through them and onward, crawling on
hands and knees over the boulders, which were getting
sharper and more jagged. Everything around me was wet and
half-dark because of the fog. The mountain got blacker and
steeper, and the wet cliffs glistened. In some way or other I
was at the same time inside the mountain. The darkness
became thicker and dread settled around my chest and neck.
I was completely surrounded by stone, fog, and mountain. At
the same time I was outside the mountain, but I had no sense
of the sky above me. This lasted for a period which felt like
many nights and days, and my strength waned until I could
hardly manage to go on. Time after time I fell down, but got
up again and crawled on, now it was straight through the
mountain, and it was all darkness, nothing but darkness. I
knew that the last of my strength was going now, but dragged
myself on a little more before collapsing. I knew that I'd
never get there, that several yards of black, impenetrable
mountain wall were shutting me off forever from the other
side. The cavern I was lying in closed tightly around me now,
and water was dripping inside the darkness. It became nar-
rower and tighter, and I felt the roof of the cavern pressing
down on my back as I tried to turn on my side. I couldn't do
it, but just lay there, wedged inside the mountain. I laid my
head down on the stone under me, knowing that it was all
over.

    At the same moment the wall of stone slid aside, or the
rocks were lifted up—in some way I myself had sprung them.
The light before me wasn't just daylight, it was blinding, flaming sunshine filled with the whole spectrum. The sky shone
over everything. But I saw nothing of earth or the landscape,
only light and sky. I crawled forward to the opening and
raised myself halfway up. The abyss below me was unbeliev-

ably deep; miles down lay a fertile landscape stretching out to
the ocean, which sparkled in a deep blue color. Never have I
seen such splendor as this sea and land below me.

I stood way out on the edge of the abyss, while dizziness
and dread stabbed at my body. It was thousands of feet down
to the land, and I was hanging over the ledge. This whole side
of the mountain was as steep as a wall, but still had chinks
and footholds for climbing. A few yards down the face of the
cliff my dread mounted to many times what it had been
inside the dark cavern. To turn back was impossible. The
only thing left was to hang over the abyss until I plummeted
down into all the wondrous splendor below me, or to manage
the climb down.

The dream had the force which some dreams have: it sat
lodged in my body for several weeks afterwards. It was clear
and unambiguous and will always pursue me: the cliff and the
narrow ledge in the warm dry sunlight which went straight
through me, the sight of the luxuriant, ancient-heroic landscape and the endless glittering sea far below—it all gave me
the strongest feeling of loneliness I've ever known. It was the
Mediterranean, I knew, which was down there: the
Mediterranean of Antiquity.

Is there anything which awakes such a strong dread in me
as freedom? Who is mature enough to bear it? And who has
trained us to fear the light, space, the face of the cliff, and the
ocean?

A tamer can make a dog of a lion, but never a lion of a dog.

Still, there are people who grasp freedom at once, who
don't doubt, don't hesitate—but accept themselves as the
measure of themselves and of everything, and who don't
seem to show any dread. In some cases these are people who
have the strength to do it and the innate wisdom to understand what the price is. In other cases they are people who
have no idea what they're doing, who choose freedom out of
ignorance and lack of understanding—they know nothing
about any price, and they go under when the price is

demanded. It means ruin to choose to think for oneself if one can't think.

In Stockholm I studied with Isaac Grünewald. One day in his studio I had just packed up my things when he came over and looked at the nude I was trying to paint. After awhile he pointed to a part of the picture.

"This here. . . ." he said.

I was aware of it, and replied:

"Yes, I know. I was going to fix it tomorrow."

He stood still for a moment, then he said:

"But suppose you died tonight? Then what would people think of you?"

I felt dread after he'd said that. Not because he had reminded me of an unlikely thing: dying tonight. But because he had put the knife to my throat: Do it now! You know the truth, and you put off acting on it till tomorrow, because you prefer to wait as long as possible to draw a conclusion on your own. You have freedom in your hand, but you don't dare to grasp it. You don't dare to be alone in this!

He could have said: You don't dare to paint your own picture.

At the thought of finishing it, of painting it in accordance with my own perception, I felt fear like a hand around my throat, as when I was a child and was ordered to dive into the sea from a much higher springboard than I was used to: of course it was simply a matter of *doing* it. Every step toward deciding for oneself what the world looks like is a step away from others, away from others' opinion, others' judgments, others' morals.

To finish painting the picture—*here and now*—without waiting until the morrow in hopes that I would have become wiser by then, in hopes that I would have learnt something from others—that would have meant painting my own picture.

Only many years later did I understand what happened inside me when he said: But what if you died tonight?

Freedom always means a *choice here and now*—and without advice and help.

I've received a letter, from a long way off—from a person whom I don't know, but who is soon to die. This stranger writes in his letter to me (and *I* have received the letter at such a time as this!):

"There's no reason I shouldn't die . . . I come from a fine old cancer-family . . . but anyway the time has come. I now see clearly what I had vaguely known before: that I have never lived *my* life. I've lived my spouse's life, my father's life, my siblings', my children's, my neighbors' lives, *other* people's lives. I have filled the role which others expected or demanded of me. This I lived up to, and I would rather have been the greatest criminal, but committed my crimes myself.

"It has dawned on me that for almost fifty years I've lived a life which has not for a single day been my own, but the one which those around me arranged and stage-managed for me; in other words first my parents' life and later everybody else's—the teachers', the school's, the community's, the church's, the life of morals and politics—a bungling and consumptive life, not because it was necessarily a bad life, but because it wasn't mine.

"Now, as the moment approaches, they naturally come marching in again—with priests and sacraments—to arrange my death for me as well. They want to make a pattern for that too, so that I'll die in the way that the others think is correct. But no. These last weeks, they shall be my own. I shall die in peace (for them), and in my own way. The vision of death makes all standards and norms ridiculous, and in the face of these last days there's only one thing that counts: what I myself am. I have one last chance to get to know myself, to know who I was . . . what I could have become. And this is what it took!"

This is what it took. In the moment of freedom one has Death on one's side; one has Him as one's last trump card, the last irrefutable argument. But one pays for this freedom with one's life. It is said that parting is death, and freedom means separation from all which can give advice, help, and support; it is choosing here and now, alone.

It's no accident that my good teacher back then had to conjure up the possibility of my dying tonight in order to force me—which he didn't succeed in doing—to paint my own picture. At that outermost, lonely moment, at the leap out into freedom, one has Death as a friend by one's side—but one feels His presence as dread.

Those who don't know this dread are either born as kings, or they don't know what they're doing.

This is one side of freedom. Another is to become irrelevant to oneself, to become a stranger to oneself. But that's a new chapter in the protocol about the concept "Freedom." It comes right after the chapter on "Evil," which in turn comes after the chapter on "Dread."

The dream about the tunnel through the mountain, out toward the sun and the sea and the dread before the abyss, is of course connected with the dream about the rebellion and the boy Ivan. These dreams are the two greatest experiences of dread I have ever had in my life. They were stronger than the dread of mortal physical danger, which I've experienced several times.

✧ ✧ ✧

At the last stage of alienation, that of becoming irrelevant to oneself, freedom arises: to evaluate everything, a murder or the saving of a life, anew and independently of any code of laws: according to one's own reckoning, here and now. It's a revaluation of all norms, on one's own responsibility.

The dream of coming through the mountain was an exact prophecy of the unbelievable significance the Mediterranean has had in my life. It is two things: the red town and Tuscany on the one hand—the catacombs and Antiquity on the other.

It involves two levels of experience: Praiano and the catacombs. The latter experience is the only one which has given me concrete information about reality without space and time, and it has therefore at the same time given me an understanding of the words "here" and "now."

Of course I know that *everything* is impossible to describe,
and everything is an escape: my forty-six years have given
me such a boundless sum of experiences that even in my state
of perforated consciousness and mutilated, bleeding memory,
a description of my mnemonic content would fill not books,
but libraries. Ten more years—and my knowledge of the
world will be so appalling that it can only destroy.

❖ ❖ ❖

The Roman catacombs aren't the only ones, but in this
connection they're the most important. Today I've forgotten
their names, but I know them all, even if I haven't set foot
down in those passageways for seven years. It isn't fear which
keeps me away, for the same thing wouldn't happen over
again. My last visit under the earth contained everything.

❖ ❖ ❖

Around ten years earlier I began my exploration of the
catacombs, and I got to know them rather well. Although
nobody becomes an expert. There are so many hundreds or
thousands of miles of underground passages around Rome
that few people know them, if anybody does. The air and the
smell of the catacombs, the strange winding passageways in
the tufa—from the first visit they made a powerful impression
on me. They lie around Rome on all sides. I believe those to
the south and the north are the best known.

Every time I came to Rome I'd go walking in the catacombs, I got to know the clear symbolic motifs of the chalk
paintings in the small white chapels which are scattered
around the passageways, and I became familiar with the earliest Christian saints. I usually stuck to the small, cheap
brothel-hotels in the city; only a couple of times did I stay
anywhere else.

In the evenings I'd usually walk around in the streets, find
a cheap *trattoria*, drink wine, eat, wander around the city some

more, drink more wine, look at the faces in the streetlight, and finally end up over in the slums. Around midnight I'd head home to the bordello and sleep, heavy with wine—full of pictures from the catacombs and from the streets and *trattorias.*

The catacombs encircle the whole city, in many places several stories deep. I no longer remember how many miles of these curved, rhythmic, dancing passageways there are around the city, but it's a lot. And on both sides of the corridors there are ledges hollowed out for the dead, three or four deep, like the bunks in an old-fashioned ship's cabin or in a third-class sleeper on a train. There are bones or remains of bones all through the passageways, on both sides three or four graves on top of each other, for mile after mile. This says something about *the dead's enormous numbers.* In some places there are larger rooms dug out with higher ceilings, often with skeletons and skulls by the hundreds and thousands, skeletons of holy virgins, martyrs, and consecrated holy men. The air in subterranean Rome is fresh, comfortable in temperature, and has a summery, flowerlike aroma. The walls in the soft tufaceous rock are brown, with a faintly reddish undertone. One of the strange things about these graves with their remains of millions and millions of dead is that there's no melancholy or sadness about them, but on the contrary a holy gaiety, something which lies beyond all time. They've been dead for so long.

Because the passageways are so labyrinthine, and above all so endlessly long, ordinary people aren't allowed to walk alone in the catacombs; a stranger could disappear without a trace here. You have to follow a guide or a cicerone, a monk who walks ahead with a burning candle and delivers his routine spiel for the flock of visitors following after him. For every batch he recites the same pious wisdom. I knew several of these guides, and some of them were just as addicted to drink as I was, so we'd sit together in front of the entrance to the graves drinking wine or grappa while they waited for a new batch of guests to gather. When there were eight or ten people wanting to go down, one of the brothers would rise

and lead the way into the adit. The lectures were held in
Italian, French, English, or German—whatever the visitors
wanted. The brothers were great linguists. I seriously considered settling down there and getting a regular job as a custodian: I was thinking of my own benefit and of the
Scandinavians who occasionally turn up without knowing any
foreign languages. At that time it would have suited me to get
such a pious job.

I knew the saints' lives well, some of them very intimately,
and besides orienting people about the particular catacomb I
was put in charge of, I could also have told the guests almost
all the saints' legends of significance. Many of the dead had
been martyrs, and the legends thus brought me into contact
with material for my later work. The one circle of motives
intersected with the other.

I never got as far as becoming a custodian, but I got to
know the catacombs and the brothers well enough to be
allowed to wander alone around the passageways and
chapels, in this life-giving, flowering darkness from another
world. The meeting with the past and with so many dead had
a soothing and restorative effect on me, and actually it was
also for reasons of health that I went down there so often.
Sometimes I'd stay under the earth for hours. When I came
up again from all those holy and blessed, the sun and the air
were new and divine to come back to.

I'd often get hungry down there, and would eat right afterwards. I remember a Roman artichoke of which everything,
practically every fiber, was edible.

Also I developed definite and rather simple eating habits
during this time. Often I'd just go into a grocery store, get one
of those small white loaves of bread and cut it lengthwise. I'd
sprinkle some olive oil over the insides and buy a few ounces
of filling which I distributed on the lower half, so that there
was first squid or tunafish, after that sausage, then ham, and
finally a piece of cheese. Then I'd put the other half of the loaf
on top, and get a glass of wine at the counter. I'd begin eating

the bread from the fish end, either standing inside the shop or sitting on the steps outside, occasionally refilling my glass.

Another method was to finish making the sandwich—or a little packet of food— inside the shop, then go to a *bottigleria* and get the wine there and find a place at a table, as the workers do. In such places everybody talks together during the meal, they eat and laugh and the wine is cheap.

After eating I'd often go down into the underworld again to feel the enormous stillness which reigns there. After a few hours I was calm, the lights were burned out. It gave me a feeling of life and health, but like so many medications the cure perhaps contained elements of addiction and depravity, of narcomania. Also the imagery in the catacomb paintings meant a lot to me.

Naturally I knew not only the custodians of the catacombs, but also other people.

One night I formed a lasting friendship.

I'd been walking around the city much longer than usual, and was sailing on the wine I'd drunk. On the way home I found one of those places which are open all night, and where only taxi drivers and whores and once in awhile a tired policeman come in to relax a minute in a round of cards with whoever is already sitting there.

On the tables there were plates of hard-boiled eggs and salt, and set into the white tiled wall in the back were huge brass wine spigots, so that the wine from the barrels on the other side of the wall came out of a faucet as in a bathroom. I said hello and asked for a can, which I got immediately. It was big and wide-mouthed and well adapted to the lovely spigots. Then I sat down at the long table and began on an egg, which I dipped in the salt dish as I ate. It's an excellent midnight snack, this: hard-boiled eggs and a quart of wine to sleep on.

Right afterwards a couple came in and sat down more or less beside me. It was a pretty blackhaired girl with her pimp. He was an Ethiopian and black. They were both very friendly and we quickly got into a conversation. He was very slim and finely built, with a thin melancholy face, but I no longer remember what we talked about.

After awhile we went out onto the street and walked together through the still, nocturnal city. The girl didn't meet any customers, or perhaps she was finished with work for the day. We told each other about ourselves and where we came from. She wasn't Roman either, but was from a town near Naples. We ended up in an all-night café at the railroad station, where we partook of a new meal and drank wine. We smoked and talked and finished by drinking a couple of grappas.

He insisted on paying, and it was no use my saying that I wanted to be the host for them. They saw me to my hotel, which wasn't far away. The girl came up to the room with me. I threw on my clothes afterwards and accompanied her down to the street, both to see her safely off with the pimp, and because she wouldn't accept any money I had in mind to settle with him. When we came down, he was sitting on the staircase, looking lonesome and melancholy. But he smiled and shook his head. It was all just for friendship's sake, he said. They both laughed over my living in this hotel.

I stood looking after them—they disappeared down the street, hand in hand like brother and sister in a forest.

Afterwards I often met them again at night, either in the night spot where we'd met the first time, or on the streets around there, where she had her beat.

They were always the same, but it was painful that I was never allowed to pay for what we ate or drank together. Perhaps it didn't matter so much; she was a charming girl who earned good money, and he was a decent person—both were well-dressed.

Then I also went a lot to the oldest churches in Rome, mostly to see the mosaics of scenes from the Gospel or from the lives of the saints. Likewise the subterranean grotto of Mithra under the church in back of the Colosseum was a place I visited often. It provided a strong reminder of Antiquity, sometimes with a tinge of something light and green, something easy-going and heathen which has disappeared. I never found anything in Rome of the same sort as from ancient Naples, with the carefree, benevolent lewdness and the jolly pornographic sculptures. For me Rome is and will remain the nocturnal streets or a harsh Antiquity, power politics, the Colosseum, and the catacombs. It is empire and world domination, but it flowed right into the blood in my veins.

It gave me that ration of past which was necessary for my nourishment at that time, and which I couldn't do without. I don't know what it was, but it gave me a feeling of having a home and an origin. There was something which came together in me.

Many years later I drove up to Rome from the south. I had left Naples late in the afternoon of the preceding day, and had spent the night in the car en route, out by a green meadow near a brook. I was well-rested and fresh after my morning coffee when I came to the outskirts of Rome around eleven in the morning. It was Sunday.

I stopped on the highway right near the San Callisto catacombs, locked the car and went over to the entrance. It was a bit of a walk. I'd been there often before, and knew the whole area both because I had followed the old Via Appia toward the Campagna many a time, and because of the burial places here.

The whole thing was normal for me, and I waited a while until the next batch was ready to be led down into the passageways. After a few minutes we went down, and because I knew it all well from before, I lagged behind the visitors by myself, without listening to what the guide was saying. I noticed only that he was speaking German.

I walked by myself in the semi-darkness and heard his voice like a faraway hum which had nothing to do with me. I felt that I'd had a dream in the night, it was unclear and behind a veil or a wall of glass. Gradually I understood that the dream was important, that I was dreaming it now. It was immensely difficult to get hold of and hang on to, but the fleeting images began to move visibly before me. At the same

time I heard the guide's voice in German and English. It was
a complete, perfect simultaneous translation. I didn't know
where or by whom; but that didn't bother me, I found it natural to hear the words in two languages at once. Far more
important were the pictures in the dream, which now went by
me so fast that I couldn't manage to grasp them or to remember them. Despite my efforts to hold onto the pictures it was
still an immensely pleasant feeling; all bodily sense was gone
and replaced by a yielding warmth which surrounded me and
filled me, a mental or spiritual sunshine. The images glided
past me, swift, supple, and very lovely, there were people and
ancient buildings, temples, tombs, monuments, colonnades,
and houses. It was as if the people were moving in a dancing
procession, always agile and swift, a little too fast for my eyes,
which were simultaneously following what was happening
around me in the catacomb and the two languages which the
guide was speaking at once with no difficulty. I saw the people around me just as clearly as those I was seeing in the
dream, or in the pictures. The dancing, leaping people among
the temples and the colonnades began to sing, and it turned
into a song which was a hum as of many flutes and voices, in
an unknown and incomprehensible language. Slowly the catacombs disappeared, and I was only in the pictures, moving
among the people, life ran through me, and many of the people were friends and acquaintances from other countries and
places, from Germania and my homeland, from Stockholm
and other cities. There were also relatives there. It was all
luminous pictures and song.

All at once I was standing in the daylight in front of the
entrance to the catacomb. Someone was standing beside me,
and I felt that there was something familiar about her. Where
I was, or who I myself was, I had no idea. There was a hum
inside me, and the echo of the pictures was so strong that I
could see them all the time. Above all I still had the soft and
distant feeling of sunshine in my body.

I looked at her who was standing beside me.

"Who are you?" I said to the young woman.

She mentioned a name, but the sound was entirely unfamiliar to me, and yet there was something about her face and figure which wasn't strange, something vague and unclear which reminded me of things which were far away, which were impossible to remember. At the same time I was alert enough to observe the expression on her face. First she smiled incredulously, then she grew serious.

"Who am I?" I said. "Do you know that?"

Again she mentioned a name, but it glided past me unrecognized. I didn't know anything. Not where I came from. Not who I was. At the same time I heard that the humming and the music were fading, and I understood that my own consciousness was changing. I felt no dread—only peace and stillness.

"Do we know each other, or have we anything to do with each other?" I said. I faintly remembered an island in a blue sea, but it had a strange kind of name, not to be pronounced. The landscape and the people, as well as the young woman beside me, were unreal and alien, far, far away. At the same time they were slowly coming closer. She told me who we were, and that we had come together from the south. I laughed loudly when I heard the name Naples, because I thought it was a crazy name, and also when she named the island we had stayed on. For that, too, she had a short name which was nothing like the one I was thinking of. Altogether I thought it was jolly that she didn't know or understand the reality. We walked over to the car together, and I understood that it was I who was different from usual.

In the car I had some bread, cheese, and a couple of glasses of wine.

A while afterwards I knew who we were, where we had come from, and where we were going. Slowly I came back—not entirely.

This experience happened toward the end of the Praiano period and must have ushered in the transition to a cooler *weltanschauung,* my life in Heiligenberg.

THREE

My first meeting with Germania took place amid sacred rites in a brothel in Hamburg. It was—to be exact—twenty-seven years ago. Actually it began at a bar in the same distinguished city. Over the bar hung a placard:

Jews are not welcome!

There was a man standing beside me, and I drank a glass and got into a conversation with him. Inside the dining room itself there was much gaiety, and people were arm in arm, singing heroic songs. I went to the door and looked in. There was a warm, billowing mass of people. Right beside me, at the entrance door, hung a new, much larger sign:

Jews are not welcome!

I went back to the bar.

I asked the man beside me if he knew where a lonely youth could go to satisfy his natural craving for feminine society. He leaned over the bar and said to the bartender:

"The young Man wishes an Adventure."

The man behind the counter nodded, and wrote a word on a slip of paper which he laid beside my glass.

"*Auto nehmen*," he said: "Taxi! Telephone over there!"

He had pointed to the doorman by the main entrance. I

drank up, paid and went to the doorman's lodge. On the wall above him hung a sign:

Jews are not welcome!

It was a very large sign. The through traffic held sway at the entrance, a revolving door turned insanely, everything was a stream of peroxide-colored hair, of uniforms and boots and happiness. People were shouting, greeting each other, clicking their heels and slapping each other on the back. The doorman telephoned, greeted people, shouted Heil Hitler, took capes and uniform overcoats, handed out packages and collected tips, as he said:

"Where to, please?"

I showed him the slip of paper, and with a frivolous, friendly grin he dialed a new telephone number. He shouted a few words into the receiver, while I looked at the paper. It said: "Kalkhof."

Two minutes later he dragged me out onto the sidewalk and over to the taxi which had arrived. The street was powerfully lit, and it glittered with peroxide curls and shiny boots. It was all movement and *joie de vivre* and uniforms. I gave him a tip and got into the cab. Screwed to the back of the driver's seat was a sign:

Jews are not welcome!

I handed the slip to the driver. In three minutes we were there. It was a new sidewalk, again uniforms and peroxide ladies. A procession of military boots and shouts and greetings which whirled through the air. I went in through an iron gate which looked like the entrance to a colossal pissoir. Inside was a street with windows, where the girls sat. I went a few paces down, then ducked in through a door; in the entrance hung a sign on the wall:

Jews are not welcome!

To an older lady I paid a fee, I think it was three marks.
Then I found myself in a cubicle with a red light, a small
table, an ashtray, and a red bed. There was a lady of uncertain age in there, clad only in her underwear. On the wall it
said:

𝕵𝖊𝖜𝖘 𝖆𝖗𝖊 𝖓𝖔𝖙 𝖜𝖊𝖑𝖈𝖔𝖒𝖊!

"Do you want to give me something?" she said calmly. I
wanted to show my *savoir faire*, and put a couple of marks on
the table.
"Do you want to give me more?" she said, nodding appre-
ciatively.
I put another mark under the red lampshade. She nodded
again, and with two motions of her hand she took off her own
garter belt and put a protective condom on me. Before I
knew what had happened I was standing on the street again. I
looked down the row of doors and display windows. Then I
shook my head and went in the next door. In the entryway
hung a sign:

𝕵𝖊𝖜𝖘 𝖆𝖗𝖊 𝖓𝖔𝖙 𝖜𝖊𝖑𝖈𝖔𝖒𝖊!

I paid the fee and again found myself in a red cubicle with
a small table and a red bed. The lady was considerably
younger this time, around my own age, and she was in full
working dress: the garter belt was off already. She smiled.
"Want to give me something?" she said.
I put a couple of marks on the table, and while she was
rolling the hygienic protection onto me, I caught sight of
something on the wall—a sign. I felt faint and had the impression that I wasn't seeing right:

𝕵𝖊𝖜𝖘 𝖜𝖎𝖑𝖑 𝖓𝖔𝖙 𝖇𝖊 𝕾𝖊𝖗𝖛𝖊𝖉!

There were *two different texts!*
I must have looked bewildered, for she looked at me and

followed my glance over to the sign.

"*Macht nix aus!*" she said indifferently. "I have nothing against Jews. Just give me a little extra!"

I put two more marks on the table. She hurriedly lay down on the bed:

"Now make it quick!"

❖ ❖ ❖

Outside the congestion and the movement were greater than before, there were still more uniforms, and trucks of soldiers were driving through the overfilled streets. People were shouting and singing, and some struck up enthusiastic fighting songs. It was a public celebration, an orgy of happiness. I didn't understand what it was about.

Only a little later in the evening did it dawn on me that the people were celebrating the outbreak of the Second World War.

❖ ❖ ❖

The rest disappeared in a roar of motorcades, motorcycles and shouts and song, in uniforms and boots. The avalanche was unloosed. Jolly red-white flags with swastikas in the middle flapped in the sun.

After my sojourn in Stockholm I saw the city again, many other cities, many, many cities, railroad stations, villages, wastelands of ruins, from Cologne and Stuttgart to Hamburg and Berlin.

The last thing I remember from Germania was the joyful flags, snow-white, rose-red and with the jolly swastika rotating and sprawling in the round white central field—flags which flapped and beat in the wind, on flagpoles slanting out from the façades of old houses in narrow streets in medieval towns, in small villages, flags which filled the streets and the broad avenues in the big cities. They cracked and banged like whiplashes, shone in the sun and danced in the wind. It was a sun-drenched, ripe and golden late summer day, with brass instruments, high children's voices, school classes which marched, women who smiled, men who sang.

The destruction six years later was worse than one could have imagined. The first thing I remember of postwar Germania was a shot-up but not wholly bombed-out railroad station at a little stop in North Germany, and the face of a trainman, gray-white, emaciated, grimy, and unshaven under a soft black uniform cap. He was standing right outside the window of the compartment, with bad teeth and his head turned to the side, looking forward toward the locomotive; he shouted something to a co-worker, which is how I saw his teeth. It was a hard, exhausted, and despairing face. It was Germany's face. He shouted again, the whistle sounded a couple of times, and the train went on—to new stations, buildings peppered with bullet wounds, and empty, burnt out houses, fallen-in houses, bombarded houses which had sunk to their knees or all the way down. The remains of plumbing standing like dead vines in the air, halves of buildings where the floor and parts of the walls remained like shelves, with the wall section in different colors. There were cities with miles and miles of rubble heaps and mountains of stone, blocks of houses had turned into hills and ridges, and broad boulevards had become narrow footpaths which wound among the rises and hills in a new nature. Whole cities had become landscape once again.

In a way it was as if nature too had been destroyed, as if the vast lowlands in the North lay in impotence and hopelessness, in affliction, guilt, and despair. It was as if the Lüneberg Heath had turned gray, as if the sun which hung over the horizon gave neither light nor warmth, but was just a lump of halfway burnt-out embers—dark red and dying.

It was as if the very earth, the grass, the trees, and the sky over this land were in the process of dying.

Everybody had lost something, people or property— nobody thought about anything but the barest necessities— some potatoes, a little bread, and a few cigarettes. I've never

met such human people as the Germans at this time among
the ruins; calm, resigned people, on the way to becoming
nature, they too—philosophic, thoughtful people, content and
almost happy, if naked want were kept away. There was a
kind of lethargy over the land, something which resembled a
coma, a languor and a quietude as after one has lived through
a severe illness. In all the misery there lay a peace over land,
cities and people.

I didn't know that this was due to only one single thing:
that the paper mark was worthless. Teutons who have lost
faith in the eternal worth of money simply no longer believe
in anything on earth. When paper money has no buying
power, life has no standard, the world no meaning. This I
didn't know.

But two days after the dirty, greasy, worthless slips of
paper were traded in for new, strong currency with purchas-
ing power, then I knew it.

I happened to be in Germania when the exchange took
place, on the new national day itself, W-day. *Währungsreform.*
Why isn't this day celebrated as New Teutonia's birthday?—
Whatever may have been in the making before the day of
exchange was killed in a few hours.

There was something brewing in Germany before the currency reform; I'm not the only one who saw it. There was a
new humanity present, a brotherliness, a depth—a first seed,
an infinitely weak and tender germ of something new, of
something non-Teutonic in Teutonia. This one night,
between the worthless currency and the strong hard currency,
decided Germania's new development, and thereby the fate
of Europe in the years which are to come.

The rest of Europe ought to observe *Währungsreform* as a
day of mourning, a day of calamity for European countries: if
the statesmen in Europe had any sense, they would agree that
we should all fly our flags at half-mast on Mark Day.

The change which took place in this country in the course
of those few hours in which life got back its meaning was
more fantastic than any bombing attack.

Until the evening before W-day all the shop windows were empty, hardly any goods of any sort were to be had. The country gave the impression of an incredible scarcity of goods, a gray and endless poverty.

In a few hours it became evident that the poverty was a garnish, used to beg free cigarettes from foreigners; the misery was a camouflage. The next morning the day dawned over a New Germania bulging with ham, sausage, and bread, with butter, bacon, eggs, cheese, shoes, clothes, furs, shiny new furniture, refrigerators, and ready-made, gleaming, brand-new models of cars. The new elite streamed forth the very next morning arrayed in chamois skin, gloves, silk ties, and a new, happy look on their faces.

They had sat there hoarding their wealth until the buying power of the mark was in order again. Let me tell the story of Schweinehund.

Schweinehund wasn't his natural-born name, he was only called that because Schweinehund was the word he used most often. He was a prison guard in my old fatherland during the five years before the war ended. He was an unrestrained absolute ruler over others.

He wasn't even one of the worst. In his own way he had both humanity and good temper, there was a kind of soul in him. The trouble was just that Schweinehund had a sense of humor.

He held sway in a little prison camp in a little town, and everybody, both in the camp and in the town, knew him. He was round and burly, a bit stout, and he had a big dog on a leash. Schweinehund set great store by this dog, and he gave it meat and cod-liver oil and sausages.

Schweinehund's humor consisted of two things: he used swearwords and he kicked. The swearwords weren't really so bad, for he didn't have a big vocabulary. He had only "Schweinehund." When he had said Schweinehund, he'd laugh heartily. The kicking part was worse. Of course a kick *dann und wann* isn't the worst thing a human being can be exposed to—so it's true that he wasn't one of the worst. He never hit. But he liked to kick in a joking way, from behind, in the rear—not in the belly or in the testicles, which are the most usual targets for kicking Teutons. Schweinehund was a good fellow underneath, and he kicked people from behind. The joke about the kicks was that they were supposed to come as a complete surprise, and land like a shot. They were thus rather forceful, and they befell the just and the unjust prisoners alike. Unfortunately it happened a couple of times that he kicked off a vertebra, but that wasn't the intention. It was the kick itself which was the joke for Schweinehund, the surprise—that was his form of wit, of satire and humor. Only a few became cripples.

When Schweinehund had kicked, then he was like to split his sides laughing, he'd lean back and laugh with all his good heart. When he'd gotten in a good kick from behind, he'd laugh with all his good nature, with all his hearty humor. Then he'd say:

"Schweinehund!"

When he had said Schweinehund, the laughter would take over completely, he wheezed, he whooped, he choked, he got convulsions and was like to be strangled with laughter. No, he wasn't one of the worst.

All the same it went badly with him for awhile.

In the first place Schweinehund lost the war in his own way, and that was bad enough, for he was fond of his Führer and of his superiors. But he had done his part to win; as I said, the prison camp was small, and the town was small, so after five years a large proportion of the inhabitants had been inside this little camp. In short, there weren't very many who hadn't sooner or later got their kick from Schweinehund. Nevertheless he lost, and ended up in a camp himself.

To be sure he wasn't allowed to kick anybody in there, and that was a deprivation. But "Schweinehund" he could say as much as he liked. He didn't have it so bad in the camp.

The misfortune was that he was sent back to Germania, to a gray and impoverished, war-torn, bombed-out Germania. He found it dreary in his homeland, and the food situation

was bad. He pined and longed back to the time when he had
been a prison guard, had an abundance of food, and at any
rate could allow himself a kick or two every day. He longed
for the north.

Many of his prisoners he remembered by name and address.

Finally the longing for the north became so strong that
Schweinehund got himself some paper, a pencil, and an enve-
lope. He wrote a letter.

He wrote at length, and he committed to paper all the
nameless sorrows of his Teutonic soul, his longing for the north,
for butter and sausage, for the light Nordic summer nights,
ham, rich cheeses, and the northern lights. He described his
longing for the ocean, for more ham and more sausage and for
the fjords in the north, carved between the mighty mountains.
He wrote of his longing back to the old days, to *Freundschaft,*
beer, bacon, and aquavit. Back to the freedom of the prison
camp. He wrote all this and more to one of his former prisoners, and he ended the letter with a moving description of his
present depressing, disheartening circumstances; all was gray,
sad, and hopeless. The nutrition miserable.

When the addressee got the letter from Schweinehund, it
was *he* who laughed. He laughed more heartily than he had in
years. And he stuck the letter in his pocket and went around
showing it to people. And all Schweinehund's old clients
laughed too.

The letter contained a PS:

Some people here have it better than I do, because they
have friends abroad, and they get gift packages of food, of
coffee, tea, sugar, cheese, butter, cookies, sausage, ham, and
canned fruit. Couldn't you also remember me with such a
package, as a greeting from the good old days in your beautiful and hospitable country.

Eventually the whole little town knew about Schweinehund's
letter about the good old days and the gift package.

One of the town wags hit upon the thought that it
wouldn't take much to make the joke complete: *Schweinehund
should get a package.*

✧ ✧ ✧

There was an acute food shortage in my fatherland too at this time, but the town grocer, a ship-chandler, a cheese specialist, and a butcher got together on the project—they got help from others, and together they assembled an enormous gift crate which was nailed together and smuggled out of the country, sent by ship to Hamburg and from there on to Schweinehund.

In the last analysis he wasn't one of the worst, and a good story is worth its weight in sausage. It was worth more.

Before the gift package had been smuggled safely to its destination, Schweinehund had had a conversation with his own grocer about the complicated economics of world trade, and the grocer had said: Food and money are *Scheisse* which either get eaten up or sink in value, while on the other hand real property is a permanent asset.

These words Schweinehund concealed in his heart.

One day he got a dispatch from an inland railway express; he expected nothing, but received much. On top of the butter and the sausage and the cheese lay a greeting from twenty-four former prisoners who all thought that well, he could have been worse. He could not have been worse.

The first thing Schweinehund did was to write back with thanks, mentioning his four (or five?) hungry children, his brother's and his two sisters' children, along with his own misery.

He didn't touch a thing in the gift package, not a piece of cheese, not a sausage. Nor did he sell anything. He traded. By preference he traded off his food to old, formerly well-situated people, and he was a hard businessman who didn't trade things away cheap, and only for genuine, lasting values—for silver, gold, and precious objects. The gift package was his starting capital; he lived on his rations and on begging from foreigners, and after gift package number two, which was also the last, Schweinehund had a tiny but thriving black market business.

He had one principle: real property is a permanent asset.

When the *Währungsreform* came, he belonged to those who didn't lose on it. The old currency was waste paper, but his numerous small objects of value amounted to a minor fortune. While other people were allowed to pay out—or "exchange," as it was called—a few old marks for the same number of new ones, Schweinehund had a capital to start with. It grew rapidly now, and a few months later he was able to buy a bombed-out and almost worthless city lot with his savings. Then he got a job and waited.

He had calculated rightly: after W-day came a construction boom, the town was cleared, cleaned up, and the rebuilding proceeded rapidly. The lot grew in value at about a hundred new marks a day. When he eventually sold it at a scandalous profit, he could buy, in an even more leveled and bombed out, considerably larger town, three new ruined city lots. He continued in his old subordinate position, but he took a business school course in the evening, and learned the difference between debit and credit—which also resulted in his moving up two grades in the firm where he worked. In the city where he had frozen down his assets the price of land skyrocketed, and he looked around for a town which had been even harder hit. He found it, and when he had sold his three old lots he could buy a block in the third town.

Schweinehund was thrifty, sober, and industrious.

After the rebuilding of town number three he began to put his money into industrial tracts outside the big cities; later he built on them himself, so that the next time around he could sell whole stretches of finished row houses or parcels with single homes.

How much Schweinehund owns today is something only God and Schweinehund know. But Schweinehund is as if spit out of the national soul:

His story is the story of Teutonia.

My first protocol I began at this time, a long and heavy and depressing labor, as well as an unpaid one. For me this was the beginning of my downfall: in fourteen years I've recorded a total of about 8000 folio pages, and every line, every sentence has led me further into the darkness from which I first awakened in this Alpine valley.

When you see what the protocols led to, it's easy to perceive that I had to begin writing them down in Teuto-Germania: no other region in Europe is so suffocatingly sick and false—and no other place has manifested the truth so frighteningly.

The choice of material for the First Protocol already shows that I was condemned by nature to be a born Servant of Justice: I immediately went to work recording documents from the Doctors' trials which took place in Germany shortly after peace had broken out.

Sometime after W-day I came into contact with a certain Dr. Ignatius Feuermann, later known for his historical-philosophical work *Die Geburt des Nationalsozialismus aus dem Geiste des Judaismus,* with the subtitle: *Ein Buch über die Ausrotting des individuellen Denkens.*

Doctor Ignatius gave me the judicial documents from the case, and next the medical ones; after that I miraculously came into direct contact with the intimate family background for the crimes which—along with the crimes of Vietnam, Dresden, and Hiroshima—are the greatest of our time, and I simultaneously got on the trail of the blood lust's schizophrenic origin. All this is entered in the introductory chapters of the First Protocol.

The content of the "Doctors' Trials" was the series of medical experiments which a number of Teutonic doctors in certain social camps had carried out using the little bears installed therein as laboratory animals: it dealt with little bears' scientific experiments with other little bears. The experiments included injections of infectious material for a number of diseases such as tetanus, etc., etc., castration of men and women by radiation, research with freezing and with lowering of air pressure (commissioned by the Luftwaffe), research on pregnant women, surgical experiments with the transplantation of limbs, etc., along with a

large number of nutritional experiments. For the laboratory
bears most of the medical experiments had a fatal outcome or
resulted in lifelong disability.

The doctors who carried out the medical experiments
were without exception privately well-adjusted, conscientious,
healthy, normal and decent people—and in the performance
of their work efficient, precise, and of course highly qualified
professionally.

Despite the vast extent of the research and its highly exact
and scientifically irreproachable execution, it nonetheless
failed to produce any results which have since proved signifi
cant for the air force, the navy, the army, or the further development of medical science.

During the trials the accused doctors showed no guilt
feelings of any magnitude, but pointed to the local laws and
to their superiors, who in turn pointed to their own superiors, who again pointed to *their* superiors as those actually
responsible for the carrying out of painful and insalubrious
scientific research. Likewise they could all produce testimo-
nials to their excellent, faithful and normal conduct, in their
free time as well as during working hours. In addition the
defense had the great advantage of being able to point to the
normal practice within military organizations, where subor
dinates are obliged to follow the orders of their superiors,
because otherwise all war would automatically end—or at
any rate prove rather ineffectual.

This didn't help the doctors much, but it gave their case
significant moral support.

It was worse that the corresponding research-mad scientists, the American little bears who had conducted mass experiments with the two heavy elements uranium and plutonium
on an impressive body of research material selected by the
hundreds of thousands from Japanese little bears, weren't
called before any court in this connection—despite the fact
that their experiments had had a fatal outcome for many,
many more little bears, and likewise led to the permanent dis-
abling of an immeasurably greater number of laboratory bears

than that caused by the corresponding, more conventional investigations in the Teutonic social camps in the years immediately preceding the uranium and plutonium experiments.

That the American research was regarded as exempt from punishment, while the Germanic and Central Teutonic researches were regarded as punishable, naturally had a morally catastrophic effect on the respect one would otherwise have accorded the conviction of the German scientists.

The only explanation of the differing judgments passed on the two otherwise equivalent types of experiments must be derived from the only real difference between them: namely that whereas the European experiments were performed on a Polish, Jewish, Russian, and in part even a Gypsy public, the American researches were conducted using Japanese, and hence yellow-skinned, raw material.

In the First Protocol I nevertheless dealt exclusively with the Teutonic experiments, but in return I did it all the more thoroughly.

At any rate it's here that the darkness begins to be suffocating.

To understand this one must take into account the dark time I have lived in:

The poor streaks of blood left by Maria Rosenbaum's relatives formed not even a drop in the ocean of blood which was spilled.

Young people of today no longer know what the Moscow trials, the purges or the Hitler-Stalin pact were, but *we* know it. And the blood continued to flow after Josef the Bloody had passed on; even after his death he was almighty for awhile.

It looked dark: in East and West a night-black shadow of murder, blood, and police; the world was a slaughterhouse, a criminal asylum, where it wasn't even enough to expect the worst—for things still got worse than one could possibly expect.

I studied the Doctors' Trials and the medical documents during this time, and little by little I understood that the eclipse of the sun had come. The birds stopped singing, the grass turned gray where it wasn't bloody, and the rivers overflowed

with excrement, rotting entrails, and severed limbs, just as in
the sewers under the social camps in Mozart's land.
I continued now, with protocol after protocol.

✧ ✧ ✧

I remember one time I got into the car, drove through half
of Germania, straight through Switzerland and down the
south side of the mountains—to get to an Italian bordello: to
see if there were still any human beings left in the world.
I don't remember anything about the trip, I was drunk the
whole time. I don't remember which protocol I was working
on, and it probably doesn't matter, since it was actually the
same endless record that I was writing the whole time. The car
was full of books, documents, and paper. That's how it usually
was.
But this trip through Germany and Switzerland and down
over the lowlands in Italy, I remember the end of it. Which
city I stopped in I don't know exactly, but I believe it was
Cremona or Piacenza. I drove right to a peaceful, bourgeois
hotel, parked the car in the courtyard—I was almost sober
now—and went up and took a bath in my room. Then I went
out and ate two poulardes with a couple of bottles of wine,
and after that went to a bar for some coffee.
While I drank the coffee, I asked the bartender about the
nearest *casa di discrezione*.
"Prrroooo!" said he, throwing up his hands: "I'm a married
man and have no idea about that kind of thing. I'll ask a very
good friend, he's a taxi driver and knows his way around."
He made a phone call.
A minute afterwards the driver arrived, and we drove
around the block and were there. We got out of the car
together, and he carefully locked the car doors after him. I
paid thirty or forty cents for the ride. He took the key out of
the car door.
"We're in Italy," he said with a shrug. "People steal like
ravens."

"They do that in my country too, in Norvegia."

He brightened and smiled at me, almost rejoicing:

"Roald Amundsen!" he said. "You are a compatriot of Roald Amundsen!"

"Yes," I said, while he accompanied me across the street to the bordello.

I wanted to say goodbye, but he shook his head and said that he wanted to take a trip inside too. It was his regular house. He added that it wasn't an especially high-class bordello, but a wholly ordinary petty-bourgeois one; in the third price class, in other words very reasonable. He was still enthusiastic about having a conversation about Roald Amundsen, and we went in together.

Inside it was full, the guests were standing in line, a few were reading newspapers. Two elderly gentlemen were sitting down and reading while they waited their turn. The madam walked smilingly back and forth keeping track of the sequence in the lines and talking with her customers about politics and church matters. When she caught sight of my friend the cab driver, she greeted him very warmly; it was clear that he was a well-liked and solid customer.

He greeted her in return, then pointed at me:

"This gentleman is from Norvegia: a countryman of Roald Amundsen!"

The queue turned like a line of soldiers pivoting on command. Those who were reading lowered their newspapers. Both the two older, seated gentlemen looked up at me. Most everybody smiled, and all said or mumbled something:

"Roaldo Amundsen!"

I stood before them on the floor, receiving their applause and their good will; then I bowed. The madam took both my hands and pressed them. Everybody had a few words to say, and a rather animated conversation broke out about Roald Amundsen. I had to answer a number of questions. Then I took my place at the end of the line. A moment passed, they made room up front, and while I was insisting that this wouldn't do, I was conducted to the head of the line.

I heard the driver's voice very distinctly:

"A *compatriote* of Amundsen!"

"What kind of girl does the gentleman wish?" said the madam cordially. "Very young or very *brava*?"

A vehement discussion now broke out. Some shouted "very young," others shouted "very *brava*." Then the madam said:

"Bianca?" She looked inquiringly out over the gathering.

"Elena!" shouted the one old gentleman over his newspaper.

There ensued a most thorough discussion, but more and more shouted:

"Bianca!"

The question was as good as decided, and the madam came over to me smiling. She gestured toward the brothel parliament which had taken care of my case and my interests:

"Bianca," she said approvingly. "She's the best one here."

I looked over to the cab driver. He nodded eagerly, smiling; agreeing, recommending with large eloquent eyes.

"Bianca," said the madam.

"Bianca," said the men, more and more of them nodding at me.

"Bianca," I said.

❖ ❖ ❖

Not long afterwards I was again in Germania. I wrote down protocol after protocol, a demeaning, annihilating labor, and again the darkness oozed in over me, steadily stronger and more impenetrably thick and suffocating.

While I was writing my tenth protocol I stayed in Berlin.

The record keeping now concerned penal codes, prisons, the usual means of carrying out sentences, disciplinary punishments, physical chastisement and prolonged isolation and confinement in a small space for extended periods of time—along with the immediate and long-term effects of these actions on the delinquents. My conclusion was that none of these measures leads to the desired and intended effect: to resocialize the delinquent—in other words after confining, iso-

lating and sometimes putting him in chains, to return him to
society as a man who is now better suited to a normal life
than he was before.

In substantiation of this I had collected an unusually large
amount of documentary material. This protocol had an
extremely depressing effect on me in the long run, especially
because I was now sure that this whole long and painful
record would be written down without producing any effect.
All I could do was to put everything in, word by word, line
by line, page by page.

Despite the fact that I had treated, analyzed, filtered,
worked through, and recorded considerably more bestial stuff
in earlier volumes, this tenth protocol had the most oppressive
and disheartening effect on me of them all. Possibly because
the material showed an endlessness and a degree of eternal
repetition which surpassed all else in hopelessness, but possibly also because my strength began to come to an end.

The work showed a steadily stronger inclination to come
to a standstill, not to want to continue.

At this point I discovered with full clarity that all of the
records I had written actually formed parts of a larger whole,
and that they—read and evaluated each by itself, volume by
volume—only show a meaningless and incoherent chaos. Only
seen in conjunction did they have a meaning. I finished protocol ten under an enormous strain on my strength and will.

In Berlin I have a fixed lodging which I always go back to.
On the floor below there's a night club, or—what shall I call
it—a bar, which is open around the clock, and where at any
time for a very reasonable price one can buy cigarettes or a
glass of something to drink. If the work on the records sometimes stretches into the night, to three or five o'clock, I can
always get some breathing room or a little conversation down
there. The girls are there around the clock too, even at seven
or nine in the morning. The place has a very narrow façade, a
small entrance door, and a few photos of naked girls and
clothed musicians outside. Some colored lamps. It's a simple
place, but it has the advantage that it lies outside time: inside

the dark, red and black rooms it's always night.

The girls' hair is coal-black or peroxide white. I know several of them, although I've never had anything to do with them personally.

In my mature years I've never had anything to do with Teutonic brothels, I think because there one feels as if one is in the morgue behind one of the experimental medical institutes in the old social camps. I think the girls are dissatisfied with their work, and that they revenge themselves on the customers by treating them as if they were in a military hospital.

Of the northern cities I like Berlin better than any other.

Of course except for old towns or villages, which are always the best. But I've felt more at peace in Berlin than in other Germanic cities, perhaps because in a way the German sickness is kept in check here, where two worlds meet. When I was writing the tenth protocol, Teutonia's wealth had reached the point where the country was ready to burst, where Schweinehund had once again become master of Europe. In this little whorehouse bar under my hotel one felt as if one were in a sanctuary; in the morning the girls look grimy and exhausted, the lady behind the bar doesn't expect much in tips. One can be tired and unshaven and look sloppy in one's dress without embarrassing anyone, here in West Berlin as well.

Berlin is not really a Germanic city, every other person has a name ending in -itzsch or -owsky. The city is by character a Slavic city.

Nevertheless the most important thing is something else: Berlin has not recovered from the war. Berlin, both in the East and in the West, is still a war-torn city.

Berlin has the war sitting in her face, in her flesh.

The awful thing about the West is that everything is buried in lies and Germanic bustle and health, hypocrisy and greed.

For all I know, the gas ovens as comic strips may have become widespread long since. I don't keep up with the cultural life.

I finished my Tenth Protocol.

Then I went over to the East.

I walked through the locks, past the armed guards, I went a few steps down the sidewalk. When I'd been walking up through the city for three minutes I looked around, and at once I knew it: I was in my own world. I was home again. Everything around me was stone.

All these ruins, all this grayness, all this emptiness, all this poverty. . . . Yes, that's the way we are: this is our world. This is what it looks like underneath the plastic. This is our culture. That's how poor we are. East Berlin had this quality of truth.

When you take our world and peel all the lies off it, then it looks like this: Berlin. The city of stone. The city of ruins.

The war has left us like that. We've hardly progressed a step. If one takes away the lies, then we're just standing still. This may sound strange, but the sight of this truth about the world gave me the first feeling of freedom which I'd had in many years.

Only the truth shall set you free.

✧ ✧ ✧

West Berlin too is rather high in karats. I'm thinking of the wall behind the bar in my whorehouse: it's hung with pictures of the great one, of the greatest of all, of the clown Grock! He stayed in this district a lot, and was often inside the bar. The wall is full of his great broad clown smile, full of truth and humanity.

Or I think of a little Hungarian goulash stand on one of the vacant lots which there are so many of, in West Berlin as well. The man who mixes the pepper salad and fries the spitted meat in oil, he laughs when he sees me again. Like this empty piece of land in a city of a million, and with this ugly little stall on it—that's how Stuttgart looked after the war.

Since that time we've built up stage sets, we've lied them together, built them in the air without foundations and basements. Work proceeds rapidly in such a light material as falsehood.

I have a new memory, a man in uniform. He hit me in my face, which felt yielding and swollen. I wiped my lips and got the back of my hand full of blood. Then I hit him across the mouth.

It was night outside, raining slightly. I walked down the wet, stone-paved sidewalk. A streetlight was burning, and the street was also paved. It was very dirty and full of refuse. I felt the rain in my face.

I noticed that I was lying down, with my cheek against the stone in the sidewalk. The pavement glistened. And I had my head right by the iron post of the streetlight. I wiped my face without raising my head. My hand was just as bloody now. Then I heard steps behind me. Right by the lamppost, which had been soiled by many dogs, lay a large blob of dog excrement. A little ways from my face I wanted to get up, but it was impossible. Then the man began to kick me in the back.

I don't know what country or what city this was in.

All is darkness.

FOUR

The sunlight around me is enormous; the town here, the valley and the mountain giants above us—all lies bathed in the incomprehensibly flaming and blinding light which is spring in this Alpine valley. The wind is fresh but no longer cold, the sun has warmed and dried it. It sweeps dust and moisture out of the streets. The flags bang and gleam in wind and sun. The snowy mountains above the town reflect the sunlight, so that one can't bear to look at them for more than a few seconds at a time.

Over us, a ways above the foot of Daiblshorn, lies the Castle, the Princely Residence. The magnificent building is immensely old, and large parts of it still have Romanesque traits in their architecture. Originally the Residence was built over an even older structure, an ancient Celtic monastery. From the monastery the Castle took its name, Heiligenberg, which became the name of the town below the Residence, the capital city, and finally came to designate the whole Principality. From this it also follows that the mountain Daiblshorn, thousands of feet high, is also really named Heiligenberg. In fact this is the *berg* which is referred to.

If one looks up at the jagged peaks, one will see something which resembles a new castle, blinding white and sharp, an endlessness of clarity, death, cold. Nonetheless every mountain climber knows that in sunshine a great warmth reigns on the tops, but it isn't the same warmth as in the valleys or on the lowlands or by the sea. It's a warmth of another substance.

Likewise the Princely Residence shines in the sun, it quivers in the light, and the great structure dances in the glitter.

It's good that Spring is coming now.

The winter in the valley was dreadful. The few foehn days sent an avalanche of disasters over the town.

It's as if the suddenly hot Sahara air calls forth a melting of snow, a breakup of ice inside the human soul—as if the desert air thaws and dissolves the armor of civilization, of restraint and discipline which encases the person's interior under normal circumstances, and now lets loose the forces which live in the depths of us, in that which is our true nature. The pure bloodthirsty carnivore rises up with full strength in people and kills wildly, at random, slaughtering everything around him out of pure bloodlust and an insatiable hatred for humanity.

Hitherto it has been normal and usual among us for cider drinkers in the typical delirium of the illness, in common with ordinary foehn murderers, to perform their tragic deeds by hand—for the most part with knife or ax, now and then with a meat cleaver or more specialized butchers' tools, on rare occasions with pitchforks or scythes. Of course it has often been dreadful enough, but because of the simple and basically primitive weapons the total damage done by a single murderer has seldom included more than his nearest relatives— wife, children, parents, and siblings, whatever servants belong to the household (murders of domestics), and sometimes colleagues or others employed at the place of work. It has often been gruesome enough, and it always spreads disquiet over town and valley; for such a massacre naturally turns people's thoughts to what kind of forces there are at the bottom of human nature, forces which now suddenly break free and want to see blood. At the core of even the most friendly and good-hearted citizen, husband, father, and professional man there lives one of these tiger-people, an insatiable, blood-rutting monster, filled with just one single passion: hatred of mankind, a hatred which can only be stilled and sated by an

orgy of blood. After these attacks—which can happen to anybody, often precisely the placid, usually gentle ones—people
sit in the inns talking in low voices about the murders, and
about where these devastating carnivorous instincts come
from.

On one of the last days of November came the most disquieting outbreak we have experienced here, perhaps ever.

The mass murderer was a young man, a student at the capital's technical college. The young technologist, not more than
twenty-five years old, was an unusually good student. He was
one of those cases where natural talent is combined with industry and ambition. He was in fact a paragon of a young man,
loving to his parents, loyal to his friends and classmates and
courteous, obliging, and friendly to his superiors. He had
always been like that; as a child too he had been a model pupil.

The foehn set in early in the morning, around nine
o'clock. And only something over an hour later the temperature had risen from zero to almost ninety. He didn't go to
class that morning.

Around ten-thirty the same morning he went up to his
room and got his automatic rifle, put several clips in his pockets and went down to the kitchen, where he shot his sister and
his mother. In this principality practically all adult men have
both guns and ammunition at the ready. It's an old custom,
and most of them are good marksmen besides. This young
technologist, alas, was an unusually good sharpshooter. After
killing his sister and mother he went out onto the street,
where he shot a taxi driver at the wheel, and thereafter everybody he met: children, women, and men at random. In the
course of less than forty-five minutes he had wounded fourteen people and killed eleven. It all happened so fast that by
the time the police arrived the young man himself had been
rendered harmless by a grocer who had his own precision
weapon hanging inside his office. The grocer was the first one
to understand, and to take it upon himself to do something
about, what was going on—and if he hadn't interfered so
energetically, more lives would certainly have been lost.

He took aim against the door frame and shot the boy at a distance of nearly two hundred yards. The bullet, which was jacketed, entered at the base of the left eyebrow and went straight through the head. The student must have been dead even before he hit the ground. People have since reproached the grocer for not shooting him in the body so that the boy could have had a chance to survive and become normal again, as most foehn murderers do when the attack of rage is over.

But the worst thing about this case was that it set the pattern for the next two outbreaks.

The first one came a short time afterwards; it wasn't provoked by the foehn winds, but was a cider case.

The person involved was a cooper, and like all cider-berserks he was a man of mature years, in his late fifties. He was a heavy and powerful man, with a big moustache and with thin, gray hair on his square head. He too used an automatic weapon, like the young technologist.

Most people knew that he was a cider drinker, but no one had any suspicion of the extent of his intemperance; he was a man who drank considerably more than ten quarts a day.

Of the cooper it was known that the week before the tragic acts of compulsion he had been depressed and irascible, not himself any longer. He had been sleepless at night from around two o'clock, and had then gone down to his workshop, where he had drunk cider and made ready a dozen hand grenades which he himself had manufactured. For a number of years he had among other things been an instructor in the home guard, and in weapons technology he was a very knowledgeable man. Otherwise in his whole conduct of life he was an absolute model of a good father, an able craftsman, and an honest businessman. He was very friendly and easy-going toward his subordinates and in everything a thoroughly punctual and reliable person. He was an unusually loving and dutiful son, who idolized his old mother and took care of her with touching devotion. It can be mentioned that once when she was away staying with relatives in one of the neighboring towns in the principality, he wrote to her every single day for several weeks.

This man then, one day takes his murder weapons with him and goes out on the street. He threw four hand grenades into a schoolyard where children were playing, after which he shot a video technician on his way to work. The weapon he used was a large machine pistol of Belgian manufacture, which wasn't designed for precision shooting. Nor was he himself anywhere near as sure a marksman as the young technologist, and the result of the murder binge was many more wounded than killed. But because of the rapid fire from the gun and the loathsome effect of the hand grenades, more of the wounded were maimed and mutilated in a horrible manner. One of the victims, a young teacher as far as I remember, had almost the whole lower part of his face shot away at close range.

When the police surrounded the cooper he defended himself with his last hand grenades and with deadly salvos from his machine pistol. Like the student, he too had provided himself liberally with ammunition, and the police finally had to shoot him in the same way that the grocer had shot the technologist.

The cooper killed six people and wounded almost twenty.

The police now demanded a ban on private possession of guns, but before the authorities had been able to make up their minds to put the ban into effect, the third outbreak of murder madness had already taken place—likewise this time a faithful copy of the previous ones.

It happened during a foehn period at Christmas time, and the most peculiar thing was that almost simultaneously there were parallel cases of mass murder with guns in Germania, the United States, and England. And in them neither the foehn nor cider was part of the picture. Taken all together it seemed like a kind of human edition of rabies, a contagious bloodlust. However, Germania, England, and the United States are large societies, while our society in this principality is small, and both the frequency of the bloodbaths and the injurious effect itself therefore become much higher among us.

When the third outbreak came—a day or two after Christmas—both the people and the police had in the meantime learned from the foregoing disasters, and this time intervention came very fast. At the same time this case was the most difficult, because the mass murderer had stationed himself in a window high up in a building with a view over the marketplace, one of the main streets, and above all the main road leading into the city.

This foehn murderer was again a young man, around thirty years old. He was a former career military man, a passionate Bible reader and an avid gun collector—and like the other two murderers, also known as an unusually correct and honest person. Strangely enough he had about the same relationship to his mother that the cooper had had. During the whole inquest after the tragedy, and I was there myself as recorder, there was not one negative piece of testimony about the murderer.

He took his post in the window with a long-range hunting rifle equipped with a telescopic sight, and with unbelievable precision he hit three motorists one after another. They were all on the way into the town, and all three lost control of their driving. One was even killed on the spot by the bullet, which entered just over the left eye. After that the Biblical scholar shot two pedestrians in the marketplace. But in the still winter morning—it was a holiday and few people were out—the shots were very audible, and everybody sought cover. Several of the neighbors had seen where the shots were fired from, and the police immediately closed off the street and surrounded the house. A few hours later the Biblical scholar shot himself.

On New Year's Eve we were sitting at the table in "Zum Henker." Since it was a holiday, we were all dressed in black. We were almost the only guests in the inn; people with families usually stay home on such days. It was inevitable that we should talk about these occurrences which now lay like a nightmare over the city, and were naturally on everybody's mind. The bell ringer drank kirsch, I drank red wine, and the sexton kept to his cider, which he drank out of a big stone jug.

"Well, we still have January and February before us," said the bell ringer; "the worst foehn months are yet to come."

I'm writing this down during my lunch hour. I can see the mountains and a great part of the town. People are going to the inns now, to eat during their break in the working day. The church bells are chiming in the church where my friend was bell ringer. While this is happening, I write the last lines in my last protocol.

I lay down my pen.

Happy the one who has a room.